GRETA GOVERNMENT AND HER SNAKE-OIL-SURPRISE

GRETA GOVERNMENT
∾ AND HER ∾
SNAKE-OIL-SURPRISE

NATE ROBERTS

Mill City Press

Mill City Press, Inc.
212 3rd Avenue North, Suite 290
Minneapolis, MN 55401
612.455.2294
www.millcitypublishing.com

ISBN - 978-1-936400-85-0
LCCN - 2010940844

Cover Design by Wes Moore
Typeset by Madge Duffy

Printed in the United States of America

All of the people, places, and events depicted in this book are the product of the author's imagination. Certainly, the author has referred to real offices and institutions such as Congress, the President of the United States, the Supreme Court, and locations like Las Vegas and Los Angeles. However, those political offices, institutions, and locations are entirely fictional creations—aside from the label that has been attached to them.

While the events depicted occur within a fantastic, future America, the author uses some cultural references that closely resemble current events. Those references—as they occur within the confines of this book—are fictional. The events depicted would best be described as "cultural beaver-dams built across the author's stream of consciousness." In no instance are those references intended to convey "facts" or reveal "truths" regarding any living person or currently functioning institution. The references stem from the author's opinions about his own American experience.

The quotes and actions attributed to the story's historical figures are entirely fictional. Historical figures are depicted exactly as the author has chosen to represent them. The author gave only self-serving and superficial regard to the actual lives of the historical figures who appeared within this story.

This book is dedicated to my wife and two sons. Thank you for your support and the patience you showed every time I told you that the story was "finished." You're truly a life-time supply of holy-niceness.

Thank you, CM, DA, and JW. I couldn't have done this without your help.

Press crown' dem secular mess-i-yuh
Said all duh nations day'd in-spy-yuh
Day say day'll take duh nation hi-yuh
'Cept we still stuck down in duh my-yuh
Distort duh truth day'd often try-yuh
Duh faux-news and belov'd mess-i-yuh

Day need dear face shoved in duh cam-ruh
You see dem grace duh cuv-ruh Glam-ruh
Day was a buncha shameless scam-ruh
You had duh dream day had duh hamm-ruh
Duh iron fist it came to slam yuh
Duh faux-news and belov'd mess-i-yuh

Day knew just how to make duh ought-uh
You best believe day walk on wat-uh
Day got duh headline in duh pay-puh
Day was duh hope and change create-tuh
Day ranked right up dear wit duh Make-uh
Duh faux-news and belov'd mess-i-yuh

Day kept dear past and plans a seek-ruh
Day got in office start to creep-uh
Day come to shear you ev'ry doll-uh
Don't mind to hear you scream and holl-uh
Now open up it time to swall-uh
Duh faux-news and belov'd mess-i-yuh

'fore long compassion form duh rash-uh
It feel too good—can't stop duh scratch-uh
Day did duh Karl Marx grab and snatch-uh
You marvel at duh schemes day hatch-uh
Control your life day gonna try-yuh
Duh faux-news and belov'd mess-i-yuh

They were the secular messiahs
We dared object they called us "liars"
"Free" press then tore OUR lives wide open
OUR every misdeed was then spoken
Meanwhile THEIR background checks were token
Free press revived one day-I'm hopin'

Press crown' dem secular mess-i-yuh
Said all duh nations day'd in-spy-yuh
Day say day'll take duh nation hi-yuh
'Cept we still stuck down in duh my-yuh
To hide duh truth day'd often try-yuh
Duh faux-news and belov'd mess-i-yuh

-Old Conservative Spiritual

Messiah-mania—the cultural pandemic—was characterized by volcanic eruptions of euphoria.

Old Nick lay vanquished, and some new stars had risen in his place.

The conquerors epitomized all-things presidential. Inside their packs, they carried promises of peace and prosperity—they were magic.

Obstructionists shouted, "If it sounds too good to be true, it often is." But those who craved populist imagery over well-reasoned arguments flocked to crown the fiery comets as king.

In the aftermath of the victories—while the presidents' coronations and reigns unfolded—intellectuals, commanding generals, leading celebrities, the Spiritual Leader of the Church of Pop Culture, and the allegedly objective news-gathering machinery packed every available airwave and the tiniest fractions of column inch with glowing endorsements of their new heroes.

However, hidden safely beneath the heaps of hyperbole, an endless succession of presidential miracles, and the flood of orgasmic tingles that afflicted each new chieftains' adorers lay—the future.

–Ronald Anthony Travis, American Historian

Chapter 1

Early autumn

How much longer? Ray Watford asked himself. The fog of sleepiness slowly receded, and he began to feel awake. The morning air felt icy. He could almost see his breath. "Where's that flashlight?" he muttered while his hands groped the darkness.

He hadn't bothered to try the table lamp. The device sat within easy reach, but it might as well have been miles away. "Damned light," he hissed. Then he fought his desire to yank the lamp's plug from the socket, march outside, and let gravity do the rest. He *hated* that light.

Unfortunately for Ray, that show of anger would have only gotten him into trouble. His wife, Sarah, *loved* the lamp. He had no idea why, but she did. For him, the lamp was a monument to *Power to the People.*

Any goodwill that had been garnered by the Power to the People Resource Allocation and Monitoring System had vanished. In spite of the pre-implementation promises, reality once again failed to match rhetoric. The advent of the energy-*rationing* system meant the death of unmolested access to electricity. Gone were the days when someone like Ray could flick a switch and receive light in return.

Progressives—who had stuffed their faces with renewable-energy dog-food—waited open-mouthed and panting for the Federal Government's forests of windmills and prairies of solar panels to generate the promised energy riches. "We can no longer afford to make sensible decisions about the costs and benefits of our energy resources," the Energy Czar had stated. "We need to be *green*—no matter the price." When the Czar later stated, "We can produce all the energy we need from renewable sources. All we have to do is *allocate* those resources correctly," few in the press even bothered to read the tea leaves. The fix was in.

Days later, the Federal Government enacted a ban on the possession and use of fossil fuels. Within weeks, flora fascists had demolished every American oil rig and refinery. Not to be outdone, fauna fascists flooded coal mines and capped natural-gas pipelines as part of an energy industry witch-hunt. Even America's nuclear reactors—those gentle giants European nations had used to successfully generate *their* energy—were pronounced *guilty by association* and told to *scram*. Consumers—except those granted *special exemptions*—were told to find alternatives to meet their energy addictions. "Or better yet," the Energy Czar taunted, "feel free to go on a diet."

Once the smoke cleared, the energy infrastructure looked like it had been pulled from a cereal box. The system's capacity equaled a fraction of need. Americans hadn't gone on an energy diet—they had been sentenced to a government-imposed hunger-strike. And then they were left to sit in the dark—exactly as Ray was doing.

When he finally found his flashlight and then his wristwatch, he learned that the first of his family's two "electricity-allocation windows" wasn't due to arrive for a few hours. The two-hour blocks—one in the morning and one in the evening—were the only times the Watfords had access to electricity at home. *I can't believe we ever allowed things to get this crazy,* he told himself.

Still holding the flashlight, Ray pointed the light's beam toward Sarah's face. The dim, flickering light tickled his wife's ears and cheeks while she quietly snored. *She's still so beautiful after all these years,* he thought. Then he reached over and brushed a few strands of hair away from her face. He allowed the back of his hand to caress her cheek. *I'm going to make this right,* he silently told her. Then he swung his legs off the makeshift bed and stood.

The straw-filled canvas bag that doubled as a mattress always left him sore. This morning was no exception. His shoulders and back ached from the barely-comfortable conditions. A smile crept across his face when he realized, *I'm always free to sleep on the plywood floor.* He chuckled softly. *I guess we're free to do a lot of things we never imagined we'd be doing.*

As he started towards the bedroom door, he grabbed a robe from the floor. The garment had been made from cornhusk and recycled newsprint. After he had pulled the flimsy covering across his shoulders, he flapped his arms to get warm. "I better call the Housing Czar's office today. Maybe they can come out and fix these drafty windows," he whispered. Then he winked at his still-sleeping wife. The Housing Czar wasn't going to fix anything, Ray knew. But the joke was one of Sarah's favorites.

When Ray stepped into the hallway, a familiar voice greeted him. "Your thermostat has been set at a cool but comfortable fifty-seven degrees," *Greta Government* cooed. "If the temperature is too cool, *feel free* to put on a sweater."

"Greta Government" was the nickname the citizenry had given to the previously-unnamed, national public-address system. The system consisted of a network of loudspeakers that had been strung from coast to coast. The automated female persona made all of the system's announcements and served as de facto voice of the Federal Government. The system gave the President and Congress an excellent means of speaking down to the people.

The need for Greta had revealed itself during yet another collapse of the housing market. The Housing Czar—eager to ingratiate himself to *certain* home owners—offered subsidies, incentives and renegotiated-loan terms as part of an all-you-can-grab, free-money buffet. Unfortunately for the American taxpayer—the endangered species that always got stuck with the check—the goodies were offered to those homebuyers with the lowest likelihood of repaying their debts. Before taxpayers even had time to bus the dishes, the loan-default piles had grown taller than the California sequoias. Even worse, the spend-a-thon had trapped still more of the nation's resources in housing—the financial equivalent of a petrified nest-egg.

Though the market's umpteenth meltdown was nothing new, the events allowed then-President Handley Puppet and the Congress to reprise a familiar role. Like sugar-saturated children on Halloween night, the Demagoblicans in Washington dove into their costumes. Then they play-acted one of their favorite roles—that of the euphemistic *reluctant shareholders* for yet another sector of the economy.

Uncle Sam's holdings already boasted automakers, banks, energy companies, the faux-news industry, the health-care establishment, and nine-tenths of the motion-picture and television industries. The housing market seemed like a logical addition to his portfolio.

"We've invested billions of dollars in saving these homes," the Housing Czar later stated. "Why wouldn't we control the allocation of *our* property?" The comments prefaced Congress' decision to condemn all forms of housing—including those homes paid in full long before the government nationalized the banking system. The mass condemnation was the first step towards a law that gave nearly all Americans *equal access* to housing.

"How is it fair that some families get to spend their entire lives living in homes while others are forced to move from place to place? Having a job and income doesn't entitle you to *preferential treatment* in *my* America," the Czar proclaimed. The stirring statement came while he announced the passage of the *Welcome Home Act.*

The new law provided for the "nationalization of all of the recently condemned homes, condos, apartments, and other forms of human and canine shelter." The law dictated that access to this government-owned housing was to be awarded by lottery. No form of payment would be necessary to live in any of the *Peoples' Housing Units (PHUs).*

An inevitable backlash followed the law's passage. Protest marches and violent confrontations erupted. Homeowners torched their homes instead of turning them over to the government. The Feds turned to loudspeakers to drive away the unwelcome inhabitants who refused to leave their condemned homes. "You no longer own this home. Vacate or you will be arrested. You are trespassing on government property," were some of the first messages voiced by Greta Government. The tactic was a smashing success.

"Maybe we should install these speakers in all of the Peoples' Housing," the Housing Czar said after he'd watched the last squatter slink away. Soon, the Czar had arranged to have the public-address system installed inside all of the Peoples' Housing Units. Eventually, Greta's reach was extended to cover *all* of the Peoples' Areas.

Ray often entertained fantasies of destroying the system's dove-shaped speakers as they hung from the walls. *A few hits with a baseball bat; that's all it would take,* he said to himself. But in spite of his urges, he knew that it was a prohibited act to lay hands (or a bat) upon poor Miss Greta. So he resisted.

When he reached the bathroom, a familiar odor assaulted him.

The stink—which had embedded itself into the walls—counted back the years of *letting it mellow* between government-controlled toilet flushes. Holding his nose, he braved the stench for just long enough to retrieve a cardboard box. He'd kept the box hidden in the room's otherwise-empty cabinet. Once he'd fetched his prize, he continued down the hall.

Greta greeted him once again as he entered the kitchen. "Access to the refrigerator is restricted. Feel free to return between seven and eight in the morning; noon and one in the afternoon; and five and six in the evening. Between-meal snacking is prohibited," she said. "If you find yourself hungry outside approved refrigerator hours, feel free to remember that there are people going hungry in the world. Instead of stuffing your face, feel free to fulfill your daily exercise requirements." The admonition was largely academic. Had the locked refrigerator been opened, a few bad apples and a half-empty jug of triple-skimmed milk were the only foodstuffs to be found.

Ray walked over to the window and peered outside. A sliver of moonlight had managed to wriggle between cracks in the solar-panel array. The gigantic structure loomed over the PHU and blocked out most of the sky. As a boy, Ray had spent hours gazing into the nighttime sky. He fantasized about traveling to distant worlds. Tonight though, as he craned his neck and stared through the cracked pane of glass, the under side of the renewable-energy canopy was as far as he could see.

The monstrous solar panels had been erected as part of the *Equitable Communities Project.* The project—brainchild of the Puppetgrad City Council—was intended to provide affordable energy for all the city's residents. Council members had given every household in the city a *good fortune* score. The scores were based mostly on income and amounted to a novel form of taxation. The good fortune scores given to each household were then aggregated by neighborhood.

The neighborhoods with the highest total scores were subjected to special taxes. Those taxes funded the installation of the hundreds of lookalike solar-panel arrays that dominated Puppetgrad's skies. The panels supplied energy at no cost to those neighborhoods with the lowest scores. "This is a fair way to spread life's prosperity," Puppetgrad's mayor stated. In a fitting twist, the Federal Government seized all of the electricity generated by Puppetgrad's solar arrays and dispensed the nationalized juice via its own Power to the People.

When Ray finally stopped ruminating on the Equitable Communities Project, he walked over and sat at the table. He searched through a dozen rolls of toilet paper he'd kept hidden inside the cardboard box he had found in the bathroom before he found the correct one. He unfurled the rough, single-ply sheets onto the table and began to write.

Writing on toilet paper hadn't been easy, but he'd had few alternatives. Possession of writing paper had been banned years earlier. The daughter of a prominent U.S. Senator had suffered a painful paper cut while reading a letter. The message—sent by one her father's detractors—criticized an "Oxygen Tax" the senator had sponsored. Had the letter expressed support for the oxygen tax, the girl's paper cut might have been viewed as the price of democracy. However, opposing views were no longer tolerated in Washington, D.C.

The next morning, the indignant Demagoblican paced the Senate floor and denounced the evils of writing paper. "This product has created a public menace. Writing paper is an imminent threat to the safety of every American child," the senator wailed.

Paper-rights advocates fought the bill. "We've used writing paper safely for years. Paper is part of our heritage. You have no right to take it away," they said. As was customary, the members of any opposition group were portrayed as "nuts" and "kooks" by the Yellow Lapdog Gazette—the national newspaper—and the Demagoblican Administration Mouth Piece and Misery Exploitation Network (DAMPMEN), the nation's last cable-news network.

Within a week, President Puppet—over the objections of more than half the population—signed the measure into law.

Gun-runners and other scofflaws—concealed reams of paper bulging beneath their coats—openly defied the new law. Apparently, possession of paper was the least of their worries. Ray had tried to purchase some black-market paper from the criminals, but he quickly learned that the asking price—one thousand dollars for a single ream—was too steep.

The use of a computer had never been an option. Ray knew all about the Cyber Czar's zealous oversight of American's computers.

As if writing on toilet paper wasn't difficult enough, the absence of electricity forced Ray to do most of his work in total darkness. He had managed to keep a flashlight lit with scrounged batteries. But on many mornings, he worked with only a smudge of light to illuminate his pages.

This morning though, he thought he could see a light at the end of his tunnel. He was certain that he would finish his work. However, while he struggled to decide whether "embezzle" or "bamboozle" best described the current state of American governance, Power to the People released Watford's fair share of electricity. The flickering fluorescent lights told him that it was time to wake his sons for school.

He placed the toilet paper back inside the box and returned the container to its hiding place. *Maybe I'll finish tomorrow*, he thought. *Then I just need to find someone to publish this. If I can get my story published, maybe we can finally get out of here.*

Chapter 2

If serving in Congress *really* was an act of public service, political campaigns would have looked like ham-fisted attempts to duck jury duty instead of the well-financed brawls they'd become. Incumbents—eager to return to their *real* lives—would have emptied their war chests on bullhorns and buttons that trumpeted their *own* flaws, instead of the sins of their challengers.

Americans might have even been wary of the candidates who bowed and scraped to curry their favor. When a politician promised the moon, voters might have asked the most important question of all, "How do you plan to pay for all this?"

Citizens would have remembered that self-interested politicians posed a far-greater danger than any virus or band of neighborhood thugs. Disease or desperados might infringe upon parts of an American's life, but politicians wanted to control every moment. And members of Congress posed a special brand of peril. "We need to recast America according to *our* sensibilities," the new breed of Congress *people* seemed to imply with their actions. "Some dusty, old piece of paper doesn't mean anything to us." After all, they'd felt the lusty thrill of income redistribution, and they had no desire to go back to being ordinary *citizens*.

At the outset of an era known as the *New Dark Ages*, President Puppet—a man renowned for the ruthless streak he called upon when dealing with America's allies and citizens—ruled the land. His cranky disposition towards his *friends* came in direct opposition to the pink-marshmallow bunny of a soft spot he had for America's enemies. So while the President laid out his vision of government dominance over everything, the melody in his words landed all too sweetly upon the attentive ears in Congress.

Innovation was banned. Progress ground to a halt. Nothing moved without Demagoblican say-so.

When citizens objected to the ballooning Federal Government and its heavy-handed methods, President Puppet and Congress knew who to blame. "There's too much free-speakin' goin' on out there. How can we be expected to do our job if we can't get certain people to shut up?" a member of Congress had asked.

The Congressman's query sparked a plan. The next day, the Congressional Demagoblican Caucus (virtually every member of Congress) held a closed-door meeting. They called upon legendary spin-doctors and smooth-talkers and hoped to find a way to win over their critics. The meeting went nowhere until the first-term Senator, Charles "Magnificent" Spendini, proposed a solution. The idea harkened back to the glory days of "fill-in-the-blank" and "we'll read after we've passed it," governance. "We should pass a law that gives us the power to act in closed session whenever we debate bills that are too much for the common people to handle," Spendini suggested. "The laws we pass during those closed sessions should be kept off the books—even as they're enforced. After all, what the people don't know won't hurt them."

The gathered governors gasped. The idea's brilliant simplicity left them dazzled.

Within government circles, the *It's for Their Own Good Act* was hailed as a revolutionary means to safeguard the rights of the American people. Congress had once-and-for-all eliminated the extra-curricular influence some citizens tried to wield during the passage of unpopular laws. The law was an important legal victory for the Federal Government, but it was an even larger triumph for Spendini. He had established himself as a rising star in the only place that mattered—Washington, D.C.

Passage of the It's for Their Own Good Act launched a flurry of unpublished laws. Congress authorized undisclosed taxes, they gave themselves and their staff members generous pay increases, and they banned all activities they found disagreeable. Within the eye of that unseen, law-making hurricane, the *Eyes and Ears of Fairspeech* (EEF) was born.

Prior to the New Dark Ages, *Fair Speech Now!* had been invisible. The organization was formed by a group of community organizers who worked together to shield the defenseless Federal Government from the attacks of disgruntled Americans. Fair Speech Now! staffers wrote blogs, gave speeches and led marches denouncing anyone who dared ignore the wishes of Greta Government.

President Puppet admired Fair Speech Now! "I like their moxie," he said. "Given the right equipment and resources, they could play an important role in the new America." The off-hand remark inspired the President's Demagoblican colleagues to allocate billions of dollars to create a new Federal agency—the Eyes and Ears of Fairspeech. Congress dubbed the reconstituted Fair Speech Now! as "America's Official Fair-Speech Watchdog," and gave them a simple assignment—get the people who disagree with us to shut up—no matter what.

Congress then developed the *Community Rankings and Penalties List for the Abolition of Prohibited Free Speech.* The List, as the document became known, provided a treatise on the dangers of free speech and became the bible for EEF staff members. The List forbade offensive remarks aimed at members of protected classes, prohibited slurs uttered against people of certain races and the followers of particular religious ideologies, and banned criticism leveled against any Demagoblican in Washington, D.C.

After the List was developed, EEF technicians—also known as *cable guys*—installed surveillance equipment in the Peoples' Housing, in the few remaining businesses, and in every other inhabited nook and cranny of the United States. Once in place, those hidden cameras and microphones recorded the private activities of every man, woman and child. The recorded footage was then transmitted via encrypted cellular back to EEF headquarters. Once there, the footage was analyzed by software that had been specifically developed in order to flag those instances when Americans—according to the standards set by the List—got too free with their free speech.

Even after the development of the List and the development of the EEF's surveillance network, the free-speech crack-down still lacked *punch.* Observing speech crimes was one thing, preventing and punishing those activities was another matter altogether. The agency's first Czar howled, "The First Amendment was written to guarantee the freedom of the press. It gives *elected officials* the ability to speak without fear of reprisal. The First Amendment does not give everyday Americans and talk-radio hosts the right to say anything they want. It's not fair that they are exploiting our beloved Constitution that way," the Czar roared. He demanded that Congress let him "off his leash" and allow him to "fight a winning battle against hate speech."

After Congress opened a discussion on ways to expand their war on free speech, one of the few conservatives tried to protest. "Haven't we done enough to these people? We're already spying on them; what more do you want?"

"Wake up," Spendini hissed. "We tried to do this the nice way, but no one changed. We have no choice but to do it the hard way. You better get on board or you're on your way out."

By the time the debated ended, Congress decided that the

best answer was to give EEF a troop of thugs to use. The enforcers were intended to serve as life-coaches for any would-be seditionists and bigots. The aptly named *Teachers* not only provided a special brand of learning; they also removed any need that EEF felt to rely upon traditional law-enforcement agencies while upholding the anti-free-speech laws. The Teachers were authorized to silence and punish speech-criminals whenever and wherever necessary.

If a free-speech offender was one of the few remaining conservatives left in public office, a few doses of negative publicity in the Yellow Lapdog Gazette or via DAMPMEN—followed by a warning phone call from a Teacher—usually solved the problem. Your typical redneck, on the other hand, was likely to be assaulted outside his local bar at closing time. The next morning, he found his three missing teeth and a letter instructing him to "shut his mouth" in one of his coat pockets.

News of the Teacher's activities created the desired effect on free speech. Even the secret nature of the renamed *Eyes, Ears, and Fists of Fairspeech* (EEFF) couldn't keep word of the violent punishments from spreading. The commoners had taken to referring to the brutal thugs as *Speech Bullies*. But while no ordinary American knew exactly who authorized the string of violent beat-downs, everyone knew that they wanted to avoid the need to experience such a fate.

Chapter 3

The Eyes, Ears, and Fists of Fairspeech ensnared many ordinary Americans in their surveillance web. Unfortunately, members of Congress and staffers inside each presidential administration had their own dirty deeds to hide. That's where Agent Shawn Calder came into play.

Calder started her career at the *Department of Just Send Money (DJSM)*, formerly the United States Treasury Department. She built a reputation as a bright, young, achiever with a gift for discretion. In fact, it had been the DJSM Czar who recommended Calder for work at EEFF.

General Welfare, the EEFF Czar, was impressed with Calder immediately. Welfare knew that the woman with the bronzed skin and raven hair was destined for greatness. He'd recognized her quiet intelligence at first glance.

As the general explained the job requirements to Calder, during their initial meeting in his office at EEFF headquarters, he stressed the importance of the assignment. "You need to clean up after those in power," he growled. Then he leaned in close and stared directly into her eyes. "Make sure that every shred of evidence that depicts any sort of law-making shenanigans disappears. We can't have any of that *going viral*, now can we?"

Calder sat in stunned silence while the general invaded her personal space. She'd half expected him to end his instructions with "or else," but the general somehow avoided the B-Movie cliché. When he finished speaking, he abruptly rose from his chair, marched out of his own office, and headed for some undisclosed location at headquarters.

When Calder wasn't busy protecting the backsides of elected officials, she reviewed alleged free-speech violations like all of the other EEFF agents. The footage collected by EEFF's surveillance equipment was scanned for violations by computer. However, the process didn't end there. After a potential speech crime had been identified, a human agent reviewed the footage. The practice ensured that Demagoblican violations of the free speech laws were not prosecuted alongside the true crimes of right-wingers.

Calder rarely made time for a social life outside of work. As a result, she was still single—like most EEFF agents. Though she hoped to marry one day, she hesitated to date or even make friends outside the agency. She feared that flagged footage of a friend or lover would land on her desk wrapped in a "cracker sleeve"—the nickname given to the files of alleged bigots. She couldn't bear to face such a situation, so she kept to herself.

The case that changed her life had nothing to do with the privacy of elected officials or even a friend accused of bigotry. One of her coworkers, Agent Rachel Willis, had been assigned to monitor the activities of Buster Lafayette. Lafayette, a radio-talk-show legend, had risen to prominence following EEFF's purge of talk-radio.

The Demagoblicans had ordered the radio airwaves cleansed of any conservative presence. The politicians found the medium's capacity to inform and motivate its listeners irritating and dangerous. Once the order was given, conservative talk-show hosts—once the dominant force in the market—fell like dominos. They were subjected to bloody bouts of tutoring at the hands of the Teachers.

The one-sided battle between the Teachers and talk-radio was over quickly. However, after that battle had been won, the agency became lazy. EEFF agents left radio airwaves unattended, and Lafayette filled the void that had been left by the inattention.

Though Lafayette began his time on the air serving as a music DJ, he soon began to devote brief segments of his program to monologues that harangued Greta Government's infringements upon American freedoms. In time, he began to work interviews with conservatives into his show. The final step came when the host began to take calls from his listeners, and talk-radio was reborn.

To the aggravation of Congress and the current President, Woodward N. Mannequin, Lafayette remained on the air as the lone voice of American conservatism. Frustrated by EEFF's failures, President Mannequin demanded that the agency "give him something he could work with" in order to neutralize Lafayette's impact.

General Welfare responded by offering to assemble a montage of Lafayette's most extreme moments—all taken out of context.

"Splice his words together if you need to," Mannequin nearly shouted. "Just get it done. If we can't silence him, then we'll just have to alienate him from his audience. Then he can talk until he turns blue, and no one will even bother to listen."

Agent Willis had received the assignment and was soon buried beneath a pile of the talk-show host's surveillance footage. Seeing Willis's heavy workload, Calder offered to pick up a few of her colleague's cases, "just to help out."

Willis quickly accepted the offer, but before passing Watford's file, she grabbed Calder's wrist and said, "Don't even bother with this guy. He's just a loudmouth. He thinks he can say anything he wants and get away with it." She went on to suggest that Calder should just, "let the Teachers take care of him."

Calder glanced at Watford's surveillance record. Maybe a

quick peek would allow her to make the referral to the Teachers with a clear conscience. But after a first glance, Watford's file told her an unexpected story. *How dangerous can this guy be?* she asked herself. Then she rewound the footage to be sure she saw it correctly—*Watford's scribbling on toilet paper.*

More amused than shocked, Calder searched Watford's background. She learned that he had taken a job in local government but quickly became disillusioned. Watford thought he had been doing a public service until he saw how local government worked. The most deflating revelation was the thirst the locals showed for the Federal Government's money. The passion for that *free money* ran so hot, Ray almost expected to stumble across the county's commissioners dancing around a caldron while repeatedly chanting, "Maximize Federal revenue! Maximize Federal revenue!"

Calder felt Watford's pain. The Federal Government—and its elephantine budget—was the pot of gold at the end of every government agency's rainbow. While virtually every city, county, and state government had to balance its expenses against its revenues at the end of the year—no such rule applied to Congress. Its members could borrow, tax, and print money to finance their schemes. The arrangement ensured that Federal money flowed like water from Washington to Maine. Everyone knew, but no one dared criticize.

Though Calder might have sympathized with Watford, she still had a job to do. *What could he have written that is so damaging?* she asked herself. She'd seen nothing in her background check that resembled hate-speech. So she decided that Willis's statement had been nothing more than hyperbole.

Had she been able to see the future, Calder would have turned off the footage of Watford's case *before* she completed her case-closure report. But she didn't. Allowing the tape to run proved to be a mistake. While the images of Watford flickered across her monitor, she heard him announce, "I'm nearly done with my book."

The statement immediately caught Calder's attention. She didn't think he'd been writing a book. She had no choice but to watch.

"Really?" Sarah asked. "I'm proud of you for seeing that through. Can I read it?"

"No. I'd like you to be surprised when I get it published," Watford said. He flashed his crossed fingers at her and smiled.

"At least tell me what it's about," she prodded.

"It's just some thoughts about how America is headed in the wrong direction," he replied before a wide grin creased his face.

Calder grimaced. She rewound the footage. *Please show me that I misheard him.*

"—about how America is headed in the wrong direction," Watford repeated.

"Shit," Calder muttered. Her hands were tied. Watford had just committed secular blasphemy—suggesting that America was not all that it could be under Demagoblican leadership. The crime required immediate referral to the Teachers. *What am I going to do now?* she asked herself. *Why didn't I close his file sooner?*

Chapter 4

Austin and Justin Watford ate watery *oatmeal* with triple-skimmed milk for breakfast. The boys were both tall for their ages, but neither had any meat on his bones. Food just wasn't plentiful in the new America. Only their father's job with Compassion County allowed the family its access to foods like oat-grind. A blend of finely-shredded oats and equally-fine bits of oat husk, oat-grind provided a satisfying yet nutrition-bare rendition of traditional oatmeal when it was mixed with hot water.

Ray counted his blessings while his sons choked down the meal. The closest some other families came to real grain were the government-issued grain cakes. Grain cakes were grain in name only. Made from equal parts corn husk and wheat chaff, the *cakes* were thin, pressed disks. The crunchy food filled an empty stomach but offered little nutrition. On the bright side, the fiber content made one regular.

Both of the boys finished their meal by swallowing a vitamin. The tablets were dietary staples for all but the children of elected officials. While Ray watched his sons eat, he remembered his own childhood. American farmers had been among the most productive in the world back then. As a boy, Ray had loved to eat fire-roasted corn in the fall. On cold mornings, he braced himself with a steaming bowl of *real* oatmeal. Baked potatoes and roasted meats, salads with fresh cucumbers, lettuce and tomatoes; even exotic fruits like bananas and oranges had once been available for over-the-counter purchase in grocery stores. But that was all before the environ-mania and the rush to biofuels.

Ray never understood the celebration of Ethyl-Noleo. The
energy additive—made from corn but which tasted like butter—
could have *rightfully* been called miraculous if scientists had
taken landfill waste, lawn clippings, fallen leaves, or discarded
potato peelings and created a source of fuel. But that wasn't
the case. Scientists took two items necessary for survival—food
and water—and used those consumables to create an inedible
substance. *Even a dunce could recognize the foolishness of a plan
that used food to make poison. Why won't the Federal Government
allow the vast stores of inedible oil to be tapped to make fuel? Instead,
they insist upon wasting corn and sacrificing the chance to produce
soybeans and other grains to*—Watford shook his head and cleared
away his mental critique of American energy folly and asked, "Are
you boys ready?"

Then all three of them grabbed a carbon-dioxide-scrubbing
mask from the shelf by the back door. The masks—a mandatory
accessory for anyone who ventured outdoors—functioned like
the rebreather apparatus used by scuba divers. However, instead of
carrying a tank of compressed gas—that would have been crazy—
people inhaled regular air. The rebreather simply scrubbed the
poisonous carbon dioxide that humans exhaled before the toxins
were released into the environment. "The environment is for
looking, not for touching," the Federal Government's *Pristine
Air Campaign* had suggested. "Let's leave the earth *better* than we
found it." In addition to requiring the use of the scrubbers for
humans, the environmental campaign mandated the use of feline,
canine, and bovine rebreather devices.

Once each of them had donned his own scrubber, Ray opened
the back door and peeked outside. He needed to ensure that none
of his neighbors were about. He couldn't risk having anyone see
him as he walked his sons to the school bus. Confirming that the

coast was clear, Ray ushered the boys out the door.

The three of them walked quickly across the patch of dirt that had once been a lawn. Grass simply couldn't survive the relative drought and perpetual shade caused by the solar panels above the yard. When the Watfords reached the alley, they turned left and walked north for a few blocks until they found an open garage door. The trio stepped through the doorway into the darkened space.

Inside sat a rusted Peoples'-wagon van. The vehicle's windows were tinted and its back door stood open. Ray hugged and kissed both of his sons and then he told them that he loved them. Then he watched the boys climb into the back of the make-shift school bus. Stifled laughter trickled out of the vehicle as the Watford boys greeted their friends and buckled in for the short ride to school.

The Congressional ban on private and charter schools had driven some parents, like the Watfords, to form illegal, underground schools. Schools sanctioned by the Federal Government bore a stronger resemblance to Demagoblican indoctrination camps than to educational institutions. The para-educational institutions had been the only recourse for parents who hated the idea of deprogramming their children each day after school.

Ray waved as the rusty van backed out of the garage, turned right, and sped down the street. He considered walking home to finish his novel before work. He quickly rejected the idea. If he arrived at work early today, he could take time to deliver his novel to Kerwin Publishing tomorrow. Besides, he reassured himself, *it's not like anyone's going to find my story.*

Chapter 5

A message was painted on a sign that hung above the door to every EEFF Teacher's lounge. The quotation told people everything they needed to know about the men and women who lurked inside the dingy, poorly-lit room that always smelled of stale coffee and cigarette smoke. "Citizens of enlightened nations stand ready to sacrifice liberty to achieve equality. Our duty is to ensure that those sacrifices are made," the sign read. The quote had come from Handley Puppet's inaugural address and served as EEFF's motto.

In spite of the grand proclamation, many of the Teachers would have quickly admitted that they enjoyed inflicting pain upon others, if they'd been asked to share the *real* reason they joined the force.

Calder cringed at the thought of EEFF's *pet gorillas* smashing down Watford's door and then hauling him away. She had seen the blood stains that the janitors couldn't *or wouldn't* scrub off the floors in the basement interrogation cells.

While she walked to her cubicle, she massaged the base of her neck. She always seemed to carry her stress there. *I have to refer Watford to the Teachers,* she told herself. *It's my career if I don't.* When she reached her cubicle, she began to pace within the tiny space.

But the Teachers will kill him. I don't want that on my conscience. Why did I agree to take this case? she asked herself. She wished she could go back in time.

EEFF's field offices were designed with watching in mind.

Once you made it inside the heavily-guarded and improbably thick, concrete walls, you were afforded all the privacy you could expect in a well-lit glass house. Institutionally-white tile floors glistened like the melting polar ice caps. Spotless glass walls shined with magnificent clarity.

The see-through construction of EEFF's accommodations served two purposes. First, the glass walls allowed for easy supervision of the agency's employees. The agents were supervised by Agent Watchers. The Agent Watchers were monitored by Agent Watcher Watchers, who were in turn watched by Watchers of their own. And the eye in the sky—well, everyone knows that story. The system of supervision not only ensured that all EEFF staff received an overdose of oversight; the arrangement also swelled the ranks of the Federal Government workers union. And to Calder, it felt like every eye in the Puppetgrad field office was focused on *her.*

All I need to do is refer Watford to the Teachers, she told herself. *Go grab the form, and it will all be over.* Then she left her cubicle and trudged down the corridor. In the distance loomed a towering set of shelves. The shelves held tall piles of paperwork. Calder grimaced as she slid a single *Remedial Education for Bigots, Obstructionists, Haters, and Seditionists* (REFBO) Form from the stack. *I hope the Teachers don't hurt him too badly,* she told herself.

As she plodded towards her desk, she couldn't keep from blaming herself for Watford's fate. She knitted her fingers together and squeezed hard. She wanted the pain to purge the guilt she felt. *Protocol demands that I inform the Teachers about Watford's activities. I've flagged lesser violations without giving the offenders a second thought.*

Then why haven't you turned him over yet? she countered

during the solitary tête-à-tête.

He reminds me of Dad, she finally admitted. She had tried to deny the feelings, but couldn't. And though she knew it was a mistake, she decided what she *had* to do.

She crumpled the REFBO form and held it within her clenched fist. *I need to see what he wrote, and I need to see it today,* she told herself. Every minute was critical. She couldn't afford to have the novel discovered by anyone else.

She hurried back to her desk, took a deep breath to steady her nerves, and made a phone call.

Chapter 6

Standing outside the back door of Watfords' PHU, Calder waited while one of EEFF's cable guys worked to open the lock. Calder's nerves were already frayed, and waiting out in the open didn't help calm her. *What's taking him so long? Open the damn door already!* Calder wanted to shout as Mitch, or Rich, or whatever his name was fished in his pants pockets. *Quit playing with yourself, and get that door open!*

Squeezed tightly under each arm, Calder held an inflatable doll. The dolls—both male in form—were camouflage. The idea was that Calder and her cable-guy companion appear to be the Watford family. The dolls had been the cable guy's idea. He said that the dolls had saved him from curious neighbors more than once.

Calder slowly glanced to her left and then to her right. She scanned for any signs of activity along the block. She told the cable guy that she needed his help to investigate a hate-speech emergency. If Rich—or maybe it was Mitch—had known Calder's true motives, he might have referred *her* to the Teachers.

Calder was surprised by the number of empty lots along the block. The Welcome Home Act had created *equal* access to housing. Unfortunately, that access was equally terrible—unless you were an elected official.

Members of Congress—both current and former—and their staffs and other highly-placed Federal Government officials were exempted from the Welcome Home Act. The exception was said to be a matter of national security. "We can't have our elected officials moving around like a bunch of nomads. Now can we?" the Housing Czar had replied when he was asked to justify the preferential treatment the law afforded some.

The current state of the neighborhood clearly illustrated that the equitable dispersal of housing wasn't the only consequence of the Welcome Home Act. By the end of each lottery cycle, a significant proportion of the PHUs had been damaged beyond repair and had to be leveled. Too many of the lucky lottery winners left their prize unfit for habitation as they departed. And the cash-starved Federal Government—which had essentially stolen the homes in the first place—had no money to replace the destroyed housing. The left side of Watford's block looked more like a gap-toothed smile than a thriving neighborhood. Two or three lots in a row sat empty. The once-present homes demolished.

"Do you see anyone?" the cable guy whispered, jolting Calder back to reality. He'd finally found his PHU master key and was ready to open the door.

"Clear," Calder replied.

"Equality before liberty," he whispered as he pushed the door open and ushered Caldwell inside.

"Residents and visitors: Be advised that there is no smoking inside the Peoples' Housing. If you *must* smoke, please feel free to go to the nearest smoking reservation. It is located in southern Ontario, Canada." It was Greta Government again. "Be advised that the Housing Lottery occurs in seventeen weeks. Ensure that your belongings are fully packed on lottery day to ensure a smooth transition for the new occupants. Equality before Liberty."

I wonder if the Greta talks just to hear her own voice when no one is home, Calder wondered. She strode through the kitchen and down the hallway.

The cable guy craned his neck and peered at her. "You need

to be quick," he whispered. "We haven't tracked these people's schedules. They could come home any minute. And I'm already on probation after I bungled my last insertion."

The cable guy reached into his pocket and pulled out an egg-shaped device. He jammed his thumb onto the machine's activation button. The silver egg began to blink and emitted enough magnetic distortion to disable the surveillance equipment. While Calder's activities were technically legal, the agency worked hard to ensure that no one learned about these break-ins. The people would have been outraged if they knew about the government's snooping.

As she neared the bathroom, Caldwell paused to admire a photo that hung in the hallway. The framed picture showed a smiling Watford family, presumably while on vacation. Because she had lost her own parents, seeing the photos of Watford and his family only made her feel even more isolated.

It had been years since Calder had seen her parents. They had been traveling home from church when Calder's father accidentally turned his tiny electric/hydrogen/helium-balloon/foot-powered car in front of a pack of hostile bicyclists. "God's Favorite People," the name the environ-maniac bicycle-gang members had given themselves, bellowed, "Share the road!" as they bored down upon the floundering Mr. Calder. The frightened motorist's feet frantically slapped the pavement as he struggled to avoid the speeding peloton. Unfortunately, he just wasn't quick enough.

While all of the cyclists escaped injury, neither Mr. nor Mrs. Calder was so lucky. Their auto provided egg-like resistance to the onslaught of the fast moving bicycles. The crush of environmentally-friendly tires flattened the flimsy, tinfoil-and-tape-vehicle like it was a pan of stove-top popping-corn.

Tears filled Calder's eyes at the memory. She wanted to run

from the house and find somewhere to weep. She didn't want to feel alone anymore. In her moment of loneliness, she considered using EEFF's network of surveillance capabilities to locate her brother. *I wonder where he—*

"C'mon, Calder, you need to get moving," the cable guy hissed, pulling her back to reality. "The housing is empty. I'm going to wait in the van. If these people come home, be ready to get out fast. You got it?" he said before he made his way outside.

Calder stepped into the bathroom and found the box that contained Watford's novel. She grimaced as she pulled the first roll of toilet paper from the box and read the novel's title. Suddenly the room began to feel hot. Sweat beaded and then trickled down her forehead and cheeks. She pulled a portable scanner from her work bag and began to gently drag its infrared image reader along the unrolled toilet-paper.

The scanner, which had been programmed to flag prohibited free-speech, wailed like a teething baby. Each time a banned word or phrase appeared on the paper, the scanner erupted with a piercing squeal. By the end of the first roll, the scanner had flagged more than two hundred instances that should have triggered a visit from the Teachers.

Calder hadn't heard a scanner behave this way since she reviewed transcripts from the Reagan administration. Disbelieving the machine, she peeked at the text while she rerolled the paper. What she saw made her drop the one-ply sheets like they were on fire.

In the Hall (Reflections on America)

Chapter 1

First, some history. You could rightfully call me a genius if I could identify the exact moment the American Dream turned into a nightmare. Maybe it was the New Deal or the Great Society. The shot heard 'round the world might have triggered the end of the American experiment. After all, you know what's been said about voting oneself bread and circuses.

I encourage you to search for the answer. While you retrace America's steps, ask yourself how a nation that possessed her strengths could have been transformed from world leader to banana republic.

"Banana republic?" That's sedition, some might say. However, the teevee and the "news" papers have been telling the story their way for a long time. No one has said anything about them.

Regardless of the path that brought America to this point, the nation has been headed downhill for years. Americans somehow misplaced their ability to tell shit from shinola. As a nation, we began to suffer self-inflicted wounds each time we stepped inside our voting booths.

When Handley Puppet stepped behind the bully pulpit, the Fourth Estate—which was already on wobbly legs—took a dive straightaway. They didn't even give us the satisfaction of seeing a punch graze their chin. The peoples' watchdog wagged its tail and became the government's lap dog. And presto, the faux-news industry was born.

Reporters became so invested in the success of President Puppet, they didn't hesitate to hand their customers a pile of dog shit and then claim that the mess was *really* a slice of chocolate cake.

The Founding Fathers—those visionaries who saw fit to include the First Amendment as a safeguard against government influence on the press—must have been doing circus flips in their graves. The institution they specifically protected surrendered its objectivity and made matters worse by trying to disguise their allegiances.

Tin-pot dictators around the world must have looked on in envy, calculating the time and expense they incurred to impose censorship. Meanwhile some upstart in a democracy was able to get the same benefit for free. "I'd impose democracy in a minute if I thought my reporters would give me the American treatment," one dictator was quoted as saying.

For years, the FauxPublican Party provided a backstop against the fascination progressives held for collectivism. FauxPublicans seemed to realize that the world needed a strong and capitalist America. The world already had a Germany, a France, and a Sweden; it didn't need another. And no one benefitted from seeing the

American economic engine dismantled in favor of a welfare-driven mule and plow.

At one time, the FauxPublican Party even ran interference for those Americans who worked hard to improve their lives. Everyone in America benefitted from the protections, whether they knew it or not.

Unfortunately, as the era of Santa-Clausian politics reached full speed, members of Congress created policies that allowed more and more idle hands to claim the harvest of fewer and fewer productive workers. As the years passed, it became clear that too many FauxPublicans believed that the best way to stay in office was to act like their Demagogue Party counterparts. These FauxPublicans ran with the wolves during elections but bunked-in with the sheep when they reached Washington.

Conservatives finally decided they'd had enough. They left the flock to form a party of their own—a Brand New Party.

The FauxPublicans and Demagogues were thrilled to watch conservatives go their own way. For a while after the departure of conservatives, the two major parties maintained the illusion of separate identities. But each day, FauxPublicans and Demagogues looked more and more like a pair of bumbling twins.

FauxPublicans and Demagogues forged an unprecedented brand of legislative cooperation. Bipartisanship came to mean sweeping socialist

changes proposed by Demagogue politicians
and cosmetic tinkering by the sound-alike
FauxPublicans.

It had sounded so momentous when the
FauxPublican and Demagogue party chieftains
appeared on DAMPMEN to announce that they
were burying their gridlock-inducing hatchets.
Tears flowed and the two party heads vowed
to mend fences. However, as Americans soon
learned, the close alignment of the two major
parties ensured only one thing—the smooth
and unchecked growth of government.

Calder couldn't believe what she had read. EEFF Protocol
clearly addressed situations like this. "Possession of seditious
material is a crime. Any agent who comes across such material
must confiscate said material and arrest without Mirandization
any person suspected of seditious behavior or aiding and abetting
seditious behavior." She repeated the text of the EEFF training
manual aloud.

The other rolls in the box didn't get any better. The scanner's
wailing continued through the final roll. When she had finished
scanning, Calder knew that the moment the images reached
EEFF headquarters, someone would immediately issue an order
for Watford's remedial education. He'd be in the hands of the
Teachers before she even made it back to the field office. And
she'd be lucky to escape disciplinary action for failing to report the
infractions sooner.

Sweat poured down her forehead as she slumped to the floor.
She wanted a cigarette. All along, she'd known what EEFF protocol
demanded, but she couldn't bring herself to follow orders. From

the moment she discovered Watford, she knew she could never report what she found.

As a child, Calder sat beside her father while he talked about Ronald Reagan, the Constitution, and the Founding Fathers. The elder Calder preached the value of hard work and the preciousness of liberty. She knew she could no more betray those ideals than she could betray her father.

Instead of transmitting the images in the scanner's memory, Calder pulled the memory card from the scanner and dropped it into her pocket. Then she found a blank memory card and slipped it into the scanner. After making the switch, she laid the scanner on the bathroom floor and smashed the heel of her boot into the device's processor. The machine's lights flickered and then went dark.

She stared at the pieces of plastic and metal that littered the bathroom floor. She'd just jeopardized her career and probably put her life in danger. She planned to tell the technicians at the field office that she accidentally the dropped machine. She hoped they would buy her story.

Before leaving the bathroom, Calder reached into her pocket and pulled out a sheet of paper. She quickly scribbled a note and slipped it into the cardboard box on top of Watford's novel.

Chapter 7

Senator Charles "Magnificent" Spendini drummed his pen on the surface of his cherry-wood desk. The desk's prior owner had said the antique had been fashioned from the same tree cut down by George Washington. Spendini was fond of telling his guests that Washington's decision to cut down the tree only demonstrated just how out-of-touch the nation's first president had been. "Maybe if old Georgie had been a little more disciplined and a tiny bit tougher on his pals, the world wouldn't be facing imminent disaster." Like most progressives, Spendini's favorite pastime was confessing other people's sins.

But George Washington was the last person on Spendini's mind at the moment. He sat—his telephone receiver jammed into his ear hard enough to make it hurt. On a normal day, Spendini's calendar was packed full enough to make an air-traffic controller at LaGuardia sweat. It had not been a normal day, and it was far from over.

The senator had learned early that most people hated listening to boring facts. They wanted their heart strings pulled. Hoping to capitalize on the trait, Spendini studied with legendary propagandists in Hollywood and the master European mind-benders and learned to distort and conceal the truth with smoke screens and straw men. It had been Spendini who dispelled the accurate image of America's shattered fiscal piggy bank. Into poor piggy's place, Spendini inserted the dubious notion that American retirement funds were kept within a sturdy lock-box.

Spendini knew that if taxpayers ever examined the lock-box, they'd quickly realize that they had been fleeced. The whole system seemed more like the greatest Ponzi scheme in history than responsible governance. But Spendini and his colleagues never allowed the masses to look behind the curtain. He made sure to deflect the blame onto others—bankers, the fossil fuel industry, drug companies, and grocery stores that didn't stock arugula. He made sure that every time the people went looking for a villain, they were always looking in some other direction.

The roguishly handsome senator currently served as Senate Majority Leader. And though it was late in the evening, he was still doing the peoples' work. He rubbed his square jaw and then pulled a mirror from his desk drawer. He needed to check the state of his hair. For years now, he had worn his hair in the standard issue Congressional style—a full head of hair parted along the side. He took a moment to admire the perfect salt and pepper blend he'd struck. Though with Spendini, it was impossible to determine whether his mostly silver hair had been highlighted with black to make him appear younger or if his black hair had been laced with silver to make him appear wiser. Only Spendini and his hair dresser knew for sure.

At the moment, Spendini and his hair were waiting for Arthur Banks to pick up his telephone. Banks had served as a career bureaucrat at the DJSM. And when the DJSM staffer finally picked up the call, Spendini wasted no time before berating Banks for his inability to "grab the damned phone."

Banks stammered an apology and then tried to change the subject. He had never been an ambitious man, but he knew how to follow instructions. He had a pudgy middle, a graying patch of hair that circled the sides of his bald head, and a forgettable face. And he'd been well-compensated for the years he spent overseeing special projects—projects like the one Spendini had called to discuss.

"Where are we with the *Hand?*" Spendini demanded. The Hand was an abbreviated reference to the Hand of Equity—a device designed to increase the Federal Government's cash flow, among other things.

The Hand had been Spendini's brainchild, but the system was developed inside DJSM. The cigar-box-sized machines and the supporting network of servers allowed DJSM to process every transaction made in every American store, restaurant, and service location—right down to garage sales and lemonade stands.

Consumers made purchases like they always had. However, there was one important twist—the Hand required the purchaser to provide his tax identification number when making purchases. The buyer's number was then checked by computers at DJSM. If the buyer was wealthy, the sales tax rate climbed proportionately. If the buyer was poor, he was spared the injustice of being taxed. The network of machines allowed for a progressive taxation system that would have made Karl Marx proud. The Hand also allowed DJSM to collect its tax revenue the moment the transaction occurred.

"The Hand is ready to go, Senator," Banks told Spendini. "We've been running tests for six months now, simulating up to 8 million transactions per second, and things have gone perfectly. Frankly, I'm quite surprised. The Federal Government doesn't have a stellar track record of producing quality goods and services. Look at how long it takes to get a passport. And I've heard there are some dealerships waiting on payments from the cash for—"

"Shut up!" Spendini shouted. "I'm glad to hear things are working," Spendini said after taking a moment to calm down. Spendini had gone great lengths to ensure Banks's complete cooperation. The senator possessed a set of color photos that showed Banks engaged in various sex acts with three members of the Baltimore Bureaucrats cheer squad.

Bagging three of the cheerleaders wasn't the achievement it had once been. Instead of being part of something sexy like a professional football league, the Bureaucrats were part of the only sports league that had not been banned by the Federal Government—*The National Dialoguing, Consensus Building, and Victimhood Validation League.* To make matters worse, the members of the Bureaucrat's cheer squad weren't the smoking-hot, young women of the past. Attractive cheerleaders had also been banned. Critics stated the practice of finding women who were pleasant to look at was sexist. As a result, the Lap-Sitters—as the Bureaucrats cheerleaders were named—consisted of a stable of wrinkled, whiney, minimally-bathed, patchouli-oil-stinking former hippies, who ended every cheer routine with, "…, man."

And though the four-way depicted by the photos never took place, the evidence would have been sufficient to destroy Banks's marriage. Since Banks's wife, Mildred, controlled the couple's checkbook, allegations of infidelity would have left the bureaucrat divorced and penniless. The arrangement left Banks eager to do anything Spendini asked of him.

"Are *all* the functions ready?" Spendini asked.

"Do you mean *the Bank Balance Juggler,* sir?" Banks had seen the feature listed on the Hand's function list.

"What have you heard about it?" Spendini inquired.

"I don't know anything about it specifically. Kugler just said that *everything* was ready. He said all he needed was the green light to flip any of it on."

"That's good news, Arthur. You've really come through for us. The President is going to need this money if he's going to create the three million new jobs he promised. You are authorized to roll out the Hand immediately, but remember, all of the other functions beyond basic transaction processing are beyond your security clearance. Is that clear?"

"Understood ...Sir?" Banks paused for a moment. "Do you have time for one more thing?"

"Sure, but make it quick," Spendini replied, conveying more than a hint of his irritation.

"I received a burst transmission from EEFF," Banks began. "Actually the message originated from a field scanner used by one of EEFF's agents. The signal was an anti-tampering feature installed to keep field agents from withholding evidence."

"I see," Spendini said, even though he really didn't. "And the nature of this transmission?"

"The message was garbled, but I'm worried that we might have a field agent who has tried to conceal evidence."

"Do we have any idea what the agent was doing with his scanner?"

"Well, the agent was a woman, sir. Her name is Shawn Calder. And, no, we don't know what she was investigating. EEFF has software that can piece together garbled transmissions. I'm sure they'll conduct their own investigation."

"If this is an EEFF issue, why are you involved? And why should I care?"

"When EEFF was founded, President Puppet wanted to make sure that someone was keeping an eye on them. One of the President's aides asked DJSM to create the software that runs EEFF's portable scanners. We created a parallel-burst-transmission-function for the scanners—one burst alerts EEFF and the other comes to DJSM. EEFF doesn't know it, but it's our job to keep an eye on them."

"I see," Spendini said while he furrowed his brow. Being kept out of this loop displeased him.

"It's a realistic possibility that Caldwell destroyed her scanner to cover up seditious material."

The words grabbed Spendini's attention. In addition to serving as Senate Majority Leader, Spendini also chaired the Prohibited-Speech Oversight Committee. Spendini scowled at the idea of an EEFF agent—a guardian of free speech—hiding a seditionist. "You know how I feel about hate speech, Banks. Keep me posted. If this Calder is harboring a seditionist, I want both of their heads on a plate."

Chapter 8

President Woodward N. Mannequin and his top economic advisor, Nathan Chubbs, sat side-by-side on the Oval Office's sofa. As part of the outlandish makeover of the American government, President Puppet had authorized both the *Bailout Bonanza* and the *Succession of Stimulating Stimuli*. Mannequin wanted a similar achievement as part of his legacy.

The President and his advisor had sequestered themselves in the Oval Office for a long night of economic stimulation. President Mannequin drummed his fingers on the arm of the sofa. "Why didn't I promise to create 50 new jobs instead of three million?" he asked with the whine of a young boy who didn't want to finish his supper.

"How many jobs do we have so far, Mr. President?" Chubbs asked.

"With the presidential waste basket technician, we have eight jobs," Mannequin replied. He scratched the side of his head. He'd never run a business or created a real job in his life. *How do business people do this?* he silently wondered. *I'm smarter than they are. This should be so easy*—Mannequin's thought was cut off by his ringing telephone. He was relieved to have the interruption. The White House switchboard operator announced that Senator Spendini waited on the line. Mannequin turned and mouthed the words, "I really have to take this," towards Chubbs.

"Good evening, Magnificent," the President said after he snatched the handset from its cradle. As President, Mannequin was one of the few people who could address Spendini by his nickname. Mannequin did so to remind the ambitious senator which of them was boss.

"Hello, Mr. President. I hope I didn't interrupt."

"Of course not, I always have time for you."

"I'm going to need you to go on television tomorrow, sir. I've given the Department of Just Send Money permission to roll out a new transaction-processing machine. The device is called the Hand of Equity, and it allows us to instantly collect sales tax whenever there is a sale. This will really help our cash flow."

Mannequin's eyes grew large at the news. He began to hop from one foot to the other. "Oh, goody," he said.

Spendini cleared his throat. "*Uh*—yes. Goody indeed, Mr. President. We really need this money—especially if you want to keep your promise on those jobs. Our ability to deliver on your promise will play a big role in the election, sir."

President Mannequin had never seen a dollar he didn't want to spend. He listened intently while Spendini explained the Hand's roll-out. "I'm in favor of anything that will help us generate more tax revenue, Magnificent. You know that. But why don't we just borrow the money to fund the job creation?"

"It's a complicated situation, sir. I wouldn't want to bore you with the details."

"Bore me, Spendini. I want the truth," Mannequin demanded—his demeanor suddenly icy.

"We're broke, sir."

"I know that. We've been broke for years. I get the concept of deficit spending—I used to work in Congress too."

"What I mean to say, Mr. President, is that in the past we *were* able to borrow money. But now, no one will buy our debt—" Spendini didn't even want to say what came next, "at any interest rate, sir. We've lost our ability to borrow money."

"Oh, crap," the President whispered.

"That sums it up, sir. That's why we need to implement the Hand now." Had Spendini told the complete truth, he would have mentioned another reason for the urgent activation of the system. However, that matter was none of the President's concern.

The Hand was Spendini's trump card, but it wasn't the only issue on the Senator's mind at the moment. "Time for one more thing, Mr. President?" he asked.

"Make it quick; I have a long night ahead," Mannequin grumped.

"DJSM informed me that EEFF might have a scandal brewing. One of their agents might have tried to bury some evidence in a hate-speech case," Spendini stated.

"I thought we got rid of all of those rednecks," Mannequin said with a chuckle. He hoped the laugh covered the jolt of fear he'd felt. He had no desire to fight off a surge of conservatism. "Do you have any details?"

"No one is certain what happened, sir."

Mannequin sighed loudly to show his displeasure. He needed facts, not excuses.

"EEFF is investigating, sir, but if they even get a sense that this is a conservative conspiracy, they will crush it, regardless of whether or not they find any evidence," Spendini reassured.

"I'm glad to hear that. Silence the traitors as soon as possible. I don't want to spend my last few months in office fending off a bunch of nut-jobs. I want to go golfing. And I have my legacy to consider. You want to protect my legacy, don't you, Magnificent?" The President didn't wait for Spendini to respond. He hung up the phone and turned back to Chubbs.

"Sounded important," Chubbs said, hoping for a morsel of the inside information that sometimes only presidents hear.

"You know, Chubbs, there are some days when I'd like to feed Spendini to a pack of wild dogs. But at times like this, he's worth his weight in carbon-credits."

"The call was that big, huh?"

The President nodded but offered no details. "But on the bright side, I think Spendini just gave me an idea. What about a presidential dog feeder?" Mannequin beamed with pride knowing that he'd created his first job.

"I think you're onto something, sir. And since you have both a dog and a cat, you could have a presidential feeder for both pets."

"Even better," Mannequin said. His eyes began to glisten as his enthusiasm grew. "We could have presidential dog and cat groomers. We could even have presidential dog and cat outdoor-business technicians. What do you think?"

"It's great for the dog, but the cat uses a litter box, sir."

"So we tell people we have a housebroken cat. The News Bureau can spin the story, and we'll be fine," the President said with a dismissive wave of his hand. "And we'll need backups for all the presidential pet-technicians in case the *actual* technicians call in sick or go on vacation. It's not like *I'm* going to put the dog outside," Mannequin said as he reached for a calculator. "We'll have to pay these new Federal employees a quarter-million a year—we need to pay a living wage after all."

"Two hundred fifty thousand dollars per job will add up fast, sir," Chubbs cautioned.

"So it's a few billion dollars; no one will even notice."

"If we create three million jobs, that adds up to seven hundred fifty billion, sir. That's not chicken feed, Mr. President."

The President paused. Clearly he was busy weighing the costs and benefits of spending so much money on a host of phony jobs.

"You raise a good point," he said. "We could get some chickens for the back yard and then hire presidential chicken-technicians."

Chubbs grinned like it was ~~Christmas morning~~ winter break. "I like your style, Mr. President."

"I never realized job creation would be this much fun," the President said. Clearly his enthusiasm had bubbled over. "If I'd known this was so rewarding, I would have started creating jobs years ago." Mannequin then jumped up from the sofa and began to run around the Oval office shouting, "*Whoo! Whoo!* The Job Creation Express is on the tracks!" He punctuated his statement by pulling on an imaginary train-whistle's cord and then saying, "only two million nine hundred thousand nine hundred jobs left."

"Let's keep working, sir," Chubbs chimed. "We've got an economy to save!"

Chapter 9

The Undersecretary to the Secretary of the Press Secretary's Undersecretary's Secretary strode to the podium to announce the start of the presidential news conference. "Ladies and gentlemen, the President of the United States—"

The overhead lights in the press room suddenly went dark. A spotlight illuminated President Mannequin. He was descending from the rafters, like the man-god American Presidents had become. The stage went dark again.

A moment later, the spotlight revealed Mannequin standing at center-stage, dressed in a purple, sequined jumpsuit that shone like the sun. A microphone stood in front of him. The President shot the audience a roguish glance over the dark sunglasses that covered his eyes. He pushed the microphone stand to the left, caught the stand with his foot, kicked it upright and caught it in his hand again. He yanked the microphone from the stand and began to sing his *Presidential Anthem*.

Stop. Look.
Drop your pants now.
Reach down.
And grab your feet.
Re-lax.
Here comes the big one.
Trust me.
Won't hurt too much.

'Cuz I know betta than U do.
I know betta than U.
I know betta than U do.
I know betta than U.

Reach in.
Dig out your wal-let.
Reach out.
Pass it to me.
Bend down.
And grab your ankles.
Wor-ried?
Don't—You can trust me.

I know betta than you do.
I know betta than U.
I know betta than U do.
I know betta than U.

Click. Click.
Pull that belt tighter.
Your stuff?
Don't be absurd.
Tough times?
You'll make the sacrifice.
Think not?
Oh, yes U will.

'Cuz I know betta than U do.
I know betta than U.
I know betta than U do.
I know betta than U.

Vote me out?
Too late for that, pal.
Ice pack.
Soothes that sore butt.
Your stuff?
What U a dinosaur?
Tyranny?
Oh, no, no, no.

'Cuz I know betta than U do.
I know betta than U.
I know betta than U do.
I know betta than U.

And in the end it goes like this—
You might not like me,
But you'll respect me.
Or you will see the depth of my resolve.

You'd best become your brother's keeper,
If you expect to have any future.
In the newly-remade U-S-of-A

So all you filthy red state rednecks—
And you hairy northern mucklucks—
If you think you're gonna stand in my way—

You'd best forget your guns and bibles.
Cancel all of them there revivals.
'Cuz, I-I-I-I-I-I-I-I-I-I
Knoooooooow

Bettaaaaaaa
Than
UUUUUUUUUUU.
Yeah!

At the end of the song, the President thrust his fist into the air and drank in thunderous applause. The assembled members of the Federal Government News Bureau (FGNB) loved *their* president.

Across America, the streets had emptied and businesses had fallen more silent than usual. Both citizens and undocumented illegals (*or friends we have not yet met,* in Greta Government's parlance) had engaged in another of their patriotic duties. Watching the President perform his anthem and then share his profound observations was *required* for everyone living on American soil.

The audience then watched Mannequin catch the rainbow-colored towel that had been tossed to him by a roadie backstage. While the President dabbed sweat from his face, he sauntered over to the podium. He adjusted the microphone and whispered a breathy "Thank you."

The podium bore the redesigned Presidential Seal. The eagle at the center had been replaced by four monkeys on a rainbow field. The first monkey—hands pressed down over its eyes—symbolized the Administration's level of willingness to examine the accumulated evidence debunking their failed policies. The second monkey had been depicted with its hands covering its ears. That simian symbolized the President's willingness to hear critiques of his policies. The third monkey—hands positioned over its mouth—illustrated the White House's approach when it came to acknowledging its shortcomings. The final monkey had its hand outstretched. A cartoon bubble above its head read, "Just send money."

The arrows and olive branches had also been replaced—a hammer and a scythe were substituted. The President considered using a hammer and sickle but chose the scythe instead. "The scythe's handle gives it a longer reach," he said. In retrospect, the distinction seemed appropriate.

American *and* Mexican flags waved in the seal's background. The inclusion of a foreign flag seemed an odd choice at first. But the President's policies provided a narrative that adequately explained the decision.

As Mannequin toweled off, he'd even stepped around to the front of the podium to admire his seal. Then, as had become his habit, he turned and gazed up at the mural of President Puppet. The enormous painting watched over the proceedings from high atop the wall. The mural's creator depicted the legendary President seated atop a cloud—his benevolent hand of mercy extended downward towards an adoring throng of supplicants. The finished product was enough to make tin-pot dictators weep with envy.

Mannequin smiled at the image. He hoped that one day he would be remembered with similar adoration. He owed much to President Puppet. *But this is my time,* Mannequin said to himself. *Let's do this.*

"My fellow Americans and my friends from south of the border," Mannequin began. "We are facing yet another crisis. Our capacity for justice will be tested. And success will be our reward if everyone does his fair share." Mannequin folded his hands as if in prayer. "Better presidents before me tried to undo the devastation wrought by former President DeVille and his bandits. President Puppet tried, but neither the Bailout Bonanza nor the Succession of Stimulating Stimuli could stem the tide of the *Even Greater Depression*."

Mannequin shook head—silent reproof of Deville's criminal blunders. "Puppet inherited the worst economy in the history of the known universe. After failing to right the ship, he had no choice but to pass the burden onto his successor, Mary O'Nett.

Unfortunately, President O'Nett's *Transatlantic Swim for Peace, Prosperity and the Environment* failed to clear the harbor. Her Administration fought valiantly to clean up the economic catastrophe, but even the noble Mary failed to induce the birth of true social justice."

Mannequin shook his fist at the camera to demonstrate his seriousness before he said, "That changes today." His face hardened into a portrait of steely resolve. "To all of my patriotic, tax-paying comrades, it is my honor to announce the rollout of the Hand of Equity." With unmistakable pride, the President gestured towards the rainbow-colored metal box that had been wheeled out onto the stage. "It is my responsibility to ensure that everyone contributes to our collective prosperity. And as you have learned, the buck stops here." Mannequin punctuated the statement by pointing his index finger directly into the television cameras pointed at him.

"The Hand of Equity will recreate the way we pay taxes. The cash flow created by this revolutionary technology will *ensure* that every American receives that to which they are entitled." Mannequin waved to the assembled reporters who were now giving him a standing ovation.

"At some time today, every business across the land will receive a Hand. Every business owner must use it immediately. The Hand will process all transactions, including payroll for workers." By now Mannequin was grinning broadly at *his* innovation. "Gone are the days when business owners and citizens need to make bank deposits or worry about filing tax returns. Our whole financial process has gone digital. The Hand does it all." Mannequin paused a moment to acknowledge more applause.

"This is just another way the Federal Government is making it easier for business people to do business. We will see a rebirth in manufacturing. We will see workers get back on their feet again as we create three million living-wages jobs." More applause flowed from the reporters; it seemed as if they were being paid per clap.

Then the President paused. His eyes grew narrow, like those of a gull readying itself to pounce upon some trash. "It's possible that some business owner will drag their feet on this initiative. So we have quadrupled the number of fiscal-patriotism-compliance-officers at DJSM. Like it or not, we must *all* do our fair share to guarantee a bright future." Mannequin winked at the camera while he bathed in still more applause. Some of the reporters fainted. Glee-filled tremors raced up and down the legs of others in the gathering. President Mannequin clasped his hands above his head and shook them like he had just won a championship title fight.

After the applause faded, the President spoke again. "Before I leave you, I need to spend a minute talking about America. I'm not talking about the America of the past, when greed and selfishness were the laws of the land. I'm talking about today. This is a land where justice and equality have replaced hate and deceit." Mannequin paused to look directly into the camera.

"I received news that on this patriotic day—a day when the Federal Government has done you a favor and made it easier for all of you to do your share—a small group of money-grubbing hate-mongers want to drag us back into our dark history of racism, sexism, and homophobia. I am calling upon you to reject hate speech in *whatever* form it arises."

"And remember—your Federal Government is prepared to do whatever it takes to make America great. So if you ever wonder whether I would be willing to force a man to work twice the hours for half the pay so that others can benefit from his toil—yes, I am! If you ever despair about excessive executive pay and wonder whether I can set wages for any industry I choose—yes, I can! If you ever wonder whether I'm prepared to send all of the Federal Government's force to punish any citizen who steps too far out of line—yes, I am!" The crowd erupted again.

Mannequin pulled the rainbow-colored towel from around his neck and tossed it into the frenzied mass. "Thank you, Washington and goodnight!" he yelled. Then he dashed out of the press room and ran down the corridor toward the White House's residential quarters.

From his bedroom, President Mannequin quickly dressed for bed. While he fell asleep, he did so to the sweet sounds of the assembled reporters begging for an encore. "We want more! We want more! We want more!" they shouted.

Chapter 10

Larry Lemonpants pulled a brush through his full head of graying hair. When he finished, he buttoned his navy suit coat and straightened his tie. He had planned to spend the day at his ocean- side villa, relaxing in the sun. Instead, he found himself staring out the window of his luxurious penthouse office. He did his best to focus on the sunrise, while at the same time ignoring the contents of the newspaper that waited atop his desk. Unfortunately, he wasn't succeeding very well at either activity.

A seemingly battleship-sized conference table—hand-planed from rainforest teak—sat in the center of the eclectically furnished office. When Lemonpants' guests arrived they would all gather around the table to talk about important matters. The table, Lemonpants' most-prized possession, had been purchased at auction for more money than some nations saw in a year. The table's surface had been too large to maneuver into the building. Lemonpants had been forced to hire a crane to lift the table through the same panorama-friendly window that he had been staring out.

At either end of the suite sat one of a matching pair of sofas. The upholstery had been done using luxurious leather. The softness of the furniture made the sitter feel as if he were settling into a warm stick of butter. When his friends and guests asked about the environmentalist's unlikely choice of leather furniture, Lemonpants snarled, "I didn't kill the things. They arrived that way. And isn't it better that I have them instead of some corporate fat cat. At least I can appreciate their lives."

A radio softly played in the background while Lemonpants brooded. The neo-folk trio, Peace, Love and Joe, sang their newest song. The hit had been *number one* on the Radio Czar's top-ten list for the past 812 weeks. Lemonpants paused to listen. His level of cheer was sagging, and the ditty always helped to perk it up.

American food aid has all but dried up
Rice for Zimbabwe won't fill a small cup
Corn, rice and beans once shipped to the poor
Will never again be sent out the door

But they're saving the Earth—one death at a time
They're saving the Earth—one death at a time
If there's one human life that's precious—it's mine
You keep saving the Earth—one death at a time.

Our regrets to you Africans, we just feel so bad.
We played you a concert, it's the best that we had.
But Hollywood's sure you'll be happy to know.
They'll be wearing your ribbon at their next trophy show.

You'll be saving the Earth—one death at a time.
You're saving the Earth—one death at a time.
You get massive starvation—Hollywood gets more wine.
You're saving the Earth—one death at a time.

Welcome back you old bone saws—you're now in the game.
We tried other methods but they were to blame.
For the big-ass health crisis we found ourselves in.
Grab those lancets, those leeches, and those voodoo doll pins.

You'll be saving the Earth—one death at a time.
You're saving the Earth—one death at a time.
You don't need no treatment—Painkillers work fine.
You're saving the Earth—one death at a time.

You poor, hapless boobs with your mercury lamps
If one of them breaks, better hold your breath, Gramps
Away and in secret I've got bulbs from TE
Hey, there's millions of you, but there's just one of me.

You'll be saving the Earth—one death at a time.
You're saving the Earth—one death at a time.
Leave the progress to me—I'm ahead of my time.
You're saving the Earth—one death at a time.

Don't pick up your phone—No—Don't waste your time
Those folks in DC have your welfare in mind
They've done you a favor—turning food into fuel
You ask what's for dinner—Ethyl-Noleo-gruel

Just keep saving the Earth—one death at a time.
You're saving the Earth—one death at a time.
You gave them your freedom—you'll surely be fine.
You're saving the Earth—one death at a time.

Don't wait for one moment. We have all the facts
Trust those rock stars, those actors, political hacks
They screamed it; they sang it; they shilled for their pals
Don't doubt for a moment those green men and gals.

You're saving the Earth—one death at a time.
You're saving the Earth—one death at a time.
Use just wind and solar—You're going to be fine.
You're saving the Earth—one death at a time.

Not long ago we stood at the ready
To help those in need, we offered our aid
Our nation's in shambles, we're penniless paupers
America's broke—you're on your own I'm afraid.

But you're saving the Earth—one death at a time.
You're saving the Earth—one death at a time.
If there's one human life that's precious—it's mine
You're saving the Earth—one death at a time.

Lemonpants always wanted to applaud after he heard that song. After all, he envisioned himself as the commanding general in the war to save the environment. However, if he'd been forced to reveal the truth, he would have confessed that he felt no special connection to environmental issues. He'd simply seen the growing environmental frenzy and decided to make the beast work for *him*. The luxurious office furnishings, seaside homes, and expensive cars were all testament to his success in fleecing the sizable environmentalist flock. But instead of using a shepherd's hook, Lemonpants used fear to keep his followers in line.

The remaining news outlets—DAMPMEN and the Yellow Lapdog Gazette—might have spread the environmental news, but Lemonpants sculpted the message. And he could move his flock in any direction wanted.

But it wasn't environmental concerns that had shattered his plans for a relaxing day. A man was the culprit. But he wasn't just any man. He was Earl Garamond.

Lemonpants had called an emergency meeting of his secret society to discuss Garamond's latest treachery—an ugly rash of conservatism seemed to be spreading. Only Garamond had the resources to make that happen.

Lemonpants and Garamond had a history. They had been roommates in college. But while Garamond picked up scholarships where he could and worked full-time, Lemonpants's bank balance barely moved while he shelled out for the twelve years of not inhaling from beer bongs and protesting in support of progressive ideals.

In fact, it had been those same progressive ideals that created the rift between Garamond and Lemonpants. Garamond's gifts for mechanical engineering had been impossible to hide. As a student, Garamond had designed and built the winning entry in the intercollegiate solar car race for three consecutive years. During an interview with the school newspaper, Garamond spoke about his achievement and the potential for solar automobiles. "This contest is a lot of fun, and it's a great challenge, but solar energy just isn't a match for internal combustion engines. These cars that we build have one purpose—they travel from Alberta to Dallas. That's all they do. When it comes to transportation, solar energy is a gimmick. A candle gives off light, but it'd be foolish to rely on candlelight to perform surgery. I don't understand the rush to abandon a proven source of energy in favor of a more costly and vastly inferior option."

Lemonpants, a public policy major and the chief editor of the university's newspaper, was incensed by Garamond's comments. Lemonpants wrote a scathing editorial, calling his roommate, a "backwards, short-sighted, morally-bankrupt pig." The editorial won for Lemonpants the university's highest award for journalism.

And while Garamond and Lemonpants never had a *friendly* relationship, the editorial ensured that their interactions would remain hostile.

Even though years had passed, Lemonpants still stoked his hatred of his former roommate's successes. While he waited for the other members of the *Moral Compass Society* to arrive, he took a few stray glances at the Yellow Lapdog's lead story. He had nearly gagged after he had read the headline: *GARAMOND TAKING OVER THE WORLD*. "Who does that bastard think he is? Poisoning our planet with those ungodly machines of his?" Lemonpants asked, the bitter sneer on his face making him look deranged. "He should be put in jail for his behavior. He shouldn't be rewarded. The environment doesn't like a mess maker like him."

Lemonpants hadn't even bothered to look at the body of the story. If he had, he would have seen that Garamond was being condemned—not lauded—for the wealth he'd accumulated. The story closed with the lines, "I become fearful when any single man is looked upon as the answer to all of a nation's questions. Each day the Garamondia legend seems less like a modern success-story and more like cult of personality."

A knock at the door jerked Lemonpants away from his grousing and into reality. Edward Tramsoot, the Editor-in-Chief of the Yellow Lapdog Gazette, stood in the doorway. Tramsoot nodded a silent greeting and took a seat at the far end of the enormous table. Close behind Tramsoot followed General Welfare, the EEFF Czar. Next entered Sunny Davis—Head of the Demagogue Party. Sunny Davis' alter ego—Davis Sunny served as head of the FauxPublican Party. Sunny usually left the Moral Compass meetings at the midpoint only to return seconds later as Davis Sunny.

Next through the door came Silky Simmons. Simmons served as the commanding officer of the militant arm of the CGLBAHHTTGGCOGA—the Coalition of Gay, Lesbian, Bisexual, Asexual, Hypersexual, Hyposexual, Transexual, Transgender, Gender-neutral, Gender Confused and Organ Grinder Americans. The organ grinders had seemed like an odd fit at first, but to the CGLBAHHTTGGCOGA's leadership, any time they added a letter to their initialism, it felt like progress. Besides, the eccentric entertainers needed a group to call their own, and the monkeys were a huge hit at the group's monthly meetings.

The CGLBAHHTTGGCOGA militia, a group based in California, had become notorious during the state's fight over Proposition 8. The gang sharpened its reputation by egging, vandalizing, and assaulting its enemies under the guise of free-speech. Rumors suggested that they had considered making a flaming *equals sign* their calling card, but those rumors were never confirmed.

The Spiritual Leader of the Church of Pop Culture arrived next. As always, he came splendidly dressed in flowing golden robes, a golden miter perched atop his head. He kept his left hand perpetually outstretched so that all in his presence might have ready-access to his large, kissable ring. In his fist he held a shepherd's crook. An ever-present train of babbling sycophants followed in his wake.

At the tail of the procession came Senator Spendini and his frequent companion, Rita the Clown. Rita, the longtime Speaker of the House, was a zip code of a woman with the kindness and charm of a cranky wolverine. She dominated the lives of Americans from her Congressional throne. In fact, few Americans could even recall how life had been lived prior to her reign.

While Spendini had grown up in a wealthy suburban home—

his dreams of life as master of misdirection being encouraged by supportive parents—Rita was raised by a band of feral circus performers. The circus troupe had chosen to live as outlaws rather than yield to a Federal Government ban on circuses.

The performers had created an existence for themselves in the wild, apart from the Government's umbrella of compassion. To support themselves, the group performed in secret, remote locations.

The Federal Government Circus Police Department and DJSM agents tried to halt the illegal performances—or at minimum obtain the Fed's fair share of the take—but in every instance the authorities arrived a few hours too late. They found little more than extinguished fires, discarded ticket stubs, and large piles of elephant dung.

As an adolescent, Rita hungered for Government intervention into her life. Eventually, she chose to run away from the circus to join society. Once there, she lived out her adulthood harboring bitter resentments toward her parents. Their sin had been keeping young Rita beyond the reach of the Government's love. She never forgave her parents for their decisions, and she vowed that she would never allow any more children to be born the way she had—lost and abandoned in the wilderness, with no chance to feel the warming rays of Government's grace upon their faces.

Rita studied political science and public administration in college. She moved directly into law school after graduation. By the time she had reached the age of twenty-six, she'd already won her first seat in office—working as a state legislator. Her notion of Government as a benevolent force that had been authorized to do good works and punish evil deeds—much like a stern nanny charged with supervising insolent brats—strengthened her commitment to public service.

Over time, Rita began to wear the pancake makeup and painted face of a clown. Her showy appearance was meant to serve as a reminder of her parents' selfishness. She also carried a bicycle horn wherever she went. She honked the horn to sound the clarion call any time an American's access to Government's goodness was impeded.

Lemonpants allowed Spendini and the clown to settle into their seats before he started the meeting. Lemonpants and Spendini had their own history. The two of them had created a twenty-first century triangle-trade. Lemonpants fleeced the environmentalists via the sale of carbon credits. A portion of those carbon credits was funneled to Spendini in the form of generous campaign contributions. The deposits in Spendini's war chest allowed him to maintain a stranglehold on his seat in the Senate. In return, the senator forced passage of legislation that gave important environmental moneys—like carbon credits—favorable tax treatment. The passed laws allowed Lemonpants to keep more of what he creatively acquired. The arrangement enabled the environmentalist to maintain his high-society lifestyle without the high-tax aftertaste. The arrangement was the Mona Lisa of conflicts of interest. But it was little more than business-as-usual in Washington's Church of the Perpetual Conflicts of Interest.

Once everyone had taken their seat, Lemonpants walked to the head of the table. "Welcome, fellow members," he began.

"Equality before liberty," they responded.

"We are facing an emergency." Lemonpants paused to allow his statement to sink in. "There is news that a conservative insurgency might be underway." A few members of the group gasped. Others nodded their heads. "I called this meeting to put each of you on alert. We must never underestimate the power of our adversaries. Certainly, we could pool every ounce of brains to be found in the Midwest, and we still wouldn't muster a solo intellect that could understand our intentions—that is without offering a series of illustrations drawn in crayon—of course. But those simpletons are not my concern right now. That honor goes to French Garamond, commander-in-chief of the entire bumpkin nation. He's the one who keeps me awake at night," Lemonpants said. He punctuated his statement by slamming the day's newspaper down onto the table with the Garamond headline visible to everyone.

"EEFF has obtained evidence that an author in Puppetgrad, Minnesota, has written a novel that violates our prohibited-free-speech laws. They have reason to believe that the author intends to contact a publishing company in an attempt to sell the rights to the book. EEFF has also discovered that one of its agents suppressed her knowledge of this seditious material—material that should have already been confiscated." Lemonpants stopped speaking and glared at General Welfare.

Welfare sat motionless, a look of shame pasted onto his face. Lemonpants fought the urge to smile as those seated next to the general slid their chairs an almost imperceptible distance away from the EEFF czar in order to disassociate themselves from the man's failure.

"Now, we've all made mistakes," Lemonpants continued. "We're not here to point fingers, to dwell on EEFF's mistake, or to bemoan the agency's utter lack of competence in this matter. We're here to discuss the silver lining that this dark cloud has presented to us." Lemonpants smiled a wicked, toothy grin. "We know we are dealing with a conspiracy, and a conspiracy of this kind will ultimately involve Garamond. Rather than picking the culprits off one-by-one, I suggest that we wait and grab all the conspirators at once," Lemonpants hissed. Given the depth of Lemonpants' pockets and his financial support of Demagoblican candidates, a suggestion from Lemonpants was the political equivalent of a papal bull.

"But Larry," Spendini interrupted. "The President said he wants us to silence Watford as soon as possible."

Lemonpants turned and glared at the Senator, silently chastising him for the informal tone he'd taken. "You should know by now that the President does as he is told, *Senator*. Any president that doesn't know how to follow simple instructions won't be staying in the White House very long. You might want to keep that in mind." Lemonpants continued to stare at Spendini allowing his gaze to burn for a while. *You just have to know how to handle politicians,* Lemonpants silently told himself. *They need to be reminded who the boss is every now and then.* Then Lemonpants redirected his attention towards the group. "When the time is right, EEFF will grab the entire group—the author, the publisher, that brain-dead agent and French Garamond."

The members of the group broke into spontaneous applause. They exchanged smiles and high-fives. Lemonpants had founded the Moral Compass Foundation to provide a coordinated front in the push towards American progressivism. While none in the group had ever run a successful business or even took the time to listen to anyone with differing points of view, each of them was convinced that their insights were the key to making the United States into the workers' paradise it had been founded to be.

Lemonpants waited for the applause to fade away. Then he explained the details of his plan. When he had finished, he closed the meeting by telling the group, "By the time we're finished, every American will know that Ronald Reagan is dead."

Chapter 11

Agent Calder had watched the presidential news conference the previous day, as did all her coworkers. The entire complement of EEFF's Puppetgrad field office had gathered in the theater-style conference center on the building's lowest level. Calder tried to appear attentive during the President's unveiling of the Hand of Equity. The last thing any ambitious EEFF agent wanted to do was to appear to be disinterested in the President's vision. However, she became acutely interested when President Mannequin launched into his condemnation of hate speech.

Her guts clenched when the President openly chastised anyone who might engage in "seditious behavior." It had been years since a president had made such an overt condemnation of speech-crime.

She tried to reassure herself, saying that she was just being paranoid. But she couldn't shake the suspicion that her visit to Watford's PHU had been discovered. EEFF veterans often joked that Greta Government had tentacles spread across every inch of America. Calder wondered whether there might be more than a little truth in her colleagues' lighthearted warning.

After she arrived at her cubicle, she tried to focus on her work, but she couldn't manage to concentrate. She dared not look at Watford's file. She feared that a single peek might further implicate her in the scandal she could feel swirling around her. She almost expected one of the Teachers to walk up, slip a black bag over her head, and haul her away.

The biggest stressor was the location of the memory chip.

The chip still contained the scanned images of Watford's novel, and it sat hidden in her desk, tucked behind a stack of files. She knew that every day the chip stayed inside the field office, the risk of its discovery grew larger. She needed to smuggle the chip out, but she was unsure how to conceal it during the security scan performed at the end of each shift.

Due to EEFF's super-secret nature, General Welfare employed every possible means to ensure that the agency's veil of secrecy remained intact. This meant monitoring every agent's person and possessions each time they left the field office.

Certainly, EEFF agents working on official business could have easily revealed the agency's existence. But agents were required to file permission reports which indicated exactly where they were going, what they were taking with them, and why they needed to go. Agents also knew the exact price of treachery. None of them wanted to receive a visit from a group of Teachers.

It was the agent gone rogue—believing he could safely smuggle out agency secrets—that the scanning was intended to discourage. All staff members, including General Welfare himself, were required to pass themselves and any bags, boxes, or bundles they carried through an x-Ray scanner before exiting any EEFF facility. The machines had been programmed to locate any material an agent might be hiding.

Calder paced within her phone-booth sized cubicle as she strained to decide how she could successfully smuggle the chip out of the building. She considered hiding it in her hair, holding it within her arm-pit, and inserting it into locations she didn't really want to consider. As the list of bad ideas began to outweigh any hope for success, she nearly convinced herself to confess her crimes and beg for mercy. Then an idea struck.

EEFF's pseudo-military mission gave General Welfare a

secret rush. He believed that the uniforms worn by EEFF staffers should reflect the nature of their mission. He decided that the battle uniforms, formerly worn by soldiers, best reflected EEFF's role in American society.

The uniforms not only offered a visible reminder that EEFF agents were on the front lines of the battle against hate speech and sedition. The clothing itself offered a financial benefit for the agency.

Back during the Bay of Prudhoe invasion, a sizable force of hairy Scandaharvians invaded Alaska. The bearded marauders arrived with the intention of creating a Scandaharvian empire in North America. After the invasion force had spread across the state, the invader's commander was asked why they'd felt the need to invade. "Are you kidding?" he replied. "You Americans are so naïve. You pat yourself on the back as you pass laws that keep you from fulfilling your own energy needs. You seem to think that because you won't touch the oil that waits beneath your feet that those resources hold no value. I have news for you: you might refuse to drill that oil, but we'll be happy to do it for you."

Americans held their breath while they waited for their government's response. President Puppet refused to take military action to repel the invasion. "Alaska is a—*yawn*—important part of America," the President said, "but I don't think we're going to send troops to defend it. There's nothing in Alaska except rednecks and oil. Frankly, those Scandaharvians did us a favor by taking that mess of a state off our hands. Besides, a war would require a lot of fuel and cost a lot of money. And we have neither to spare. I guess we'll just need to get on with our lives with forty-nine states. After all, we can always replace Alaska with Puerto Rico. Then we won't have to change our flag."

After Alaska had been ceded to the invaders—and a

precedent of appeasement had been set—there seemed little reason to maintain a standing army. Ships were scuttled. Jets were converted into mobile, miniature wind turbines. Short-haired, sea faring warriors were simply told to "go make an amphibious assault on a very distant island without using any landing craft."

With the wide-spread discharge of military personnel, supplies of surplus military clothing skyrocketed. Suddenly there was a virtually limitless stash of unused combat uniforms available for use. General Welfare took full advantage of the situation and used the clothing to outfit his own troops.

On most days, Calder would have liked to wear an outfit that was more feminine than her fatigues. She thought the getup made her look fat, and it did nothing to flatter her lean, yet amply-endowed figure. However, the combat boots that adorned her feet gave her the best possible chance to smuggle out her secret cargo.

Her hands shook as she made a tiny incision in the tongue of one of her boots. The small cut, which was hidden by a slab of padding, seemed like the perfect place to hide her contraband. While she pushed the memory chip into place, she silently thanked God for the progressive miniaturization that had taken place in the computer-memory industry. She allowed herself a fleeting smile as she imagined the difficulty of smuggling the vacuum-tube-memory of a 1950's super-computer out EEFF's front door.

When the workday finally ended, Calder gathered her things and slowly walked towards the security station. She hoped to hide in the crush of EEFF staffers who were also going home. She allowed small groups of her coworkers to walk past her, believing that a long line of staff waiting at the screening station might allow her to get lost in the shuffle. She tried to relax and control her breathing. Her coworkers carried on—laughing and joking and discussing plans for the evening—as though they lacked any cares. Clearly none of them were trying to conceal evidence of sedition.

Sweat ran down Calder's forehead and her cheeks smoldered. She imagined a scene in which one of the Teachers poked his head out of the Teacher's Lounge and shouted, "Dead-girl walking," as she moved past.

When she finally reached the checkpoint, she felt as though she might faint. She fought the urge to vomit as she bent over to untie her laces and remove her boots. Panic gripped her. She wanted to run through the scanner and out into the streets, but she knew that would be suicide. Instead, she tried to steady her hands while she placed her boots into a gray, plastic bin. Then she gently laid the bin on the conveyor belt.

The scanning process bore a strong resemblance to that which occurred in airports—except without all the genital grabbing. EEFF's scanner could detect metal objects certainly, but it had to do more. The devices had been calibrated to detect non-organic material such as photos, documents, computer disks or other media that could have been used to smuggle EEFF secrets out into the world.

More sweat ran down Calder's temples and into her eyes. When her turn to be scanned had arrived, she held her breath while she stepped through the x-Ray's threshold. With her eyes tightly shut, she emerged without incident.

Her heart pounded. She could feel the beat in her ears. Then she whispered a silent prayer for the safe passage of her footwear. Another flash-flood of sweat cascaded down her face. Her mouth felt like it had been filled with sand. *Please send my boots through. There's nothing to see in them. Please—*

Then, as if her silent prayers had been answered, the boots slid out of the scanner. The plastic bin glided slowly down the conveyor belt and stopped directly in front of her. She released an audible sigh and grabbed her boots.

From out of nowhere, Calder's boss—a Special Agent Watcher in EEFF vernacular—appeared and grunted, "Hold it, Calder. I need to see those boots." Dingo Clark struck an imposing figure as he towered over his charge. He was six-and-a-half feet and two-hundred-fifty pounds of musk, muscle, and misogyny, and he was rarely in good humor.

Clark had been married during his early twenties, but his wife never quite made peace with the secrecy and the emotional distance his job placed between them. Consequently, the shaky marriage collapsed before Clark's thirtieth birthday. Though he didn't fight the separation, he never understood why his wife wanted the divorce. Afterwards, he blamed every woman he met for his ex-wife's sins. Calder was no exception. "You're in deep trouble," Clark growled. He grabbed the boot that held the memory chip from Calder's grasp. "Step out of that line," he said.

"Yes, sir," Calder said as she snapped to attention. She now was certain that she was going to barf. She wondered whether puking on Clark's boots would help her to escape or only make things worse. She closed her eyes, not wanting to watch her boss yank the hidden memory chip from of its hiding spot and shove it into her face.

"What is this?" Clark demanded while fingering the cut in the boot's tongue. Calder held her breath. "Do these boots belong to you, Calder?"

"Yes, sir."

"No they do not!" Clark shouted. "These boots belong to the Federal Government. If I ever see another cut in the lining of your boots, you are going to be mending boots in your free time. Do you understand me?"

"Yes, sir! I understand, sir!" Calder shouted as she yanked the boots from Clark's grip and ran for the door. "It won't happen again, sir."

"It better not, or I'll shove my foot so far up your—" Clark stopped speaking. He didn't need a sexual harassment beef, but he wanted to be intimidating. "I meant that I'll —*Awww*, shit, get out of here before I really get mad," he said as he shooed her away.

Clark watched Calder run down the corridor and out of the field office. Earlier that day, General Welfare had filled Clark in about the nature of Calder's crimes. Welfare had also ordered the Watcher to oversee Calder's scanning. As the large man examined the x-Ray image of Calder's boot, he smiled. The memory chip was clearly visible inside the boot's padded tongue. *General Welfare will be pleased,* he told himself. "Be a good girl and lead us to Garamond," he whispered before he turned and walked back to his desk.

Outside the field office, Calder's heart pounded. Her hands shook as she sat on the curb and yanked her boots onto her feet. She didn't even bother to tie the laces. She just shoved the strings inside the boots and ran.

When she could run no farther, she slowed down and began to walk. She kept her eyes focused down on the ground but still walked as quickly as possible.

When she reached her apartment, she opened her door and threw it shut behind her. Paranoia gripped her, and she slammed the deadbolt into place. She immediately grabbed her electronic book reader from the coffee table and inserted the smuggled memory chip.

While she waited for the scanned images to appear on the book reader's display, Calder walked to the kitchen and poured herself a glass of water. When she returned, she set the glass on the coffee table and flopped onto her sofa. She hoped to give the EEFF monitoring equipment in her PHU the impression that she was only trying to relax after a long day at work. She'd only been able to read Watford's foreword during her visit to his PHU. While feelings of queasiness danced around her stomach, she began to read more.

In the Hall (Reflections on America)

Chapter 2

Somewhere between this world and the next, stands a door that leads to the *Hall of Deceased Historic Personalities, Religious Figures, Cultural Icons, and the Like.* For the sake of brevity, I will refer to it only as the Hall. The Hall allows all who enter the opportunity to have an audience with those entities, both real and imagined, that have shaped history.

I'd been searching for a biography of Ronald Reagan when I found the Hall. After I had searched the biography section of the Compassion County Library, I'd found nothing written on one of America's greatest presidents.

Undeterred, I sifted through the American History collection. Again, I found nothing. I checked the library's catalog—again nothing. I had nearly given up when I glanced through the open doorway of the janitor's closet. There, on a dusty, bottom shelf, I saw a hastily-scribbled sign that read, "Insignificant American Presidents." After moving plungers, dirty sponges, and a box filled with four score and eight urinal cakes, I saw a dusty stack of forgotten tomes. The pile of books contained biographies on Ronald Reagan, George Washington, Thomas Jefferson, and other American presidents deemed "insignificant" by the prevailing regime. The books appeared to have gone unread for years.

I brushed the dust from the works' covers and made a stack out of the books on the floor next to me. Once I had finished moving the books, I noticed a small opening in the wall behind the shelf. Light flowed through the hole and into the janitor's closet. I decided to investigate.

After crawling through the hole in the wall, I found myself in a tunnel that had a dirt floor. A string of dim lights hung from the passage's earthen roof. Old timbers had been arranged at regular intervals to prevent cave-ins. The tunnel gradually became larger until it ended at a stout oaken door.

The door stood at least ten feet high and had golden hinges that were anchored in a wall of marble. *What on earth is this?* I asked myself. My mouth hung open as I wrestled my feelings of disbelief. Too curious to turn back, I pulled at the golden handle, and with a whisper of air, the door glided open.

My first glance left me dumbstruck. I'd never

seen anything like it. The structure appeared to have been carved into an enormous bed of marble. The floors shined beneath the light of crystal chandeliers suspended from the ceilings. Roman columns lined the walls. A seemingly endless collection of doorways dotted the corridors that stretched far into the distance.

I read the sign aloud. "Welcome to the Hall of Deceased Historic Personalities, Religious Figures, Cultural Icons and the Like." Beneath the sign sat a small stack of maps. The maps showed the locations of the countless personalities, figures, and icons who *resided* within the Hall. At the bottom of the map, two rules had been printed: "There is no speech without free speech," and "Knock before entering."

I grabbed one of the maps and began to walk down the corridor nearest me. My shoes beat a steady rhythm on the marble floor. The footfalls gave cadence to the melody of the ringing hammers and chisels that echoed across the distance. The world was constantly generating historical figures I assumed. They must have had an endless need for additional space.

I soon realized the statue which stood outside the door matched the identity of the historic figure within. I had already decided which figure I wanted to visit first. His accommodations were located near those of Ben Franklin, Julius Caesar, and Hippocrates. When I passed the famous Greek physician in the hallway, I thought I heard him chuckle and whisper, "Health care reform, indeed."

When I reached my destination, I stopped to brush the dirt off my pants and straightened my tie. I wished I had brought some breath mints. I'd never met a cultural icon before, and I had wanted my breath to be fresh enough for the occasion.

I lingered outside his door for a moment. I was nervous; unsure what I would ask him. Then I gathered all my courage and knocked.

I thought I heard someone say, "Come in," so I pushed the door open and saw him sitting there in a dingy union-suit. The cuffs at his wrists had become ringed in filth and were threadbare. "I'm here for a visit," I stammered, embarrassed at his state of appearance. I shifted my glance to the corner of the room to spare him any further embarrassment. "I'm sorry. I didn't realize— Should I come back?"

Uncle Sam sighed and rubbed a bony hand through his goatee. His fingers could have used a good washing, and his goatee seemed to be flecked with tiny globs of ketchup and cheeseburger. A bottle of whiskey and a plastic bag filled with marijuana rested on the table. "No. Don't bother," he whispered. "It's probably time people saw me for what I've become."

In a wardrobe nearby, his blue suit-coat and white shirt formed a rumpled ball, while his bow-tie dangled from a clothes-hanger. His unmistakable star-spangled top hat, its brim tattered, rested on one of the shelves.

I pulled up a chair and sat down at the table next to him. His eyes were bloodshot. Beads of sweat clung to his forehead. Occasionally one of the droplets broke free and ran down his cheek or into one of his eyes. His face was a swollen balloon. Clearly, this was not the man that I had expected to find. "Are you feeling alright?" I asked him. Secretly, I feared that he might collapse right in front of me. "Should I call a doctor or something?"

"It will take more than a doctor to help me, son," he said in a rice-paper voice that was barely audible. Yet in spite of his appearance, his eyes still held a spark.

"What do you mean? You're Uncle Sam. You're the symbol of America. You know—the land of the free and the home of the brave?"

He wheezed. Or maybe it was a chuckle. I'm still not sure. "You're a young man," he said. "You haven't been around long enough to remember what America used to be." He opened the whiskey bottle and filled his mouth before swallowing. Then he pulled a joint from his stash and lit up. I watched as he filled his lungs with a deep drag. "Want some," he hissed as he held the smoke and extended the joint to me.

"With all due respect, sir, what has gotten into you?"

He cocked his head as if to say, *what do you mean?*

"You're sitting in your yellow underwear and smoking pot. You reek of booze. Where's the real Uncle Sam?"

"Don't you dare lay that trip on me, sonny! I am the real Uncle Sam. You think I did this to myself?"

"What are you talking about?"

"I'll show you." He walked over to the wardrobe and grabbed a rolled-up piece of paper. He spread the makeshift scroll across the table top and said, "Look at me. Do you see that look of determination? I was ready to do whatever I needed to do. It didn't matter if the job was easy. I could look myself in the eye back then. Now look at me," he said before he gestured to his flabby gut and tired face. "I'm a used up shell. I'm a drunken, drug-addicted wreck." He grabbed the whisky bottle, took a pull, and then hurled it against the wall.

I watched the bottle shatter in an explosion of glass and whiskey. Some of the spray splashed our faces and clothing.

His eyes narrowed and his jaw muscles grew tight. "And there you have it. I used to stand for an America that did not shrink from doing its part. Sure, we tried to stay out of the two world wars. But when we finally agreed to go to the aid of our friends across the Atlantic, we brought free, American men and women to the fight. I was there when we helped turn the tide against the Kaiser. I was there when we fought the Nazis from Normandy to Berlin." He began to pace the floor, gesturing wildly while he spoke. "I used to stand for Americans who used creativity, optimism, and a whole lot of grit, to do the impossible." He sighed before continuing.

"But no one wants Uncle Sam around anymore. Everyone wants the Tooth Fairy or Santa Claus to take care of everything." Uncle Sam stopped speaking and pointed towards the door. "You know what? You might as well save your breath. Go talk to Kris Kringle. He's just down the hallway. Go rap on good old Santa's door, and let him solve all of your problems for you. Hell! Elect him president for all I care. It seems like your Demagoblicans run Santa in most of their districts anyway. What do you want Johnnie? Okay, here's your puppy. What about you, Janie? Okay, here's your pony."

I was startled when he strode across the room and flipped the table over onto its top. I watched while the heavy, oaken mass skidded across the floor and slammed into the far wall. He glared at me, sucking ragged breaths into his lungs. Then he leaned in towards me—his nose scarcely an inch from mine—and growled, "What do *you* think I should stand for?"

Calder shut off the book reader and laid it on the coffee table. She wasn't sure whether to laugh or cry. At another time, she might have supported this sort of free speech, but that was before she took a job at EEFF. She rubbed her temples and tried to decide whether she was ready to risk her life for this novel. But the cold fear that sat like a ball of ice in the pit of her stomach told her that she probably already had decided.

Chapter 12

Ray left home early the next morning. He hadn't been able to sleep.

The prior night after dinner, he retrieved his cardboard box and prepared to do a bit of writing. But he immediately realized that something was wrong. He'd always placed his cardboard box into the cupboard the long way. When he opened the door and saw the short end of the box, a wave of dread rushed over him.

He gingerly pulled the box from its hiding place, as if he were trying to prevent an explosion. He set the flimsy container on the bathroom floor and slowly lifted its flaps. As he peered inside, he saw a note. Chills ran up his spine. *Who could have seen this?* he asked himself.

Ray—
I paid your home a visit today.
Your story has endangered you and your family.
Get it out of your house as soon as you can.
I'll try to protect you.
Trust no one in the government.
-SC

Panic overtook him, and he slumped to the floor. *What do I do with this? I can't tell Sarah.* He struggled to make sense of the ominous note. *I've got to finish the novel tonight,* he concluded.

He was awake long past midnight before he finished working. And when he woke the next morning, he was only thinking of his family's safety.

Ray decided to stop at Kerwin Publishing on his way to work. He wasn't sure whether they would look at his story or not, but at the moment, it didn't even matter. He just wanted the dangerous pages as far from his family as he could get them.

Instead of taking the Peoples' Commuter Line all the way to the Compassion County Government Center as he usually did, Ray exited the train at the station that sat in the shadow of the Monument to Capitalism. The "monument" wasn't really a monument at all. It had once been a domed stadium that served as home to the state's defunct professional football team. The few remaining shreds of the stadium's domed roof dangled down the walls and fluttered in the breeze.

Football and other contact sports had been banned after it became obvious that Greta Government had overpromised and under-delivered on her promises of "health-care reform." The duped citizens realized that providing "universal health insurance" was a lot different than providing universal access to *medical treatment*.

"We need to cut down on the public-health risk of organized sports," the Healthcare Czar said after the Federal Government had been forced to admit its need to ration medical care. "These athletes over-consume our precious supply of medical treatment. Since they won't voluntarily restrict their activities, we need to do it for them. As always, people can feel free to choose less-violent forms of expression. This decision will lead to lower medical costs for everyone."

The ban on football—and then on all contact sports—left no need for stadiums. Kerwin Publishing's headquarters—Ray's destination—sat a few blocks from this forgotten edifice. Though Ray had been disappointed by the ban on professional football, it was old news. He was now curious to see whether any other parts of downtown had fared better than the stadium.

The changes that had occurred since Ray had last walked these streets were obvious. Steel-chain barriers now hung across all doors, windows, and other openings on the bottom few floors of every building. The metal mesh barred entry to unwanted visitors. The buildings' owners hadn't given up all hope that they might have tenants again, but at the moment their hopes seemed like little more than childish wishes.

Piles of bricks—fallen from building exteriors—lay scattered across broken slabs of concrete that were once sidewalks. Paint peeled from walls and fences in long fingers. The bony carcasses of starved rats littered the gutters alongside the refuse that they had long before picked clean. Potholes that could swallow a moose pocked the streets.

As the public infrastructure fell into disarray, the citizens demanded repairs for their streets and sidewalks. But government officials always seemed to have more pressing uses for tax receipts. One Puppetgrad city council member had even made the timeless remark, "I got into politics to *fix people's lives*, not to *fix the streets*." And the state of the streets clearly reflected the council member's values.

As Ray picked his way across the uneven, trash-strewn roadway, he heard what sounded like music in the distance. The noise came very softly at first and grew louder as he approached. He wondered whether there might be an early-morning concert. He walked toward the noise and soon recognized its source. The tinny and barely melodious composition flowed from Greta Government. Ray looked up and saw one of her dove-shaped speakers, barely clinging to the wall on rusted mountings, as it hung from a vacant office building. He paused to listen.

Go to work. Go to work. Go to work to feed your sister.
Go to work. Go to work. You know your brother needs your aid.
Go to work. Go to work. Pay your taxes. Fund your nation.
Go to work. Go to work. Keep the promises your Congress
made.

The song ended abruptly and was replaced by a message, "Attention. Attention. It is a criminal offense to avoid work. You must have written approval from the Job Czar to take time off from work. Failure to report for an assigned shift is punishable by up to 90 days in a hard-labor camp. A doctor's note is required if you exceed your five allotted sick days for the year. The Federal Government thanks you for your patriotism. Equality before liberty." As the message ended, the work song began again.

As Ray resumed his walk, he hugged the box that contained his novel tightly beneath both arms. Butterflies danced around his stomach. *What should I say when I get there? Should I tell them what's in the box or just leave it for them?* he asked himself. *What if the speech bullies come for me? What if they come for Sarah and the boys? Maybe I shouldn't even be doing this?*

Then he stopped walking. His attention was drawn to a sign in the distance. His legs quaked while he read.

"PREMATURE-PREGNANCY-INTERRUPTION CENTER:
Over three million premature pregnancies interrupted. Ask
us about our twenty-four month, Pregnancy-Lemon-Law,
retroactive-premature-pregnancy-interruption services."

Ray shook his head. "Premature-Pregnancy-Interruption? So that's what it's called these days. I guess that's easier to swallow than murder," he muttered as a flash of heat killed the dancing butterflies. No part of him felt like dancing. He whispered a silent prayer as he watched a girl—she couldn't have been a day older than fifteen—as she and the human life inside her bulging belly entered the center alone. "That poor girl," Ray said in a voice barely louder than a whisper, "she doesn't even realize that she and her baby are no more than political footballs. And they are going in to face this alone. This is wrong, and something needs to change." In that moment, Ray knew he had stayed silent for too long. "If the bullies come for me, then let them come."

Now Ray marched towards Kerwin headquarters with purpose in his step. The building steadily grew larger in his sight. When he reached the front door, he paused for an instant before pulling the door open. Once inside, he made a straight line to the reception desk. "Good morning. I've written a novel, and I'm hoping that you—well, not you specifically—but Kerwin Publishing would consider it. Can I leave it with you?" he blurted.

"I'm sorry, sir, but we only work with established authors. I'm afraid there's nothing I can do for you," the receptionist replied.

Ray stared at the woman behind the reception desk. Something was different about her, but he couldn't decide what it was. The woman was trim but not skinny. She had pleasant but not beautiful features, and she had a kind though unremarkable voice. Then Ray noticed her clothing—an orange prison uniform. It looked exactly like the jumpsuits the convicts wore on cable-television documentaries. His mind had become so captivated by the receptionist's unusual clothing, he failed to hear her say, "Publishing is a very competitive business, so we need writers with established histories."

Ray wanted to indulge his curiosity and ask about her clothes, but he knew this was his only chance to pitch his book.

So he stayed on topic. "Ma'am, I can understand your policy," he said. "But would it be possible for me to get five minutes of someone's time. What is five minutes going to hurt?" he asked. Then he removed a roll of toilet paper from the box he'd been carrying. "I spent the last eleven months writing on this," he said. He extended his arm to give the receptionist a closer look. "Do you know how hard it is to write on single-ply toilet paper? It's like trying to write your name in the snow, if you know what I mean," he said as he smiled. "Can I just leave the box with you? All of my information is on the first roll," he said before dropping to his knees. "I'm begging you."

The receptionist sighed. "I'll see what I can do, sir. Now I need to get back to my work."

"Thank you ma'am," Ray said before he sprinted around the desk and hugged her. "I can't tell you how much I appreciate this." When he finished speaking, he turned and burst out the door. "I did it," he said. Then he realized that in his excitement he forgot to ask about the orange clothes.

After his excitement had subsided, he turned towards the government center. He was nearly late, so he walked using his longest and quickest strides. Tardiness was frowned upon, and he didn't need trouble at work. But after he'd walked a few blocks, he noticed the large crowd that had gathered on the *Peoples' Green*. The "green" was really a patch of dirt that had once housed Puppetgrad's daily newspaper.

As he drew nearer to the gathering, he noticed that most in the crowd were lounging in the early morning sunshine. The smell of waste ditches overpowered the slight breeze that struggled to push away the stench. Some of the area's inhabitants had erected tents or makeshift shelters. Ray wondered if he had stumbled across a run-down military encampment. Everyone present, including the children, wore a military-style uniform. Yet, no one seemed to be in a hurry to do anything.

A man who didn't fit with the rest of the group approached Ray. Instead of army camouflage, the man wore a tailored suit and leather loafers. His face was clean-shaven, and he wore a fresh hair cut.

"Hi," Ray said "I was curious, what is this—an army camp?"

The man laughed. "Of course it's not; it's a work site. These people are Federal Parks and Greens Inspectors."

"Wow, that's a lot of inspectors. What do they inspect?"

"I'm sorry," the man said, his manner suddenly turning icy. He flashed a badge issued by the Jobs Czar and asked, "May I see your papers?"

Ray swallowed hard and reached for his pack of identification papers. The man read the pages thoroughly before handing them back to Ray. "I see you work for Compassion County. Are you on your way to work then? Seems like you might be running a little late," the man said. His raised eyebrow turned the observation into an accusation.

"I got off the train early to—"

"Yes?"

"Sorry, I had a little brain cramp there," Ray said as he searched for a suitable explanation. He couldn't reveal his visit to Kerwin Publishing. "I got off the train early to stretch my legs and fulfill my exercise requirements," he blurted. "I've been a little busy at work, and I haven't been able to get out like I should. I don't need the Fitness Czar on my case," he said with a nervous giggle. "I know I should have just gone straight work. I'm really sorry it—"

"Don't sweat it. I'm just doing my job. I had to make sure you weren't an *orange* shrugging your duties."

"What is that?" Ray asked. He wondered whether the term might apply to the Kerwin receptionist.

The man in the suit went on to explain that during the early days of the Puppet Administration, a Federal-Government researcher discovered a causal connection between American capitalism and criminal behavior. "If some people didn't have more money, better jobs, and better lives than others, what reason would there be to commit crimes?" the researcher said.

This discovery was embraced by the President. He and his Administration pressed for dismissal of all criminal convictions—except the convictions of white collar criminals. After all, they were the ones who had rigged the capitalist system to their own advantage, and they had been fairly convicted.

After the White House had given them their marching orders, the Supreme Court Justices made the necessary proclamations. The judicial body ruled that any future criminal prosecutions must "clearly demonstrate that the effects of capitalism had not contributed to the crimes that were being prosecuted."

"It's impossible for me to prove that capitalism *didn't* have an impact on these crimes," one prosecutor was quoted as saying. "I wouldn't even know how to begin."

States were then faced with an interesting dilemma: their prisons had been emptied and the prosecution of new crimes had essentially been halted; did it make sense to even operate a correctional system? In every case, the answer was *no*. Prison doors were then barred and chained to keep people *out*.

As it had been with the dismantling of the military, the closure of jails and prisons provided an abundance of unused prison attire. Seeing the surplus of prison-wear, the Jobs Czar suggested that all remaining private-sector employees wear the uniforms as a "partial atonement for their sins. The private sector has been stealing for years," the Jobs Czar stated. "It's time they displayed their true selves."

Like nearly all of his colleagues, the man in the suit—a Federal Worksite Supervisor—had zealously supported the Job Czar's decision. "It's nice to have them easily visible," the supervisor said after he'd given Ray some history behind the unusual uniforms. "After all, we can't afford to have any oranges slacking off. There's work to be done."

The supervisor's words left Ray speechless.

"So you asked about the inspectors, and as one government employee to another, I'll tell you," the supervisor continued. "These are the people who came in second-place during the last Housing Lottery. Instead of being sent away empty-handed, the Federal Government has *hired* them to observe the state of any park or green in which they choose to reside. They receive a stipend and get to live in places like this until the next lottery."

Ray couldn't believe what he was hearing. It sounded like a joke to him. This was a shanty-town and nothing more. "And after they finish *observing*, what do they do?" he asked, trying to make sense of it all.

"They don't do anything, of course. Their job is to observe," the supervisor replied.

"What do the children do?" Ray asked.

"You don't get out much, do you? They're Trainee Inspectors. Sure, it's the parents who collect the checks, but it's never too early to start preparing the next generation to take their place in society. Am I right? Huh? Huh? Huh?" he said while prodding Ray in the ribs with his elbow.

Instead of smiling, Ray could only manage a confused expression. Then the supervisor gave a free history lesson to cure Ray's ignorance. "A few years back a professor at some university did a study. The results showed that holding gainful employment and collecting a paycheck led to increased feelings of empowerment and self-esteem. These people," he gestured with one arm towards the gathered throng, "as non-winners in the last Housing Lottery, are owed some type of consolation prize. As a means to address the inequity, they were given these *jobs*. Why should it be that only people who do *real* work should get to experience feelings of self-esteem? That doesn't sound *fair* to me."

Ray blinked his eyes and shook his head. Unfortunately, no amount of head-thrashing could make sense of such a preposterous idea. So he tried to change the subject. "What's the story with that?" he asked as a semi-truck and trailer pulled up next to the green.

"Our inspectors and trainees are entitled to certain perks. They get two catered meals each day on top of their accommodations on public park land. It's not a bad deal. It's free room and board." While the site supervisor spoke, a trio of men—all clad in the orange jumpsuits—emerged from the truck and busied themselves. One of them used a hydraulic lift and lowered a coffin-sized trough to the ground. The others scrambled to find serving utensils and prepared to serve the meal.

The supervisor jogged over to the truck and quickly returned with a bowl of steaming liquid. The bowl held a smattering of vegetable slivers that swam in a watery broth. Ray listened as the man described the history of the *Snake-Oil-Surprise*. The recipe called for imitation chicken broth instead of actual chicken stock. Congress had recently passed a law prohibiting the use of animals in any meals eaten by Americans who were not a member of Congress, Congressional aide, Supreme Court Justice, or an Administration Official or Auxiliary." The soup's imitation chicken broth tasted more like Ethyl-Noleo than chicken, but the inspectors had little control over their food supply. In the distant past, a slice of bread had been part of each inspector's meal, but with the shortage of wheat, bread was a distant memory for all but the most well-connected Americans.

Ray had seen enough. These truly were the *Peoples' People*—or more accurately, Greta Government's people—it was hard to dispute that.

Ray said goodbye to the worksite supervisor and ran to work. As he ducked inside the Compassion County government center, a nagging suspicion told him that he'd come to regret what he'd seen and done today.

Chapter 13

The ocean glistened in shades of cerulean and ultramarine as French Garamond watched the gentle swells roll past. A newly formed nation, *Garamondia*, appeared on the horizon. The jet that carried him was bound for the Garamondia's International Airport. The facility had been built upon the man-made island known as *Garamondia Three*.

During Garamondia's infancy, sea planes had been sufficient to accommodate the nation's air-travel needs. A flood of commerce changed that equation as the territory grew quickly. The influx of capital and know-how—provided in large part by American refugees—triggered an industrial and economic revolution in the self-made nation. The economic tsunami made an international airport a necessity, rather than a luxury.

Garamond smiled as he reflected upon Garamondia's—and his own—miracle stories. His given name was Earl, and he'd wandered far adrift of the plans he'd had for himself as a boy.

Garamond's parents loved to vacation in the California wine country. They'd even made occasional visits to France to sample and buy wine. His parent's tastes allowed the young Garamond to take an avid interest in the exotic, dark and light-hued liquids. French pleaded for "a tiny taste" each time a new bottle entered the family's home.

In no time, Garamond decided that he too wanted to own a vineyard in France. During high school, while his friends took metal shop, French was the only boy to take French class. His friends took to calling him "Frenchy." By the time he left for college, the nickname had stuck.

Garamond's father, Earl Senior, was a farmer. It had taken only a few crop failures for French to learn that the annual harvest was far from guaranteed. And for French, a proposition with a 10% chance of failure was too great a risk.

The inherent uncertainty of raising crops, combined with his aptitude for mathematics, led French away from the family farm. Instead of following his father's example or chasing his dream of owning a vineyard, French went to college and studied mechanical engineering.

After college graduation, French joined the American auto industry. He designed engines and drive-trains for pickup trucks and eventually, sport utility vehicles. He quickly climbed the ladder at Detroit Motor Works—the auto maker owned by Greta Government—until his ascent hit a roadblock.

Amidst the environmental hysteria that throttled the United States, Garamond worked nights and weekends to develop an SUV that was miles ahead the competition. His vehicle design delivered improvements in efficiency, comfort, performance, and safety over other existing vehicles. However, the Feds had already decided to kill the SUV. No auto company—no matter how environmentally friendly the performance—was allowed to manufacture the hated vehicle. The name SUV conjured up images of wealthy suburbanites flaunting their status—and those memories had no place in a progressive America.

After the *American* auto industry rebuffed his versatile vehicles, Garamond decided to explore the Caribbean for some elbowroom. He purchased the largest sparsely-inhabited island in the region, and he built a factory. Cities bloomed on surrounding islands as jobseekers flocked to the area. The aspiring workers hoped to get jobs building Garamond Utility Vehicles (GUVs).

Many in America scoffed when Garamond threatened to leave. During his farewell interview, Garamond said, "If the people in Washington think they'll be better off without my business, that's fine. The President and Congress seem to know everything. I'm sure they can replace these jobs."

A gusher of cash flowed into Garamond Industries's coffers. Customers committed to purchase GUVs that hadn't even been built. Investors begged to collaborate with the automaker. Flush with resources, Garamond Industries expanded beyond automobile construction.

Garamond's company developed revolutionary desalination technology and new construction materials and techniques—making the advances that enabled the construction of Garamondia Two, Three, and Four. Garamond Industries even developed a line of beers with *all* the taste and only *one-quarter* of the carbs.

Riding the crest of its newly acquired wealth and influence, Garamondia filed for nation status. Virtually overnight, the country evolved from one man's vision to the "New America."

Back in the old county, the President and Congress decried the rapid ascent of Garamondia and its complete lack of a social safety net. Garamondia's first president—a former congresswoman from Minnesota who had a pair of brass balls that put most of her male counterparts to shame—stated, "French Garamond set an important example when he showed the courage to strike out on his own. We intend to build upon that way of thinking. We're not running back to the old way of doing things."

The citizens of Garamondia knew they could benefit from the low-tax policies and emphasis on liberty that their new nation provided. Soon there were more workers willing to participate in the Garamondian experiment than there were jobs. However, the men and women who had rushed to Garamondia knew that entitlements like unemployment insurance, government retirement pensions, and welfare payments did not exist. The government existed to provide for the common defense and to promote the general welfare through the rule of law, not redistributionist taxation.

Following Garamond's example, other manufacturing and service organizations left the United States in droves. In a delicious slice of irony, Americans by the thousands collected their life's savings and swam across the Rio Grande or found holes in the southern border to slip into Mexico. These former Americans fled to other lands and pursued dreams of prosperity. Over time, even native Mexicans decided the trip north was no longer worth the trouble.

The disappearance of American capital and the shrinkage of the tax base proved devastating to Greta Government. For years, the Demagoblican Administrations and Congress had dragged their feet on securing America's southern border. When Demagoblicans realized that their chances for a socialist paradise were leaking through the southern border, a complete and sturdy wall seemingly rose out of the dust. The barrier blocked all southward traffic. "We need to keep this wealth in America. We can't have these people disappearing with our hard-earned tax money," a prominent Congressman had said while he introduced a bill to "to prevent the rampant capital theft."

When Garamond learned about the new border wall, he established the *Underground Light Rail*.

The Light-Railers—as the guides and protectors were called—were mainly ex-soldiers and sailors. These fighting-men and women had sworn an oath to defend and protect the *Constitution*, and none of them seemed to recall ever unswearing that oath. The Light-Railers tended to live in border towns in the north and south. They helped to smuggle their countrymen beyond the walls and barbed-wire fences that kept Americans in.

In spite of all that had happened, Garamond still thought of himself as an American. He denied himself citizenship in his new nation. He hoped that one day his native land would return to its senses. But judging by the President's address the night before, the odds seemed stacked against America's return to sensibility.

Garamond's jet rocked gently as it made its final approach to the runway. When the landing gear made touch-down, Garamond pulled out a cell phone and made a call. Feelings of anticipation welled in his stomach while he waited for his long-time friend to pick up.

"Hey, Frenchie, how you been?" asked Milton Kerwin as he answered the call. The two of them first met when Kerwin was assigned to interview the industrialist years earlier. The men became fast friends following their first meeting. Though the interview helped to launch a long-term friendship, Kerwin's article featuring Garamond was rejected by his editor for the blatant "pro-business bias" of the story.

"I'm doing well, Milt. It's rough down here—eighty-five and sunny every day. I don't how much longer I can take it."

Kerwin groaned. "That *does* sound rough—you jerk. But I know that someone like you doesn't call to talk about the weather. What can I do for you?"

"I need a big favor, but I promise I'll give you anything you need to do the job. I was listening to Mannequin yesterday—all that stuff about hate speech—and it got me thinking. Have you heard if there's something going on?"

"It's strange that you should ask. I got the same impression, and then this morning a guy walks into my lobby and leaves a box with the receptionist. At first I thought it was a joke, but then I started to read what he'd written, and now I'm wondering if the Feds don't already know about his story. I have no idea how they *could* know. This guy isn't an established author or anything. But they seem to know." Kerwin sighed before he continued. "And it's bad omen when the President makes a big deal about hate speech the day before you receive a package like that. Maybe it's just some tough talk before the elections. The Gazette has been speculating that McLaughagain is getting ready to retire any day."

Kerwin was referring to current Vice President Chuckles McLaughagain. In addition to giving the Administration comic relief with his malapropisms and tall tales, McLaughagain had become a *designated Vice President* for the Demagoblican heads of state. For years, each successive president had chosen McLaughagain as a running mate. Once the Demagoblican presidential candidate won the election, McLaughagain kept the people in stitches until the final few months of his president's second term. McLaughagain then abruptly retired. McLaughagain's sudden departure allowed the president to name a new vice president.

The replacement vice president served for a few weeks and then the lame-duck president also retired unexpectedly. The sudden departures of both the sitting vice president and president allowed McLaughagain's newly-named replacement to slide straight into the White House.

The political maneuvering had two key benefits. First, the tactic allowed the newly sworn-in Demagoblican president to run in the election as an incumbent. However sparse it had been, the new president could claim that he had on-the-job experience. The abrupt changes also allowed the new president to direct the activities of the FGNB during the final, critical days of the campaign.

Given the success of the Demagoblican technique, the presidential election ballots no longer included a specific candidate's name. The ballot simply read "Demagoblican Candidate for President," to give the party maximum flexibility when naming their candidates.

Washington buzzed with speculation as pundits and other insiders tried to guess the identity of McLaughagain's (and ultimately President Mannequin's replacement). Mannequin was entering the final few months of his second term, and he was preparing for his departure. Many suggested that Senator Spendini would be the next Demagoblican contender to ride the vice presidential fast-track straight into the White House.

Garamond had read the same rumors over the Internet, and he knew that it was time to act. "I don't blame you for being nervous," he said. "You're there, and I'm here, but you know the stakes. If we're going to make this happen, it has to be right now." He paused a moment. He hated asking Kerwin to risk his business's reputation and possibly a lot more, but it was the only way. "Is the novel any good?"

"It will ruffle some feathers, but it won't make a bit of difference if the Feds won't allow people to download it."

"Please just get the rights and make the novel available. I've got a feeling about this. This could be our last chance for a long time. I'll worry about the Feds. What do you say?"

After Garamond stopped talking, the silence lingered for what seemed like hours. Milt stared at his feet, grateful his friend wasn't there to see him wavering in the face of the decision. "I'll do it," Kerwin muttered, "but if things go badly, I might need some of your friends to come and save my ass."

Chapter 14

Agent Caldwell now feared for her life. She couldn't confirm her suspicions, but the field office buzzed with whispers about the hate-speech conspiracy. Even while she sat at her desk, she could feel the stares of accusing eyes against her back. When she turned around to see who was lurking behind her, she often found a knot of agents who then exchanged sheepish glances and dispersed. If she tried to start a conversation with a coworker, the conversation ended quickly. Then her colleague seemed to flee. She felt invisible *and* naked while she walked the building's harshly lit corridors. The walls felt like they were closing in on her. But in her heart, she still nurtured hope that the conspiracy rumors were true. *If they think this is a vast right-wing conspiracy, maybe they'll try to grab the bigger fish. Then I might be able to slip through the net.*

Even while she sat in her apartment, she couldn't focus on anything except her fear. She blamed Watford for her troubles, and she hated herself for sheltering him. She hadn't been able to bring herself to read any more of his novel even though part of her was still curious. The things Watford had written reminded her of her father. And the uncertainty made Calder miss her dad more than ever. She wiped a tear that had formed in the corner of her eye and grabbed her book reader. *Maybe reading will help*, she told herself.

In the Hall (Reflections on America)
Chapter 3
I pressed my ear against the door. Anxiety
gripped me this time. I'd been eager to meet

Uncle Sam, but this man—not so much.

Through the door I heard the Boom! Boom! Booming of a bass drum beat. I knocked.

As the door opened, the sounds of protest greeted me. I never would have imagined I'd hear the ungentle strains of Protest Vigorously in Opposition to the Mechanical Apparatus' music flowing from inside the room. An antique record player—its speakers turned to full volume—blared at me from the corner. Apparently Karl Marx preferred vinyl.

Marx wore a broad, toothy grin as he opened the door. For a moment, I thought I'd entered the wrong room—he looked so much like Santa Claus. His gray hair and beard, the mischievous twinkle in his eyes, told me that he had more in common with Kris Kringle than I had originally believed.

"Hello, Mr. Marx. I—"

"I know why you're here, and you can save your breath."

"What's the problem? Cat got your tongue? I come to ask you about your philosophies, and you don't want to defend them?"

He ignored me. Then he walked across the room and settled into a plush leather recliner. He reached over to a side table and grabbed a pipe. He shoved a pinch of tobacco into the pipe's bowl and struck a match. Marx then offered a gesture of his friendship as he held up his fist with his middle finger extended towards me.

"Face it. You blew it on the nature of human

nature," I said. "Your idea of paradise is a land where people of your choosing get to sit around and wait for others to do all the work. You would have been more accurate if you called your dream world a beggar's paradise. Maybe it's time you issued a retraction."

"I don't care what *you* think," he snorted as he rose from his seat. "I'm more popular than ever. Take a look around when you get back home. Virtually everyone in your government has come around to my way of thinking. Your *independent* media members think I'm a visionary. Why in the name of Joe Stalin would I throw that away?"

"You've got to be kidding me," I shot back. "The original Soviet Union didn't even last a century. That's not much of a track record. I'm betting that this crop of American Socialists isn't going to fare any better."

Marx smiled and shook his head. He was the wise master. I was the ignorant child who had been raised by chimps. "The Soviet Socialists didn't implement my ideas *correctly*. Your American socialists are doing a much better job." He grinned at me and then walked back to his leather recliner. He grabbed a bottle of cognac and poured himself three fingers of the amber liquid.

"So it doesn't bother you that Marxism can only be implemented through force? Weren't you supposed to be the great humanitarian thinker of your age?"

"If it ain't broke, don't fix it."

"Your theories seem to run contrary to some of history's top economic thinkers. What do you say about that?"

"Adam Smith couldn't carry my pencil in a wheelbarrow."

He was unflappable, a true gentleman. I had to get him to show his true colors. "Do you ever run into Uncle Sam?"

Marx's expression grew dark, like a storm had begun to brew behind his eyes. "Why would you ask me about that drunken fool? He's probably sitting in a puddle of his own puke."

"I was just wondering whether you felt any jealousy about seeing the Soviet Union collapse. After all, the United States is still standing. Aren't you a little worried about your inability to close the deal?"

In an instant, he crossed the space between us and wrapped his fleshy hand around my throat. His calm demeanor had been replaced by that of a deranged killer. "You're Uncle Sam isn't going to be around much longer, you naïve twit," he growled. "Give me a few more years, and he won't rate a poster for jock itch spray, let alone war bonds. He's finished! America's finished!" Marx released his grip and pushed me away. "Now get the hell out of my room!"

I rubbed my now-reddened throat as Marx whispered, "I'm going to enjoy watching America drown. Once people realize they can turn their lives over to the government, capitalism is finished," he said with a sneer. "When you reach the bottom line, success as a capitalist requires too much responsibility and hard work. By contrast, Marxism is *readily accessible* to the people," he said as he jabbed his finger into my chest.

I opened my mouth to reply, but he interrupted.

"Take from the rich, give to the poor!" he shouted. "What could be easier than that?" Then he laughed maniacally and began to dance around the room. "All I need to do is convince one generation that they are victims. Then, like birds flying south for the winter, they'll know exactly what to do. They won't even give their decisions a second thought, as they flock to the polls to keep the Demagoblicans in power."

Without warning, he grabbed me by the shoulders. His grip was stronger than I'd expected. He guided me slowly and steadily across the room. When we reached the doorway, he threw the door open and shoved me into the hallway. Stunned and speechless, I stood motionless while I was broadsided by his final salvo. Amidst a cascade of spittle that he'd launched from his lips, he shouted, "Suck on that, bitch!"

Then he slammed the door in my face.

"What have I done?" Calder asked herself aloud. She dropped the book reader and flopped down onto the couch, burying her face in the cushions. She cried with heaving sobs. It wasn't a matter of whether the Teachers would visit her; it was only a question of when.

Chapter 15

Ray fought his way through a jungle of placards that had been suspended from the ceiling. The safari had become a necessary ritual. Compassion County administration had decided that fragrances, cell phones, caffeine, religious imagery, non-recyclable plastics, fatty foods, and a laundry-list of other items "were unsuitable for residents of the county." The items named on the list were banned.

To ensure that county employees had been duly instructed, the county board decreed that warning signs be "suspended from the ceiling by cord of not less than forty-eight inches in length and of recycled hemp construction." The display was required for each cubicle and office in the building. The placards conveyed the letters of the law in 16 languages—including an audio track composed entirely of human whistles and mouthed clicks.

As Ray settled into his chair, his telephone immediately rang. When he picked up the call, it was Milton Kerwin. Ray felt his legs turn rubbery.

"I'd like to publish your book, Ray," Kerwin stated after he'd introduced himself.

"Thank you, Mister Kerwin. I don't know what to say."

"All my friends call me, Milt. You can start there. But before we get too far, you need to realize that things might go rough on you, if you decide to publish," Kerwin warned.

Ray stayed silent a moment before replying. "What do you mean?"

"I think the Feds already know about your book. I think the President's little speech on sedition was somehow aimed you, but don't ask me why. I just have a hunch."

"So what does that mean?" Ray asked.

"It means that I hope your past years' taxes are in order," Kerwin gave himself a courtesy chuckle to cover his discomfort. He wasn't joking, but he didn't want to make Ray any more paranoid than he probably already was. "What it really means," Kerwin began again, "is that we are going to start selling licenses for readers to download your book. I wish I could tell you what you're going to be paid for the rights. I really don't know. I can only say that I plan to run a payment of ten million dollars through the Hand of Equity. The problem is that the Hand's instruction booklet states that the Federal Government 'reserves the right to adjust all wages paid at the discretion of the Administration'. So it's anyone's guess how much of the advance will make it to your bank account."

"I appreciate you going through all of this."

"Don't sweat it. Hopefully this will help my company too."

"Thank you, Milt. I'll try not to let you down."

"You can't let me down. No matter how this turns out, it will still be a win." Kerwin paused as he tried to decide how to proceed. "When I made that bad joke about your taxes earlier, I was trying to tell you something else. A number of people aren't going to see your book as a funny story with an opposing viewpoint. They're going to call it sedition. Then they're going to call both of us a bunch of names and try to intimidate us. We need to meet—soon. I want to give you a phone number. The number will connect you to a good friend of mine. He's someone you want to know if the Feds get too frisky. He runs an organization that can help people like us if that happens."

"I understand," Ray said quietly, thinking back to the note that "SC" had placed on top of his story.

"You've heard about the speech bullies—they're not to be taken lightly. Keep your eyes open. Don't go out at night by yourself. Get a good set of locks. And pray that I'm wrong."

"I knew what I was doing when I gave this to you. I worry about my wife and my kids, but I have to do this."

"I understand." Kerwin was a widower. His wife had been judged too old to merit treatment for breast cancer. "I don't know what I would do if I were in your shoes." Kerwin cleared his voice as he thought about his wife. He felt a twinge of regret as he thought about Watford's family before he said, "Let's just both be smart, and everything will work out fine."

"I really am committed to going forward with this. I'd feel like a coward if I didn't."

"Sounds good, Ray," Kerwin said. I'm going to route your advance as soon as I hang up. We'll talk soon."

When the conversation ended, Ray almost leapt to his feet. He shoved the dangling disclaimers out of his way and then hurried to the elevators. He worked hard to hide his exuberance—he still had one hurdle to jump before he could leave the building.

As the elevator descended to the bottom floor, Ray readied himself for his performance. When the elevator doors opened, he trudged out into the corridor and dragged his feet as he walked. He needed to convince the guard that he was ill.

"Papers, please," the security guard grunted.

Ray slowly reached into his pocket and pulled out the pack of papers. He mustered a phony sneeze and aimed it at the officer. The agent of the Jobs Department clacked the keys on his lap top. He quickly discovered that Ray was trying to take his fifth sick leave day of the year. "If you leave the office, you'll need to produce a doctor's note when you come back, or it's a stint of hard labor," the guard said, a smile appearing on his face.

"Yes, sir, I am aware of that, sir," Ray wheezed.

The guard inspected Ray through narrowed eyes. He searched for any evidence of malingering. Following the brief examination the guard said, "Carry on then," and waved Ray forward.

Ray fought the urge to run from the building. But once he was outdoors, he ran to the commuter rail station.

Nearly an hour later, he arrived at the BELOV'D UNITERS Curio Emporium. He pushed the front door open and tried to hide his smile. Sarah was standing behind the counter and reading the Hand of Equity's user manual.

A handful of customers browsed the shop. One of them admired busts of the BELOV'D UNITERS. Another thumbed through a calendar that commemorated the BELOV'D UNITERS' many wondrous deeds. A third customer vigorously sifted through a box of *Secular Messiah* trading cards.

Ray and Sarah had taken over the business when Sarah's parents became too old to run the store. Sarah was the only employee, and she also served as the manager. Over the years, the curio, knick knack, and odds-and-ends store hadn't made them rich. It had allowed Sarah to carry on her family's business. "Hey, pretty lady," Ray said, causing his wife to notice his presence. While he looked at her, he realized that his Sarah had never been required to wear the orange jumpsuit of a private-sector worker. *Maybe there are some benefits to running a shop devoted to the BELOVED UNITERS after all,* he told himself.

"What are you doing here? You didn't get fired did you?" she asked.

"No such luck. But I did get my book published."

"Oh, that's nice—" she said. "You're joking, right?"

"I just got the call."

Sarah ran around the counter and hugged her husband. She was thrilled that his work had finally paid off. "When's it going to be published?"

"That's the funny part. The publisher told me the book would be available today. Then he said he didn't know how much I'd be paid for the rights. He said something about a ten million dollar payment and the Hand of Equity and told me to wait and see."

"Now I know you're kidding me." She gave him a playful shove.

"I'm serious. It's weird. Mr. Kerwin said something about the government setting wages. I never knew the Feds do that. Maybe they passed a law without telling anyone," Ray said, laughing at his own joke.

"Speaking of the Hand, I don't think ours is working. I ran a few of the transactions and—"

"The transactions didn't arrive in the bank?"

"No, payments arrived, but the amounts were off. The deposits barely covered our costs. If there *isn't* something wrong, we're getting *ripped off*. We've been receiving enough to pay for our costs but that's it. The deposits don't leave any profit margin at all," Sarah said.

"That can't be right. What sort of business person would keep their doors open if they couldn't even make a return on their investment? That would be like working for nothing."

Chapter 16

Rita the Clown wore a baggy, rainbow-colored clown suit as she barged into Senator Spendini's office. She slammed her leather portfolio down onto the reception desk, and shouted "Where's Spendini?" Her face had been slathered with pancake makeup, and a red ball covered her nose. She immediately pulled her horn from her pocket and began to squeeze the ball end—offering an overt display of her malice. *Honk! Honk! Honk!* "I'm here to do the peoples' business!" she shouted.

The receptionist, hoping to defuse the tirade, mustered her calmest tone. It was the voice typically reserved for muggers and unfamiliar dogs that seemed ready to bite. "I'm sorry about the delay, Madam Speaker. Senator Spendini is on his way right now. Can I get you anything?"

"Ice water," the angry clown growled as she shot the hired help an icy stare.

Spendini poked his head through the door and smiled. "Rita, I'm sorry to be late. Are you a little edgy today?"

"What did that tart say to you?"

"She didn't *need* to say anything. I heard you from my office. I appreciate you coming over, but maybe next time you can keep it down a little? You're scaring my staff. And I need them. We have damage control to do over the Hand. Let's go sit down." Spendini took Rita's hand and led her to a conference room.

Hulking oaken bookshelves, laden with the hundreds of volumes of Certified Federal Registers, United States Codes, and other similarly bound volumes, lined the room's walls. Other books contained thousands of pages of statutes, rules, executive orders, rulings and Supreme Court opinions. Spendini always felt a sense of pride when he entered the room. He'd helped to shape the content of every page. However, his revelry was short-lived. "I've heard that DJSM is getting a ton of calls. At first I thought we might have some glitches," Rita said as she took a seat at the table. "Now I'm wondering if there's something you should be telling me." She eyed Spendini and brandished her bicycle horn like a truncheon.

Spendini offered a weak smile. "That's where we *might* need to do some damage control. President Mannequin said the Hand was only going to *process* transactions, but his statement was only partially true." Spendini raised his hand and held his thumb and index finger half an inch apart to indicate that the President had only fibbed *a little bit.*

The clown honked her horn into Spendini's face. "What do you mean by partially true?"

"As DJSM developed the Hand, they developed a number of other functions. The transaction processor was meant to be the beginning—a test drive of the system. Staff over at DJSM must have *mistakenly* activated another of the Hand's capabilities," Spendini lied. He had authorized the activation of the progressive-tax-code function.

While Spendini explained the situation, Rita pulled a long, red balloon from her pocket. She stretched the balloon and began to inflate it. "Does progressive mean what I think that it does?" she asked. Then she began to twist and turn the balloon and revealed a twisted balloon that looked like a tower in Paris. "*Voilà,*" she said.

"Yes. A progressive tax code has been imposed upon everyone who makes a purchase. The good news is that the take has been impressive."

"How impressive?" Rita asked as she leaned in towards Spendini.

"Twenty-five percent increase," Spendini whispered.

"So what's the downside of more money?"

"Uh....we haven't really passed the laws authorizing the progressive taxation. Unless—"

"Unless what?'" Rita asked wide-eyed with anticipation.

"Unless we pass a retroactive law *authorizing* the progressive taxation."

Rita the Clown rubbed her hands together and smiled. "Is that all? I was worried you were going to say that we had to hold town meetings with those ingrate voters. Retroactive law—piece of cake." Rita had waited her entire career waiting for a day when the prosperous would be brought to heel. It was finally time to teach them who was boss. "We can have a bill through the House by sundown."

Spendini nodded in admiration. "There won't be any problems in the Senate."

"But what if the conservatives figure out what we're up to?" Rita asked with mock horror.

"All three of them?" Spendini laughed. "What are their constituents going to do, vote libertarian?" Then they both had a chuckle.

"Speaking of brain-dead conservatives, have you read that book yet?" she asked. She refused to say the novel's title.

"I've heard some rumblings, but I haven't read it yet. So some redneck has written a novel—big deal. Lemonpants and the FGNB are going to twist the publisher's arm. The book will be retracted by this time tomorrow. Kerwin has to know that we can make his life miserable." Spendini walked over and began to massage Rita's shoulders. "This book won't amount to anything. Conservatism died when Reagan left office. His whole presidency was nothing more than a capitalist fart, the stink of which has finally died away."

Spendini looked over Rita's shoulder and saw the frown on her face. "Trust me. Once the Bureau gets its hooks into Kerwin, he'll beg for the chance to retract that bucket of sludge."

Chapter 17

Milton Kerwin paced inside his office. Part of him felt like a caged lion silently waiting to gouge his prey. The other part, overtaken with an anxiety that nagged at his guts, knew that he was on the menu for the faux-news jackals.

Years earlier, Kerwin had been a news man too. He still remembered the argument he'd had with his dearest friend, Edward Tramsoot. The two of them had been discussing the future of the news media. Tramsoot, the newly promoted editor-in-chief of the Yellow Lapdog Gazette, tried to convince Kerwin to stay on at the paper following the wave of Federal Government bailouts. Kerwin hated to part ways with his friend, but he couldn't stay. He'd tried to convince Tramsoot to leave the paper and go into publishing.

"You know that the news has been my life forever, Milt. I can't leave it," Tramsoot said.

"But it won't even be news anymore. Not with the government as your reluctant shareholder. They can't even be trusted to manage their own affairs," Kerwin countered.

"You're over reacting," Tramsoot pleaded. "We've been assured by key members of Congress and the Administration that the bailout money is only meant to help us stay viable. Even *they* recognize the importance of an independent news-gathering apparatus. They have no plans to interfere with our work."

"C'mon, Ed, since when has the Government ever given away anything without attaching strings to it?" Kerwin asked.

"I know it's a risk, but we can make it work. We've been in

this together for this long. Stick with me," Tramsoot pleaded.

"I'm sorry, but I can't. Our job is to be the public's watchdog. How are we supposed to keep an eye on the rule makers once we've taken their money? I guarantee there will come a day when your *reluctant shareholders* want you to report a certain issue in a certain way. Maybe it will seem insignificant, but at that moment, when you give in and tell the story the way the government wants it told, the free press will die," Kerwin said before falling silent.

As they stared at one another across Tramsoot's desk, both men realized they had no choice but to part ways. Kerwin left to run Kerwin Publishing, the company started by his grandfather. Tramsoot stayed on at the Gazette. Though he was hurt by Kerwin's decision to leave, he understood.

Kerwin's upset stomach told him that Tramsoot would be among those in attendance today. Tramsoot had been stung by the truth of Kerwin's prediction, regarding the media's loss of objectivity, following the bailout. Over time, Tramsoot had even assembled a list of rationalizations to justify his actions. After a while he even began to believe the reasons he'd listed. "Our budgets are stretched so thin, we can't do reporting like we used to do. The Federal Government News Bureau has a vested interest in making sure that the news gets spread accurately. Otherwise, how would they have any idea how the people feel about their performance in office?"

Kerwin rubbed his temples. He'd heard all of Tramsoot's empty justifications before. He didn't want to wade into the mess again. He just wished that this whole thing was already over. Then he took a moment to daydream about his childhood. He remembered the first time he told his father that he wanted to be a newsman. The young Kerwin had scribbled the word "PRESS" on a sheet of paper. He then slid the paper into the band of his father's fedora. Then, he interviewed both of his parents until they finally shooed him away.

After Kerwin retired to his bedroom, he composed a single-sheet newspaper which he left at his parents' bedroom door the next morning. The memory made him smile as the clock took its time in ticking down the wait's final minutes.

When the time arrived, Kerwin left his office and walked down to the building's lunchroom. The chairs had been arranged in orderly rows for the event. At the front of the room sat a table with a single chair. As Kerwin waited outside the cafeteria doors, he listened to the babble of cross-talk between the assembled reporters. He peered inside and saw that every chair in the cafeteria was full.

He pulled at his tie and suit coat and then strode into the room. Conversation stopped upon his entry. The sudden silence made it feel as if the air had been sucked from the room. Kerwin fought the urge to look for Tramsoot. *I'm sure Ed will let me know where he is,* he told himself.

The clatter of Kerwin's shoe heels echoed across the silent space. When he reached the table, he was grateful to find a glass of water. His throat felt like it had been coated with dust. After a sip of water he asked, "Can all of you hear me at the back?" Murmurs and whispers were the only reply. "Thank you all for coming. I didn't expect so many people. I guess I should have known better." He paused and knit his fingers together to soothe his nerves. Sweat glistened on his forehead. "My receptionist told me that she wished that she'd had a few more arms and a few more ears to help with all the calls that she's been getting about the book." He mustered a faint chuckle to cover the silence. "I supposed we should get started. What would you like to know?"

"So Mister Kerwin," one of the reporters began after he'd shot

out of his seat—doing a perfect imitation of a jack-in-the box. A
sneer adorned his face. "Given the subject matter of this book,
I'm guessing that you have ties to right-wing hate groups. Isn't
that true?"

Kerwin smiled. *I guess they're not going to waste any time.*
He took another sip of water. *This could be a long day.* "Wow,
a toughie right out of the gate. You'd think I was running for
president or something—oh, my mistake. If I was a Dem running
for president, you'd ask me if I wore boxers or briefs. But since you
asked, I'll share a little secret with you. If you think I'm going to
be intimidated because you disagree with my views on individual
liberty and personal responsibility, you might as well pack up
your pencils and go home. Next question please."

A chubby, bald dude wearing an Hawaiian shirt and flip-flops
stood. "This book just encourages grid-lock. Why don't you want
to see a move toward the center, man?"

Kerwin grinned. "Are you talking about the center between
Socialism and Soviet-style Communism?" he asked. "We passed
the mid-point between Capitalism and Socialism a long time ago.
If we want to find that center, we need to undo a lot of what's
been done."

"What about people who can't fend for themselves?" This
time it was a female reporter with brown hair. She looked like
she'd just stepped out of the '60's with her bell-bottoms, sandals,
and tie-dyed, "What about Peace?" tee-shirt.

"What about those people?" Kerwin countered.

"It's not fair to deny them the help they need."

"I don't deny that sometimes people need help, but the
current solution is unsustainable."

"But the Government needs to make things fair for everyone,"
the peacenik countered.

"Let me ask you something. How does it help the poor—or anyone for that matter—when the government passes laws that drive up the cost of food or energy? When the economy goes into the tank and people can't find a job to make ends meet, how does that help the poor? You progressives care nothing about the poor or you would never have started down this road of phony compassion. This is nothing more than a power-grab. In the end, everyone will be forced to do as you say. And in that state of *hyper governmental bliss* that you desperately seek to attain, not a single breath will be drawn without your consent." Kerwin then banged his fist on the table. "And that's exactly how you want it."

The reporters began to grumble. Some of them shouted threats or told Kerwin to "Shut up." Then, in the back of the room, a solitary figure rose, cleared his throat, and said, "Hello, Milt." Gasps and uneasy chuckles preceded an eerie silence. Many in the group knew the history between Kerwin and Tramsoot. "You've always had a gift for the dramatic, haven't you?" Tramsoot asked. "Clearly, your life in publishing has made you wealthier—but not smarter."

Tramsoot hated the plan that Larry Lemonpants had suggested. He hadn't wanted to stop at ridiculing Kerwin and Watford. He wanted to see the Teachers beat some civility into them. But his feelings about Lemonpants' plan wouldn't keep him from using this opportunity to embarrass his former friend. "That novel—something that all of America's children are able to see, I might add—is filled with disparaging remarks about the President, the Congress, and revered icons of human history. How do you counter charges that this book is seditious and filled with hate speech—that the book defies the intent of the First Amendment?" Tramsoot asked.

"You're work defies the intent of the First Amendment,

Edward. The Constitution specifically guarantees your freedom to do your job, yet you and your *comrades* have hopped up into the master's lap. You *voluntarily* censor yourself. You dig deep enough to find a story that suits your template, and then you stop digging." Kerwin winked at Tramsoot.

"I'll have you know that the Federal Government News Bureau scrutinizes our work very closely." Tramsoot had already begun to get angry.

"Sure, they scrutinize your work to make sure that it matches the script that people—like Larry Lemonpants—have written."

"It sounds like you're not going to apologize for and retract that book. So you leave me no choice but to say that no matter how many copies of it are sold, it will never earn a place on the Yellow-Lapdog-Gazette's bestseller list. That list is for novels, not right-wing propaganda."

"You want to talk about propaganda, what about your support of the *Motorized Voter Law* that Congress passed?" Kerwin referred to the Federal election law that banned any form of identity check at polling places. And because Congress had passed the law, no state could have passed a law that superseded the federal law, even if it had wanted to do. The ban on verifying voter identity was only the beginning. The historic voting-rights act contained other damaging standards.

Congress decreed that a single "election day" was too big a hardship for some voters. States were then required to conduct elections over a two-week span or forfeit all forms of Federal funding. In the aftermath of the law, elections became a spectacle to witness. Caravans of voters drove from state to state and coast to coast to cast their votes. The Demagoblican party gave these *professional* voters two meals a day and promised them the chance to see the country. The traveling electoral circuses were treated to appearances by rock stars, movie stars, and often, the current Demagoblican President, as they made their rounds.

In one particularly egregious example of the election law's impact, the conservative governor of Arizona was defeated following a landslide election loss. Though the incumbent conservative received nearly two million votes—a figure that accounted for nearly 80% of Arizona's 2.5 million registered voters—he still lost by twelve million votes.

Instead of calling attention to the fishiness of an election with five times more votes cast than registered voters, the Yellow Lapdog Gazette praised the "spectacular exercise of electoral vigor" by Arizona's citizens. Year later, Tramsoot still refused to even consider that something might have been amiss in that Arizona election.

"How can you not call your support of Motorized Voter propaganda?" Kerwin continued. "That law not only opened the door to election fraud, it laid out the welcome mat and left a house-warming gift for it. If a conservative group had been accused of the same voter fraud as the Oak Seed Foundation had been, the Demagoblicans would have shoved their own mothers aside as they ran to start the investigation. But now, even years later, we still haven't seen any kind of federal look-see. What gives?"

"All you conservatives want to do is disenfranchise poor voters and make it harder for them to be heard during elections," Tramsoot argued.

"And all your statist rag tries to do is bully people so they believe that if they call 'bullshit,' they are the ones who are guilty of a crime. Can any of you say with a straight face that life is tougher now than it was two hundred years ago? Certainly it might seem tougher now because people have Greta Government to do everything for them. But do you really believe that it's harder to cast a vote today than it was in the past?" Kerwin asked.

"You're just a typical conservative. You have *yours* and you want to make sure that no one else can get it."

"And that just shows how intellectually lazy you can be, Ed. It's all a scam. Have you ever noticed how government *wants* more money whenever times are good? Then it *needs* more money when times are tough. But there's never a time when it can do with what it has or one penny less. And God forbid any of us dare to raise an eyebrow or object. I have news for you, Ed. We're not going to take this any more."

"Don't kid yourself, Milt. You're so greedy, you'll take anything you can get your hands on, and this book shows it." The gathered reporters erupted into applause and shouts of support. Tramsoot waited a moment for the noise to fade. "How do you sleep at night? You should be ashamed of yourself and you know it."

After Tramsoot's verbal *Coup de grace*, the gathered reporters joined in the rant. Insults, threats, and a few of the cafeteria chairs were hurled towards the front of the room. Kerwin had little choice but to flee the angry mob. The reporters cheered when they saw Kerwin disappear from the cafeteria. They'd played their role to perfection. News of Kerwin's decision to retract Watford's novel was imminent—or so they thought.

Chapter 18

While he rode the elevator to his office, Larry Lemonpants was curious to hear how the Kerwin Publishing news conference had gone. However, that news would have to wait for a while. After running from the elevator, Lemonpants threw open the door to his office and rushed to his desk.

Since its inception, EEFF had successfully erased all traces of prohibited-free-speech from the American publishing industry. And though the tight censorship fulfilled an important role in the progressive, American democracy, it made for boring reading. Every novel that hit the shelves mumbled the same tired tales about the government's benevolent goodness and the super-concentrated evil that sloshed within the hearts of businessmen. Lemonpants could scarcely remember the last time an unapproved novel had been published.

Real books were scarce. The major publishing houses didn't even bother printing books on bound paper pages. Too few could afford the expense. So Lemonpants, and those like him, were forced to pay extra for exclusive printings—a process that took time.

The bound, paper copy of *In the Hall (Reflections on America)* that rested on the center of his desk was a rare treat. The book was an unexpected gift from Edward Tramsoot. A sticky note, attached to the book's cover, read: "Here's a chance to see how Kerwin spends his days. You'll probably be interested in Chapter 4."

The cover art showed the book's title and an illustrated depiction of Uncle Sam's red, white, and blue top hat. Instead of showing the hat in pristine condition, the headwear looked tattered and soiled. Lemonpants laughed at the elementary-school imagery. "If that's the best this guy can do, I'm not sure what's got everyone so worked up," he said. When he finished laughing, he opened the book's cover and ran his fingertips across the pages—caressing them. He lifted the book and pressed it to his cheek, savoring the smell of the paper.

He allowed himself to read a passage here and there while he allowed his anticipation to build. He decided to go straight to chapter four as Tramsoot had recommended. *I can always come back to those later.*

When he found the correct page, Lemonpants took a deep breath and began to read.

In the Hall (Reflections on America)
Chapter 4

My visit with Mother Nature started poorly. I found her sitting in a rocking chair, a heavy, woolen blanket wrapped around her. As she shivered beneath her wrap, she whispered, "I'm so feverish…so feverish," in a voice almost too quiet hear.

"So you're not feeling well," I said. "You certainly don't sound well."

She turned her head to face me. She gazed as if she were trying to place my face. She pulled at the blanket causing it to nestle her even more tightly. "I've had such a fever since you humans arrived. Your SUV's and lawn mowers and barbeque grills have done this to me. I don't know how much more I can take," she rasped.

"I would have thought you'd be feeling a lot better. Internal combustion engines have been outlawed—well, except for a select few in Washington, California and New York. I would have imagined that you'd be feeling a lot better."

A fleeting look of anger crossed her face. "I fear those changes were too little, too late," she said. She followed the remark with a sneeze. It was the phony type of sneeze children perform when they hope to stay home from school. It looks cute on a kid. It's pathetic when Mother Earth is faking sick. "Maybe if you humans would stop cutting down the forests and burning my hair, I might be able to recover." She wheezed and coughed some more.

"Exactly what hair would that be, ma'am?"

"The grasslands and the forests are my hair. You go on covering them with roads and parking lots and convenience stores. When does it end?" A coughing jag erupted. I fully expected to see one of her lungs dangling from her lips given the force of the coughs.

By now, I'd seen enough of the performance. "We both know that earth warmed and cooled long before anything even resembling an internal-combustion engine was invented. What caused the end of the last ice age, wooly mammoth farts?" I asked.

Mother Nature stood up from her chair and threw off the blanket. "How dare you!" she roared. "I'm Mother Nature!"

"I know who you are—you narcissistic hypochondriac. You're so desperate for attention, you allow people to spread these half-baked fairy tales just so you can get some ink. You've been cooling and warming since long before humans. You just can't stand it when God gets all the attention for creating you. I've got news for you, baby. My eleven-year-old son was able to figure out that the polar ice caps melt during the summer and reform during the winter. And he didn't even need a grant to do it."

I was standing now too. I'd been force-fed at the all-you-can-eat buffet of environ-maniac-hysteria for long enough, and I was full to the gills. "You stayed silent while environmental groups scared the hell out of everyone so they could sell their filthy carbon credits. Then they used that money to finance the court actions that pulverized our economy into shattered bits and pieces. Meanwhile, these fanatics virtually guaranteed that all future generations of Americans will get to know exactly what it feels like to live in poverty. Human beings are starving in the streets because your disciples are working overtime to ensure that there are no factories to employ workers and create goods, and there are no businesses to sell anything. And all of this is happening to *solve* a problem that was never even a problem. Back in the 1970's, that same group of block-headed scientists cried wolf about cataclysmic global cooling. But fortunately for the environ-maniac movement, people like Larry Lemonpants realized that tales of rising seas, melting glaciers, and catastrophic storms made for much better television than warning people to stock up on long underwear. Where is your sense of decency?" I demanded of her.

She turned her back to me and faced the wall. "I don't answer to you. If you've got issues, go take it up with my PR department."

I struggled to contain my laughter. "Larry Lemonpants is a two-bit phony. He's only interested in making money. But finally, the joke's on him. There's barely a dime left in the economy for him to suck out. His gravy train's been derailed. Soon, he'll get to see how the rest of us live."

"I need you to leave," Mother Nature told me.

"I'll leave, but I won't stop telling people that you're a liar. And I won't stop telling people that if you dig to the bottom of any of these environmentalist movements, you'll find a bunch of Marxists looking to get even with people who still believe in capitalism. The climate-change legend was advanced by people who saw it as a golden opportunity to fill their own pockets. Lemonpants can quote me on that."

This time *I* slammed the door and stormed out into the hallway. "This is a friggin' mad house," I shouted before I nearly ran over a man in a white suit. "I'm sorry," I said. "I wasn't trying to bowl you over."

The man ignored my apology and handed me a familiar-looking helmet. The device was nearly identical to the helmets worn by race car drivers—with one curious difference. Instead of a visor, a thick metal plate had been welded into the space where the visor should have been. I stared at the man, as if to say, "You're kidding me, right? I might as well put a bucket over my head."

The man said nothing. He only waited for me to take the helmet.

I continued to gaze at the stranger. He was no historical figure that I remembered. I struggled to decide whether I should trust him and do as he'd asked or not. Then I really began to *see* him. His face was beyond handsome, and his hair was cut and styled perfectly. I had no idea how I had determined that he had perfect hair, I just knew. Beneath his clothing, the man's body was a temple. He was neither overly muscular nor thin. He was just unbelievably fit. All told, he looked like the shoe-in for the title "World's Greatest Model," for the next three thousand seasons.

Then I noticed his suit. If you have ever seen a human creation that appeared so perfect you refused to believe your eyes, imagine that experience multiplied by ten billion. The coat and pants hung where a suit should hang and clung where a suit should cling. The material itself seemed to emit a soft glow, making me feel happier and calmer than I could ever remember feeling. I would have bet my life savings that the entire ensemble could have been crumpled, soaked in water, and then buried for a week under a pile of sweaty, sumo wrestlers, and on the seventh day, the suit would have come out looking and smelling as though it had just been pressed using lilac water.

While I stared at him, dumbfounded by his appearance, the man intently pressed the crash helmet into my midsection. Finally, I relented. *I'm sure this is part of some hidden camera show*, I thought as I slid the helmet over my head. Next, I felt a heavy covering as it was draped over my body. It felt like a lead blanket. I struggled to remain standing, but the weight dragged me to the floor. *What now?* I wondered.

The answer came immediately.

I felt Him before I saw Him—though in truth, I never actually saw Him. The purpose of the full enclosure helmet was clear—the device ensured that I couldn't look upon the face of God. I tried to speak, but no words came. When I spoke and when I heard Him, the words flowed—not through my ears and mouth—but through my heart.

Is that really you? I asked.

Yes, it is.

Wow—I don't know what to say. I've prayed so many times, it's weird to hear you talking back—uh, no offense.

I thought I heard the Almighty chuckle before He replied, **No offense taken. I get that a lot.**

You caught me by surprise. I never expected to find you here. I figured that you'd be up in the sky.

I don't live here. I thought I'd stop by and say hello. I wondered whether you had anything you wanted to ask.

Why are we here? I blurted, regretting such a childish question the moment it escaped my lips.

Everyone is here for their own reasons. Beyond that, you need to reach your own conclusions.

But why don't you reveal yourself to us? I asked.

Who says I haven't revealed myself? I created everything. How much more revelation do you need?

I mean in human form.

I did. He was the stone that the builders rejected.

But I mean every day. Why can't you come and manifest Yourself among us?

That would be too easy.

Too easy for whom? I was confused.

Which is the greater act of faith, believing in something that you saw with your eyes or in something you searched for with your heart?

But that makes no sense. You allow such inhumanity to occur here. Why don't you stop it? If you would just reveal yourself to the world, it would all stop.

Would it really? Did it stop after the descendents of Jacob left Egypt? Did it stop after Jesus of Nazareth was born or crucified? Did it stop after the Qur'an? Did it end after Buddha or Darwin?

No. I guess not.

Why do you think that I always refer to you as My children rather than My friends or My partners?

I don't know.

It's because you're not My partners or My friends. I created you, and I love you, but I didn't give you the capacity to see and know everything. Most of you have your hands full doing your own job. No offense, but you can't help me do mine. I certainly could have put a V-chip into all of you. That would have made things a lot easier for all of us, but it wouldn't have made things better. Life has no meaning if you aren't free to choose how you spend it. No amount of forced love or forced prayer or forced devotion means anything.

But what about all of the suffering in the world? Why do you allow that to continue?

You humans are so self-centered. You act as though you, specifically, are the only ones

who have ever had to suffer. There has never been a time without suffering. Suffering is a part of life.

But it seems like you look the other way at times. Look at the genocide in Africa and violence in the Middle East. Why do those people have to suffer and die when people in America has such a good a life?

There you go again, judging me by your own reasoning. Do you think that just because Americans have acquired more material wealth than a lot of other nations that it's a sign of my favor for them? I can assure you that it isn't. Sometimes possessions are more trap than treasure. It's easy to fall in love with money and things. And remember when you talk about death, none of you are leaving your world alive.

But how are we supposed to know what to do?

Ask me, and I will help you see the way.

You mean like you're doing today?

I'm pretty sure I heard God chuckle again. **I can't promise that we'll have another conversation before you leave your mortal existence. However, when you pray, I promise that I hear you.**

But why don't you ever answer back?

I always answer people's prayers, but they don't always get they answer they're hoping for. Free will is free will after all.

But what does that mean?

Some people ask me to intervene in ways that I simply won't do. Am I supposed to directly intervene on behalf of the followers of Jesus and cloud the judgment of atheists? Am I supposed to allow the descendants of Jacob to choose their own actions and manipulate Hindus like puppets? Should I create a paradise on earth for Muslims and leave those who don't share that faith in a state of misery. I am not willing to do any of those things. If I did, I would be crushing the free will I intentionally gave to you.

So why should we even bother to pray, if you don't give us the answers that we're looking for?

Prayer gives you a direct line to Me. Listen, if you are going to pray for something like chocolate pudding, you might want to get ready to be disappointed. But if you ask for my help or guidance, I'm always here. You could say I lay out a trail of spiritual breadcrumbs—except that my guidance is more durable and a lot harder for birds to steal. I illuminate a path for you to follow if you choose. It's more a case of helping you find the faith and courage to follow what you believe is right, than it is guiding you in the direction I want you to go.

But what about people that deny your existence?

I love you humans, you always keep me laughing. Some of you work so hard to deny my existence that I've begun to feel a little sorry for you. It's like watching a dog chasing its tail. It's hilarious for a while, but when it goes on and on and on, it becomes...well, pathetic. You see scientists rejecting one of their most sacred principals—Occam's razor—when they refuse to consider the simplest explanation possible: creation has a Creator.

Then these scientists run around like they own the joint. They acquire the tiniest bit of knowledge and figure they know everything there is to know. But do they really believe that just because they discovered quantum foam that they've got the whole universe figured out? They might want to pack a lunch if they think they're going to unlock all my secrets because they'll be at it a while. My creation isn't a Chinese finger trap.

Then you get the people who seem to believe they are going to defy death. They stop eating meat and they don't smoke and they run five miles a day and go hiking instead of driving a car. But instead of being happy and satisfied with their lifestyle changes, those people decide that everyone else must act the same way as they do. Suddenly, it's you who also needs to stop eating meat, stop smoking, run five miles a day and go hiking instead of driving a car.

I didn't give humans free will so that a bunch of patchouli-oiled yahoos could force their habits upon everyone else. My guess is that it makes progressives feel validated when everybody is forced to adopt their habits. But forcing everyone else to do as you do doesn't make you right; it only makes you a bully.

Then God, the Almighty, stopped speaking for a moment. *You know, you look a little worn out,* he observed. *It's probably time you were on your way.*

But I have so many questions to ask.

I don't blame you. There's a lot to know, but you've had a big day, and you still have a few more stops to make.

Could I ask you one more question? It gets so confusing sometimes. I just don't know what to do—

Love and humility.

Come again?

If you want to select two guideposts in your life, make them love and humility.

"But what do you mean?" I asked Him. Then I realized could hear my voice again. I slapped at my arms and legs and discovered the heavy covering was gone. I got up off the floor and looked around. The hallway was empty.

I was surprised by how dark the passageway seemed after I had spent a few moments in

God's presence. And the weight of my worries sagged down upon me once again.

I sighed and began to trudge forward, knowing that it *was* time to go home—until I saw Nicholaus Copernicus, that is. I shuffled towards him hoping that he'd speak with me.

Copernicus was standing in the solarium. He wore a Renaissance era robe and sandals, but he carried an MP3 player—a solitary nod to the modern era. I would have guessed that he would have adopted a modern hairstyle. Surely there was at least one hairdresser in the Hall. But that assumption would have been incorrect. His hair still looked as if he'd cut it himself using a medieval pair of safety scissors and a salad bowl.

The sunshine of daytime had given way to night, and Copernicus gazed into the sky using a telescope mounted to the floor. When he saw me, he motioned to a nearby chair and pantomimed his request that I have a seat. A moment later, he smiled and sat in a chair next to mine.

"I would imagine a lot has changed since your time," I said.

"You could say that, but I'm guessing that you aren't here to talk about my time. How can I help you?"

"I was just wondering how it felt when you were trying to convince people that the sun was the center of the earth's orbit, rather than the other way around?"

"This wouldn't have anything to do with global warming would it?"

I smiled. "How did you guess?"

"I was pretty amused when people began to equate skepticism over global warming with the resistance that I encountered. Back then, I was truly torn. I had a model that could accurately predict the movement of the earth in relation to the sun. I knew I was correct, but I also knew that the facts contradicted what had been understood to be infallible knowledge. That wasn't an easy situation. I had nothing to gain by announcing my discoveries, and in fact I had a lot to lose. These global-warming activists have nothing but anecdotal evidence, a tiny sample of temperature data and a collection of models that can barely predict short-term weather patterns. Apparently, they've managed to conceal the vast sums of money to be made in the field of climate-change research. It's amusing that no one ever questions the money-motivations of *today's scientists.*"

"Isn't it crazy? It reminds me of the time when the International Panel for the Preservation of Bigfoot began to push for laws and new taxes to restore and maintain skunk ape habitat. I was shocked that no one cried foul. But they ran a ton of ads and away they went. Now we have millions of acres of Sasquatch sanctuary and not so much as a single Bigfoot to live there.

There's a brand of crazy running around that you just can't make up."

"Careful with the Igfootbay," Copernicus whispered out the corner of his mouth. "Tall, dark, and hairy likes to come down here at night. I'd hate to see you leave in a wheelchair."

"But Bigfoot doesn't even—*gulp*"

"Remember where you are."

"And the Roswell aliens?" I asked, my eyebrows raised.

Copernicus nodded.

"Well then, I guess we better get back on topic. I'm a little shocked by the lengths to which scientists will go to sell their services," I baited him.

Copernicus shook his head in disgust. "I hear you. I can't imagine trying to work as a scientist today. Everyone is scrambling for grant money. Did you see what they tried to say when some of their colleagues got caught using crappy data?" Copernicus shook his head. He was pissed. "One of them had the audacity to say, 'It wasn't bad science, it was just sloppy data.' Was he crazy? Data is the bedrock upon which the foundation of science has been built!" Copernicus turned suddenly and delivered a karate kick to a planter. The force of the blow sent the clay pot skittering across the floor until it shattered against the wall in a spray of dirt and fichus. "These charlatans can't find any data that supports their global-warming models, so they fudge their models and focus on compelling

imagery like polar bears stranded on ice floes.
And they call themselves scientists—"

Lemonpants had seen enough. He slammed the novel down onto his desk. His face resembled a ripened, organic tomato. "Who does he think he is?" he demanded of no one. Flecks of spittle sailed from his mouth. "How dare that peon criticize me? I'm going to destroy him now! I don't care what the President wants. Mannequin answers to me—"

He turned and hurled the novel against the penthouse window. A shower of glass and a copy of Watford's novel fell to the sidewalk below. Before the book even reached the ground, Lemonpants had picked up his telephone and was screaming for blood.

Chapter 20

Rita the Clown barged into Spendini's office. She neither bothered to call in advance nor knock upon arrival. Not many of Washington's inhabitants could pull off such brazenness—Rita was one of the few.

Though surprised by the interruption, Spendini kept his focus on the page. He too had heard the news of McLaughagain's retirement, and he wanted to be ready to accept the vice presidency. Once he'd finished the note he'd been writing, he lifted his eyes to greet the clown. Instead of rising, he remained seated behind his desk.

"Do we have anything to worry about with this book?" she demanded as she stood directly across from Spendini and tapped her foot on the floor.

Spendini had become concerned about the Watford situation himself. The last thing he needed was a surge in conservatism. They'd worked too hard to bury the troublesome ideology the last time. No Demagoblican wanted to see it rise from the grave.

But as much as he feared the rednecks, Spendini had little need for an agitated clown bent on terrorizing the countryside. "This is just a little bit of novelty steam." Spendini tried to reassure Rita. He had to demonstrate his loyalty to Lemonpants. The environmaniac was the only big-money player left in the game. No one made it into the White House without the environmentalist's deep pockets paving the way. *And if Larry wants to snare Garamond, Larry gets to snare Garamond.* "Give it another week," Spendini then said. "This book isn't going anywhere."

"That might be true, but I got a call this morning from our mutual friend. It appears that he's changed his tune. He warned me that if I wanted to keep my job, I had better find a way to destroy this Watford." She shook her horn in Spendini's face.

"Really?" *I wonder what caused Larry to change his mind,* Spendini wondered.

"Teachers—Teachers—we should send the Teachers," Rita chanted in a sing-song voice.

Ignoring the clown's rant, Spendini began to analyze the angles, looking for the best of them. *I finally find my own upside of allowing Garamond to make his play, and Larry changes the plan. But can I reason with Rita? Or has she turned into a time bomb that's more liability than asset.* "Sure, we *could* send the Teachers after Watford and Kerwin right now. But there's audio that shows Garamond begging Kerwin to publish the book. We're making the right decision to wait for the big fish. If we can get to Garamond, we end the whole thing—Watford, Kerwin, Garamond, the Underground Light Rail—everything."

"No! No! No—no—no—no—no—NO!" Rita threw her horn to the floor and yanked a balloon from her pocket. She stretched the latex savagely, punishing the balloon for the treachery of the conservative traitors. "But it took us so long to get people believing that we knew what was best. This book will destroy everything," she said while she inflated the balloon.

Spendini was torn. He knew that soon *he'd* be president. If EEFF could deal with the conspirators during Mannequin's term, he could transition smoothly into his own administration. But as he watched Rita—the closest thing to a friend that he had in Washington—he pitied her. Her face was a mask of rage. Tears and pancake makeup ran down her cheeks and chin. She twisted and turned the inflated balloon in spite of its cries for mercy.

But there was no quarter to be found in the hands of the pitiless clown and—*Bang!* The balloon exploded and tiny rubber shards fell to the floor.

"This is making me crazy," Rita said before she slammed her fists on Spendini's desk. "*We* run things. People like Watford don't amount to anything. I don't want that to change."

Spendini sighed. The exploding balloon gave him an idea. *Maybe we should try to put a little bit of pressure on Watford. It would give Rita something to keep her occupied.* "Fine, put together some talking points and send them to the FGNB. Tell them to spread the word about *Watford* this time. It's worked before."

"I'll trust you for now, but—" Rita stopped talking. She didn't want to say anything to alienate Spendini, her most trusted ally.

Spendini walked over to Rita and hugged her. The embrace created a pancake-makeup smear on his lapel. "Don't get me wrong. I would love to see how smart that dusty, old fossil, Kerwin, thinks he is when he's strapped into a chair with the black bag over his head. But he's been around the block. Watford's new to this. If we put the squeeze on him, he'll go away on his own. Meanwhile, if we can just wait for Garamond to show his face—"

"*Waaaaaaaaaaaaaaaaaaaaaaaa!* I don't understand why we can't haul them both away," Rita wailed. Tears rolled down her face again. "We've passed laws against this stuff. It's not fair." Then she crumpled to the floor and beat her fists against the ground.

"Rita, c'mon—you know that we need to keep the Teachers a secret. We don't want people to think we're a bunch of fascists, burning books and throwing people into jail for political speech."

"But we've been doing that for years."

"But we don't want to *advertise* that fact. Trust me on this one. If one of them is going to disappear, we need them all to disappear, or people are going to think we were involved. We want the people to look at us as friends—not their enemies." Spendini helped Rita to her feet. He gave her a reassuring pat on the head. *I know you don't understand the rules, but we'll get through this. I promise.* "Get the talking points to the FGNB. Let them take a run at Watford. Meanwhile, I'll work on my own little surprise."

Chapter 21

Less than an hour after Rita met with Spendini, she'd forwarded a set of talking points to the FGNB. The information was well-suited to Watford's destruction. By dinner time, the message was in widespread circulation.

DAMPMEN was given the honor of dropping the first shovels of dirt. They'd received the distinction as a reward for their years of loyal service to the Demagoblicans. The network even rejected its customary "news kitten" format to break the Watford story on its popular news-magazine show, *Nuanced Worldview with Sheena Glitzy.*

Only the biggest stories were shifted away from the network's fuzzy news-breakers. The industry owed its survival to the four-legged creatures.

The first news-kittens had burst onto the scene at a time when the faux-news industry teetered at the edge of financial ruin. Even the windfall of the government bailout had been insufficient to pull them from their budgetary abyss. Networks tried to raise the price of advertising. They replaced their existing production staff with illegal immigrants to avoid payroll taxes. They even cut six hours from their broadcast day and told their viewers that they were experiencing technical difficulties, but nothing worked. Faux-news chieftains were even forced to use the "nuclear option." The last-ditch, SOS strategy called for firing all of the expensive and superlatively-attractive talent and then replacing them with cheaper, less-attractive hosts.

None of the ideas staunched the industry's bleed out. Then,

when all appeared to be lost—even as the faux-news-industry's obituary and a host of pink slips were being written—a simple telephone call saved the day.

DAMPMEN's CEO and founder had just finished his final pink slip when his 41-month-old daughter called to tell him about the "funny kitty." The girl laughed as she explained how the family's kitten had climbed the drapes in the living room and them jumped off and ran away. The story, and his daughter's laughter, brought a smile to the executive's face and gave him an idea.

When the head man finished his conversation, he ran down DAMPMEN's hallways calling for an emergency staff meeting. "We know people love to see puppies and kitties. And we know that we get all of our news from the FGNB anyway. Why don't we marry the two?" he asked. "We can use images of puppies and kittens as a backdrop, and then we'll use a bottom-scrolling banner to report the news. All we're doing is running the same stuff repeatedly anyway. And we can get out the news at a fraction of the cost."

The few remaining employees sat motionless. The simple brilliance of the idea left them stunned. A round of applause erupted for the man who had just saved the faux-news.

The use of news-kittens revolutionized the industry and quickly became a huge hit. Not only did the new format make delivering the news cheaper, but it also made unpleasant stories go down more easily. After all, who could be angry about government waste or excess while they were watching a fuzzy, orange kitten playing with a ball of yarn? And while the news-kittens didn't keep DAMPMEN from milking misery through the use of spectacular footage depicting disasters and gut-wrenching personal tragedies, the animals offered some much-needed variety.

But even with the wholesale transition to the news-kitten format, DAMPMEN chose to hold onto one member of their talent pool—Sheena Glitzy. Her show, *Nuanced Worldview*, became the network's last faux-news-magazine show not hosted by an animal. The offering had long been DAMPMEN's crown jewel.

So it surprised no one when Sheena Glitzy appeared onscreen to launch the first smears directed at Watford. "I'm Sheena Glitzy, and this is Nuanced Worldview. Tonight's topic: *In the Hall (Reflections on America).* Is the novel free speech or hate speech? We'll tell you what to think about Ray Watford and his seditious novel when we return."

The host—formerly Ingrid Precious Skilicki—had been raised on a hog farm in the formerly-pungent, yet aptly-named, Slightlybetterthanadirtnap, Iowa. Slightlybetterthanadirtnap had once been dubbed the "Fertilizer Capitol of the World," owing to an abundance of hog farmers. In fact, Iowa had long considered adopting the slogan, "If you're looking for a load of pig crap, you'll find it in Iowa," as their state motto. However, they abandoned those efforts when they learned that Minnesota had already adopted the words as their motto—though for a slightly less-literal reason. But that was back in the days when family farmers were allowed to raise hogs.

Environ-mania meant that all governing bodies lined up to follow Greta Government's lead in environmental policy. In most instances, the words "environmental stewardship" didn't end with the ban on fossil fuels. A glut of farming-related laws was passed to protect Mother Earth.

In Iowa, the environ-maniac group, *Friends of the All Creatures Great and Small and of the Sky and of the Ice and the Seas and of Mother Earth and of the Children (as long as they're vegan, quiet and belong to someone else)*, spent limitless sums lobbying against the environmental damage inflicted by pigs. Eventually their efforts paid off, and Iowa farms that produced anything except Ethyl-Noleo-ready corn vanished like snowballs in Death Valley.

Ingrid, who made the residents of Slightlybetterthanadirtnap forget the other eighteen Skilicki children, had been born the improbably attractive daughter of two ordinary hog farmers. "She was kissed by the stars," some said. And her beauty left the townsfolk to wonder whether a vagabond male model had sewn Ingrid's seed as part of an unlikely, yet sordid, tryst with mama Skilicki.

In spite of the future rewards it would bring, Ingrid's beauty did nothing to save her place in the family's home. Though homes classified as family farms were exempted from the Welcome Home Act, they weren't sheltered from the ravages of capitalism.

Just weeks short of Ingrid's sixteenth birthday, Helen and Hal Skilicki—Ingrid's mother and alleged father—sat their lovely daughter down at the kitchen table. "We can't afford to keep you, Ing," her *father* began. "We have twenty other mouths to feed, and the bankers are going to foreclose on the farm—those bastards!" Ingrid hadn't planned to stay in Slightlybetterthanadirtnap forever. However, the bankruptcy of her parents' farm pushed the timetable for her departure forward by five or six years.

A perceptive Ingrid asked, "But wasn't it the laws outlawing pig farming that caused the problem?"

"Don't argue with your father, dear," Helen chided.

"I know this is a difficult thing to hear, but we're going to have to ask you to leave."

"But, Daddy, where will I go?" Ingrid began to cry. The thought of leaving everything she'd ever known terrified her.

"Don't worry, baby girl, because—" he paused for a moment,

letting the drama build, "you're going to Hollywood!"

Helen leaned over and embraced her daughter. "Aren't you happy? I've always dreamed of going there." Her mom began to clap her hands and chant "Hollywood! Hollywood! Hollywood!" Hal joined in the chorus until they both abruptly stopped—"your bus leaves in an hour. Here's your ticket."

Helen handed Ingrid a hastily packed a suitcase. "Now say goodbye to your brothers and sisters," she instructed.

Ingrid choked back tears and tried be brave. She said her farewells and then trudged down the gravel drive that split the fields of her family's former farm. As she neared the end of the road, she heard footfalls behind her. It was her mother. "Honey, this might seem harsh, but I know you can make it on your own. You might have to do certain things that you never wanted to do on your way to the top, but just remember one thing: selling your soul gets easier every time you do it." Then mother's and daughter's eyes filled with tears as they shared a long embrace. "I know you'll make us proud, dear," mother whispered to daughter before turning and running back to the house.

On the bus ride west, Ingrid decided to change her name to Sheena Glitzy. It allowed her to leave the memories of Iowa and her family behind her forever. Once she arrived in Hollywood, Glitzy frequently relied upon her mother's advice. In fact, she'd sold her soul more often than she cared to remember. She'd lost count of the happy endings she'd provided for the men and women who had advanced her career.

The words, "stunningly attractive," were an *understatement* of hyperbolic proportions when applied to Sheena. Her brunette hair, piercing green eyes, and magnificent cheek bones reduced men to quivering puddles of jelly. When her smooth-as-silk voice—with just a hint of rasp—was thrown into the mix, she could have read mechanical manuals and still left her audience harboring terribly-naughty fantasies about her.

A local television-station manager spotted the young Glitzy during a dinner-theater performance of "Greed, Greed, and More Greed—American Capitalism in the '80's." He left Sheena a business card with a scribbled invitation to "call."

The station manager then tried to use Sheena on remote-site reports, but she just couldn't muster the spontaneity that type of report demanded. Even Sheena couldn't explain the failures.

Unwilling to waste a face like Glitzy's, the station manager then tried her as evening co-anchor and struck gold. The station's ratings soared overnight as stories of the gorgeous, new anchor-woman spread across Los Angeles.

Seeing Sheena's untapped potential, three film-industry executives tried to steal her away from the news station. "We can make you a star," each promised. But in all three instances, aside from getting Sheena into bed, the efforts ended in failure. In every film role, she froze the moment she needed to deliver her memorized lines.

Inside Hollywood circles, Glitzy became known as the *Wooden Goddess*. Movie directors loved to use her as background scenery, but those roles would never lead her to the stardom she craved. Sheena knew that she needed a change after she played the trophy wife of a populist politician in the epic tale, *If You Have One Dollar More Than I Think You Should Have, You Must Be a Crook*. She butchered the single line she'd been given, and it appeared that she'd be laughed straight out of town.

Fortunately for her, she landed at the Demagoblican Administration Mouth Piece and Misery Exploitation Network. The network's founder and CEO fell in love with her the first time the two of them met.

In spite of Sheena's pathetic performance in cinema, the DAMPMEN boss knew he could capitalize on Glitzy's potential as a news anchor. He boasted that he would "build an empire" around his new star. But before he could do that, he had to resolve Glitzy's inability to retain dialogue.

DAMPMEN then paired Sheena with a team of analysts, writers, and a lightning-fast keyboarder for every show. The analysts and writers assembled an outline of tightly-managed content for the show. As the show aired, the keyboarder fed Glitzy material that was crafted by the analysts who looked on from backstage.

For Glitzy, it felt as if she were being fed scripted comments. DAMPMEN even built a special studio to air Glitzy's show. Multiple trademarked devices—machines that allowed a person to read scripted material while at the same time appearing to make eye contact—were positioned behind the heads of the live guests. In that way, the hostess gave the illusion of conversing with her guests even while she read the prepared script displayed by the trademarked devices.

In those rare instances when the show's content slipped beyond the outline, the director cut to a commercial break. Sheena's team addressed the variance in content and then resumed with a new script following the break. To the viewing audience, Sheena appeared to be in total control—wise, informed, and confident. Only DAMPMEN insiders knew the truth, and every network employee was required to sign a confidentiality agreement designed to protect the secrets behind Nuanced Worldview.

Sheena couldn't recall the last time she'd felt this nervous. She tried to burn off the anxiety by pacing inside her dressing room. It had been a long time since Nuanced World had dealt with such an important topic.

When show time arrived, Sheena sat behind her microphone and flashed her intoxicating smile. The cameras ate her up. "I'm Sheena Glitzy, and this is Nuanced Worldview—the show that allows you to see exactly what we've chosen to show you. Then you can judge for yourself. Joining us via satellite is our guest, Edward Tramsoot, editor of the Yellow Lapdog Gazette. Welcome to the show, Edward."

Tramsoot smiled directly into the camera. The expression on his narrow, bespectacled face oozed a greasy form of condescension. "I'm happy to be here tonight, Sheena." He flashed a smile stuffed with affection for the show's hostess. Tramsoot secretly wished he had been invited in-studio. He wished he could have gotten a first-hand look at the hostess and her world-class rack.

"Watford's novel, I assume you've read it," Glitzy began.

"Regrettably," Tramsoot said before he offered a made-for-television sigh. "As you might guess, we take our book reviews very seriously at the Gazette. I had heard many troubling opinions from our book reviewers."

"And what did you think of the book?"

"I found it to be very disturbing. It's no more than a foul rant from the opening page. It was, dare I say—seditionist."

"Would you care to share a passage that you found most disturbing?"

Tramsoot smiled the greasy smile again. "I wouldn't read one letter over the airwaves. Any bit of publicity the author receives is too much as far as I'm concerned."

"And you have taken some steps to back up your stance on the book, haven't you?"

"Yes, we have. As everyone knows, the Gazette took over the bestseller list that used to be such a source of pride for the deceased titan of the newspaper industry." Tramsoot paused to allow for a solemn moment. "The Gazette will never allow that novel to be included on the bestseller list. It doesn't matter how many copies it sells. It's trash, and it is only trying to capitalize on these very difficult times. It foments anger. It plays upon the worst in people at a time when we need to appeal to the best in them." Tramsoot paused and took a sip of water. "We are doing everything we can to stop the spread of this greed-induced virus. For some writers, Sheena, writing is about a lot more than cash. For some of us, it's about *creating a better world.*"

Sheena smiled at Tramsoot's last comment and then cooed, "We'll be back in a moment with Edward Tramsoot, editor-in-chief for the Yellow Lapdog Gazette." *It's a shame he's not in-studio. I could rock his world,* she thought—*he looks a bit like a weasel though.*

After the break, the show flowed quickly. Host and guest shared jokes at Watford's expense. "It's not even a novel. It's just a collection of essays, really—and none of them are any good either," Tramsoot sniffed. About Watford's decision to compose fictional conversations with Uncle Sam and God, Tramsoot joked, "Watford probably believes that they're both real."

"What about the guy who stares at himself in the mirror?" Glitzy asked while she laughed. "He's not even an icon. He's nobody. What was Watford thinking?" Then both hostess and guest chuckled.

At the final commercial break, Tramsoot pulled a folded piece of paper from his pocket. He scanned the punch list he'd received from the FGNB before the show. Satisfied that he had covered everything, he smiled. He had time to deliver one last shot before the show ended.

"We're back to wrap up the show with Edward Tramsoot," Sheena began after the break. "Do you have anything else to say?"

Tramsoot sighed and shook his head. "I feel pity for Milton Kerwin. Clearly greed has gotten the best of him. He's not the kind of American that America needs today. And someday soon, I hope, he will get what he's got coming." *And I hope the message comes tattooed across one of the Teacher's knuckles,* he said to himself as he pulled off the tie-clip microphone and prepared to leave.

Chapter 22

Kevin Meadows loved California. Sunshine, beautiful women, and the ocean all caused his rapid fall into love with the state. He knew the moment he arrived; California was where he needed to be.

Meadows had been born in Oklahoma, and by the time he was twelve, he knew he wanted to be a movie star. The day he graduated from high school, he packed his bags and set out for Hollywood.

During the bus ride—a trek made longer given the bus's need to stop to refuel at every greasy spoon in its path—Kevin decided to change his last name from Culhagen to Meadows. With environ-mania running at full throttle, he decided the new name might give him the hook he needed. Unfortunately, everyone else in Hollywood had reached the same conclusion. The credits for a typical movie read like the script of a nature documentary.

The obstacle-ridden path to stardom revealed itself the instant Meadows stepped off the bus. The muscular arms, square jaw, and chiseled cheek bones that caused Oklahoman women to lose their minds were little more than a decent start out west. Virtually everyone within 200 miles of where he stood—except those poor residents trapped in some of L.A.'s often-deadly neighborhoods—plotted their own path to movie stardom. For every Kevin Meadows you saw on the sidewalk, ten more lurked inside run-down apartments or lived under freeway bridges while they awaited their big break.

Kevin found work here and there. He had the quintessential

tough-guy look when he sported a few days' facial hair. His resemblance to the legendary cinema tough-guy, Tony Cojones, helped him land a handful of non-speaking roles. But it wasn't until he worked in the film, *Soaking Wet,* that his career started to ascend. *Soaking Wet* told the story of a band of courageous terrorists who dared defy the DeVille Administration. The movie also starred Mike Flower-Power, Alex NoNukes, and the reanimated corpse of Adolph Hitler—cast as former President DeVille. Meadows earned critical acclaim for his performance as the courageous leader of the terrorist cell. One of the film's highlights came when Meadows's character pelted the hated American President with both shoes.

Soaking Wet propelled Meadows into leading-man status. He soon landed the lead role in a five-picture zombie-thriller franchise. None of the movies had been big hits, but Meadows sold tickets.

Since he had secured his future financially, just making money was no longer enough. Every few months, he launched himself into some type of crusade. As often as not, his focus usually wandered before any *real* effort was required. Meadows liked the idea of being change agent. He just didn't like the heavy lifting which accompanied the role.

Today, Meadows lounged by his swimming pool and waited for fellow actors Mick Boyle, Jimmy Forest, and Will Williams to arrive. Meadows hoped to enlist the others in a plan that could help jump-start all their careers. The plan—if carried out correctly—could give him the measure of gravitas he so desired.

As the trio of actors strolled onto the deck that surrounded the pool, Meadows beckoned for them to take a seat. "This might be coming out of left field, but I've been doing a lot of thinking lately," Meadows began. "We're all kind of stuck in our careers, and we can't seem to get back in the mix. I think we need to get ourselves in the news," he said.

For months Meadows had been watching Nuanced Worldview to "get in touch with what's going on out there." He'd seen Glitzy's interview with Edward Tramsoot the night before, and the experience had left him energized. "Can any of you identify the main issue facing us today?" he asked the others. He liked to play guessing games with them. He thought the approach made him appear smarter.

"I don't know—the collapse of the movie industry," Mick offered. Mick was the prototypical coattail jockey. He had been dubbed "Kevin Meadows's shadow" by Hollywood insiders. No one really knew the basis of their relationship, but everyone knew that you never saw a Kevin Meadows film without seeing Mick Boyle's name during the credits.

Meadows offered a patronizing smile for his protégé. "No, it's the environment. Everyone is worried about the environment. Look at that one political dude. He won some kind of prize for working with the environment. How cool would that be?"

"Are you suggesting that you're going to help us win some kind of prize?" It was Will Williams asking. Will was the newest member of the foursome. He'd only been in Hollywood for a few years, but he was already mentioned as a potential superstar.

Meadows tossed the morning edition of the Yellow Lapdog Gazette onto the seat between Williams and Jimmy Forest. Like Meadows, Jimmy Forest had started his career playing bit-part tough guys. After some modest success, he tried to make the leap to more serious roles but struggled. In one independent film, he played the sensitive husband of a woman experiencing an identity crisis. One reviewer suggested that Forest's work had been "literally statuesque." The critic went on to express genuine surprise that the actor "hadn't attracted pigeons during filming."

"Can either of you see the perfect opportunity in that paper?" Meadows asked Forest and Williams after he'd given them a few moments to browse the Gazette.

Again with the questions; why doesn't he just tell us? Forest wondered while he picked up the local news section and thumbed through it. He saw a story about the Demagogue Mayor of Los Angeles. The Demagogue Party was still the gold standard for state and local governments. The local politicians felt little need to cloud their loyalties by joining the Demagoblican movement.

L.A.'s mayor was mired in a corruption scandal. He'd protested his innocence and the FGNB had sent its L.A. beat writer to talk to the mayor. The Yellow Lapdog Gazette had run the subsequent article in its attempt to help clear the mayor's name.

In the story, the mayor was quoted as saying, "Why would I think anything was wrong when I found a plastic bag containing $42,000 dollars on my porch? This kind of thing happens all the time. I have a sizable garden behind my house, and I sell vegetables to raise a little extra money. I've had a bumper crop this year."

The mayor's opponent in the upcoming election took some photos of the incumbent's back yard and sent the photos to the Yellow Lapdog Gazette. The photos showed that the mayor's back yard held a few trees and a row of flowers but not so much as a single carrot. Curiously, there was no mention of the missing garden in the newspaper's story.

After flipping through a few more pages, Forest wanted to bring the silly assignment to an end. "Do you want for us to plant a vegetable garden in the mayor's back yard?" he asked.

Meadows laughed. "It's this guy. He pointed to an article in the Entertainment section. The headline read, "Too hateful for the Gazette."

"What about him?" Forest demanded.

"Why do I need to do all the thinking for this crew?" Meadows smiled after asking the rhetorical question.

"Go ahead and be the smart guy. Just quit dragging this out," Forest growled.

"Screw you, Jimmy!" Mick said as he jumped to Meadows's defense. "I don't hear you coming up with any brilliant ideas. Let Kev tell us his plan."

"Thanks, Mick," Meadows said. "I think Jimmy is just eager to hear what's in store. He hasn't had a successful film in a while, and he wants to get to the top just like the rest of us. Isn't that right, Jimmy?"

Forest clenched his fists and his jaw muscles quivered in response to the verbal slap. "You're right like always, *Kev*," Forest mimicked.

"Enough," Williams said. He always seemed to be called upon to play the peacemaker. Meadows and Boyle usually paired off against Forest. Williams tried to stay out of the fray but often felt obligated to come to Forest's defense. "I'm curious about your idea, Kevin," Williams said. "We all want something to get our careers moving in the right direction. You've had some really good ideas in the past," he lied. "Let's hear what you've got."

"Thank you, Will. I appreciate the vote of confidence." Meadows grabbed the paper and read the news story about Edward Tramsoot's appearance on FNN. When he finished reading, he folded the paper and smacked it. "What do you think?"

"About what?" Forest asked.

"About his idea, dumbass," Boyle hissed.

"I'll come over there and smack you." Forest slid forward on his seat to back up his threat.

"Go ahead and try," Boyle shot back.

Jimmy flung himself across the divide between the two seats and a flurry of slaps ensured. Williams pushed himself between the two and stopped the brawl. "Both of you sit down!" he shouted. "Let Kevin finish his idea. If we start fighting, we'll never figure this out."

When the fight ended, Meadows took fifteen minutes and outlined his plan. By the time he finished speaking, everyone believed they could make the plan work. If they succeeded, they could make some very influential friends.

Chapter 23

Back in Washington, the political aristocracy celebrated a day filled with revolution. Glassed were raised and warm feelings held sway. Cigar smoke filled the air giving it a thick, blue haze. The FauxPublican and Demagogue Parties had shared expenses to rent Washington, D.C.'s, Diverse Stallion restaurant for the gathering.

While the rest of the nation observed smoking bans and dined on a supper of watery Snake-Oil-Surprise, these members of Congress feasted on prime rib, strip steak, pork chops, fresh carrots, cucumbers, arugula, tomatoes, and other vegetables grown on the hidden government farms located across the fruited plain. Warm loaves of bread and butter and rich crème brulee accompanied the feast. Lagers and wines washed down the meal.

After the fare had been devoured in gut-busting quantities, the assembled public servants reclined before a blazing hearth and sipped liqueur. Tonight, they cared not for which of them used to be an elephant and which a donkey. They had taken a stance against their common enemy, and this was the spoils.

As the evening of merrymaking and good cheer neared its wine-soaked conclusion, a lone voice cut the noise. "Ladies… Gentlemen…" Senator Spendini called to the group. He wanted to deliver his message before everyone was too drunk. He tapped a knife against the side of a crystal tumbler a few more times and then began to speak. "Everyone knows why we're here tonight. We face the greatest threat American democracy has ever known." The raucous babble grew silent. "I'm not talking about terrorism or our long standing budget issues. I am talking about Buster

Lafayette and Ray Watford and everyone who tries to chip away our authority."

"Tomorrow, when we cut the snake's head off, the rest of its body won't know which way to turn," he said.

A few hours later, the full bodies of the Senate and the House of Representatives—many members hiding bleary, bloodshot eyes and nursing hangovers from the night before—refused to allow discomfort to prevent the swift passage of a long-awaited law. Spendini had organized a day-long retreat the day before. At that retreat the Congressional Demagoblicans had hammered out the law they were about to pass. Spendini was certain about the bill's passage. He'd proclaimed his victory to his FGNB contacts before an official vote had even been taken on the measure.

At a news conference a few hours after noon, Spendini strode to the podium, his face beaming. "In the spirit of true bipartisanship, I am here to proclaim the passage of the *Reclaiming Our Fairwaves Edict*." He pumped his fist and waved at the gathered reporters. *People like Buster Lafayette have obstructed progress for too long*, he told himself. *Now they will get to see the true power of the Federal Government.*

Spendini gripped the sides of the podium, his face a stone mask. "Our public airwaves have been polluted for far too long. Starting today we will demand an even-handed treatment of all points of view and those airwaves truly will become fair-waves." Wild applause erupted.

"A new day has dawned in America," he continued. "It is a day of hope. It is a day that promises change. Beware—I say to any who tries to impede our progress. Beware!"

Chapter 24

Somewhere between Stark and Lake City, Florida, a bearded trucker and his beer gut eased the big-rig to a stop. Outside the cab sat an abandoned gas station. Stringy weeds grew through cracks in the station's refueling apron. The tiny hut that had once housed an attendant, a rack for smokes, a tiny fridge, and a few shelves, still stood. However, the structure's windows looked like jagged-toothed smiles. Dirt and leaves littered the floor. The door had long ago been ripped from its hinges.

An observer might have laughed when the trucker exited the cab and removed the rig's fuel cap. Any rational person would have been surprised to see the driver reach into his pocket and pull out a key—a key which unlocked a still-functioning fuel pump.

The abandoned gas station provided the perfect camouflage for a fuel depot. At a glance, the site was dismissed as a relic from the past. But in truth, the ground concealed a nearly-full tank of fuel. The private refilling station had been constructed as a hedge against the fossil fuel ban. This location was one of a dozen such sites that Buster Lafayette had established across Florida.

The network of hidden fuel depots served as a vital tool in Lafayette's struggle to elude the speech bullies. Once EEFF discovered that Lafayette had reestablished talk radio, they targeted him for attack. The talk-show host's homes were routinely vandalized. His broadcast studio had been ransacked on a weekly basis. A car bomb succeeded in killing his former driver. Finally, Lafayette decided that mobility was the only path to safety.

He purchased a diesel rig and semitrailer. Then the trailer was configured to serve as a mobile broadcast studio and living quarters. Five days a week for three hours a day, Lafayette rode the Florida highways and offered solitary opposition to the FGBN and its lackeys.

The mobile studio's daily route was known only to Lafayette, the rig's driver, and the show's producer. The strategy had been successful in keeping Lafayette free from harm in the past, but the talk show host wondered how the Reclaiming Our Fairwaves Edict might change his situation. He suspected that the efforts to locate him would only intensify. All he could do was keep driving and hope to evade the law.

A thick stack of faux-news articles, opinion pieces, and hand-written notes sat on the broadcast console. Lafayette spent the final moments before show time reviewing his materials. He planned to lead the show with a monologue lambasting the radio broadcast edict and the urgency Congress had shown while passing the closely-guarded law.

Though no one mentioned him by name, Lafayette knew he was the new law's main target. No one else had more than a fraction of his audience—or his clout. However, in spite of his efforts to find the new law's actual language, he had no clue what Congress meant when they referred to "fairness" or what the exact consequences of breaking the law would be.

As he cleared his voice and began to speak into the microphone, the studio door flew open and slammed into the wall. He'd expected to see the show's producer enter. Instead, it was Rita the Clown. And she announced her presence with a series of blasts from her bicycle horn.

Rita had eschewed her typical clown suit in favor of blood red coveralls today. Upon her forehead rested a pair of protective goggles. "I brought you some more show prep," she hissed. The clown lifted her left sleeve, lifted her right sleeve, and then reached behind Lafayette's ear to produce an egg. Rita tapped the egg on Lafayette's head and cracked it open. A single sheet of paper fell from the shattered shell. "Read it and weep," the clown said before she watched with amusement while Lafayette's expression changed from mild irritation to genuine concern.

Lafayette read the press release carefully and quickly realized that the information on the pages had not even been shared with the faux-news outlets. The release explained that the Reclaiming Our Fairwaves Edict had picked up where the Fairness Doctrine left off. However, the new law expanded upon the old legislation in a few critical ways.

While the Fairness Doctrine ostensibly sought to balance the content of talk-radio shows between two opposing viewpoints. The Edict considered the slightest deviation from the Demagoblican definition of "balance" as a demarcation point where free speech ended and punishable hate speech began.

The legislation also authorized *Designated Victims* to monitor the airwaves for any content they deemed "hateful." If hateful content was observed, those victims were free to deliver corporal punishment to any offender.

Congress considered the use of tire irons, chains, baseball bats, racquets, lengths of timber with and without nails, firearms, and folding chairs as "instruments of social justice." In the end, the law's authors decided on restraint and imposed limits over the edict's enforcement. The final version of the law specified that punishment could only be inflicted with "cane poles" but none "larger than 1 inch in diameter or longer than five feet in length."

Rita the Clown savored the moment while she watched

Lafayette read the release. Not even the red frown that had been painted across her mouth could disguise the malevolent grin on her face. She hopped from one foot to the other while clapping her hands as the press release dropped from Lafayette's hands and landed on the floor. "Are you ready? Are you ready? Are you ready?" she sang, clapping her hands furiously.

"Ready for what?" Lafayette asked, clearly confused.

"Are you ready for some justice, you bastard?" Rita spat. Her face twisted from smile to snarl in an instant. "C'mon in everybody," she shouted. Then a stream of the government-deputized Designated Victims (DV)—truncheons in hand—flowed into the converted semi-trailer.

Lafayette watched as these members of the so-named *Fairwaves Compliance Brigade* stood in the now-cramped studio. A rainbow-clad gay-rights activist entered first and gave Lafayette a government-sanctioned glare of hatred. Next, a member of the environmental group *All Creatures Great and Small...*, strolled in through the door. Clearly he hadn't bothered to shower for the past few days. A member of the *Primates are People Too Foundation* arrived next. His tee-shirt had been decorated with a photo of a chimpanzee poking its head through a mansion's door. The caption on the back of the shirt read, "Housing is a right for us too." The parade of victims continued until fourteen of them filled the tiny space. Each of them hoped to be the first to strike a blow against their despised enemy.

Seemingly undaunted, Lafayette grabbed his microphone and began his show. "Ladies and gentlemen, today is a big day for me. As some of you know, our diligent Congress worked overtime to pass a law dubbed the 'Reclaiming Our Fairwaves Edict.' Until only moments ago, it was impossible to find any specifics regarding the law. I now know why. Allow me to paint a picture for you," Lafayette said before he described the scene within his studio.

When the host finished his description, he pulled a cigar from his briefcase, lit it, and enjoyed watching the smoke fill the studio. "I am not one to disappoint," he began speaking again. "I can't predict where things will go, but I didn't create this program to allow these fascist Marxists to come in here and intimidate me—" He clenched his teeth and tightened his shoulders while he waited for the blows to rain upon him. Instead of feeling the bite of cane poles, he only heard the whispers of the DVs.

"Hit him!" Rita hissed.

"He hasn't said anything yet," the gay rights activist replied.

"What do you mean? He called us fascist Marxists," the environmentalist said.

"I can't speak for anyone else, but I am a Marxist. And if it takes fascism to make that a reality, I have no issue with that," the activist for poor Americans replied.

"Me too," came the whispers from a few of the others.

"I hate to break this up," Lafayette said while he watched the discussion unfold, "but I have a show to do..." Then he shooed them outside.

"Oh, sorry—" one of the activists replied. Lafayette watched the group file outside into the Florida sunshine. Their argument continued past the end of the broadcast.

Chapter 25

Persistence had propelled the newly appointed *Vice President* Spendini up the political ladder. That and pragmatic problem-solving. But none of that mattered tonight. He stared out the upstairs window of the vice presidential residence and felt helpless. He'd been ensnared by his own trap.

After Chuckles McLaughagain announced his retirement earlier that day, Mannequin wasted no time in naming Spendini as the new vice president. For Spendini, the door to the White House was now impossibly close. Incredibly, the entrance had also been left wide open for him.

But while Spendini contemplated what it would like to be president, Lafayette, Watford, and the rest of the redneck termites threatened to bring down the White House on top of him. *Those bible thumpers aren't going to stand between me and the Oval Office*, the new vice president told himself. *But how can I get the initiative back on my side?*

The situation with Watford was clearly out of control. No one knew how to shut him up without revealing EEFF's Teachers to the world as the squad of jack-booted thugs they were. And worse, the situation with Lafayette had become a running joke.

Congress passed the Reclaiming Our Fairwaves Edict, but the Designated Victims had only managed to argue about whether or not the talk show host had violated the law. *We passed that law so they could go in and whip Lafayette's ass, not deliberate for weeks.*

Some people suggested that the Demagoblicans should, "fight fire with fire," to silence Watford, but Spendini knew they needed a different solution. No one could shout down Watford's words about liberty and individualism. What was required was a weapon more powerful than freedom. And only one thing possessed greater appeal than liberty—free money.

When Spendini authorized DJSM to build the Hand of Equity, he had envisioned a day like today. The progressive tax code had delivered ready cash to feed the starving government machine. But the tax code was never meant to be the game-changer he needed now. Only a miracle could save his aspirations for the presidency. He knew that it was time to swing for the fences. *I haven't gotten this far by hoping that things would work out for me. I've gotten here by making things work out.*

Spendini picked up his telephone. He heard the chirping rings of an encrypted cell phone. Spendini had given the cell phone to Neil Kugler, DJSM's best software engineer. Kugler—a computer software wizard from boyhood—quickly answered the call.

Some people were born to be athletes, others had gifts for music; Kugler had been blessed with an innate understanding of computer languages. He'd constructed nearly 30 variants of existing languages by the time he reached high school. When he graduated from college, hardware manufacturers from around the country had courted him. The corporate fat cats offered him illegally-large salary and benefit packages in hopes of luring the future star to their team.

Astute as he was, Kugler realized where the real power rested—with the government. He saw the explosive growth in the Federal Government's control over individuals and industries and wanted to be on the winning side. So instead of joining a single company—the survival of which could be arbitrarily terminated with the stroke of a government pen—Kugler went straight to the top—DJSM.

Kugler arrived at the agency's headquarters on a warm July morning. The young man asked for a meeting with DJSM's Czar, but could not gain an audience. Instead, it had been Arthur Banks who noticed the reed-like twenty-something sitting near the reception desk inside DJSM headquarters. Kugler had dressed for success in his torn jeans, flip-flips, and a dingy tee-shirt that read "Slacka."

Banks took Kugler to his office and listened while the applicant shared his story and sold his exceptional skill set. Initially, Banks found the young man to be full of bluster and little else.

Sensing Banks's skepticism, Kugler offered to demonstrate his talents. The two of them found a computer terminal that had connections to both the Internet and DJSM's own computer network. Within an hour, Kugler had shown Banks nearly three dozen trap doors, back doors, side doors, and screen doors that led into the networks of more than twenty other government agencies. Kugler lied when he told Banks that DJSM's network was "hack proof." After all, Kugler told himself, *I might need those openings some day.*

Banks hired Kugler immediately and gave him the largest compensation plan that he could wrangle. The new man's impact was immediate. Kugler designed ground-breaking software applications that improved DJSM's ability to monitor business-tax compliance. DJSM receipts grew overnight with no additional human oversight.

Tales of Kugler's talents spread throughout Washington. Soon, the reports reached Spendini's office. Within days, the Senator had shared lunch with DJSM's software genius and asked him for some specs to build a system necessary to implement a progressive tax code.

Kugler had not disappointed. Within days, he offered

Spendini a detailed network diagram including server and node capability requirements.

Spendini immediately contacted Banks and put DJSM to work in the development of the Hand. Of greater importance though had been the hush-hush conversation Spendini and Kugler had shared regarding an extra feature to be embedded within the Hand.

It was this extra feature—the *Bank Balance Juggler*—that had prompted Spendini's call on this day. Kugler smiled when Spendini said the words, "Launch the Juggler," in his matter-of-fact style. Kugler fought the excitement as it welled within his gut. He wanted to cheer or talk or ask what made today special enough to launch his baby into the world, but he did none of those things. "Yes, sir," was all he said as he worked to tamp down his emotions. "Are you sending me the exemption batch file?" he then asked.

"I'm sending it right now," Spendini replied.

"Excellent. When I get the exemptions, I'll run the Juggler. Things will look very different in the morning, sir."

"I'm counting on that, Neil. I'm also counting on being able to trust you. I hope I can trust you," Spendini said before he ended the call without waiting for a reply.

Chapter 26

When the Federal Government nationalized the banking industry, Greta Government gave each of America's banks a semitrailer load of red tape as a "Welcome to the family" gift. Banking industry executives scrambled to hire compliance officers who had had experience wading through the muck and mire of Greta's command-and-control, micro-managing methods.

Like most of her colleagues, the compliance officer that worked for the Puppetgrad Federal Pseudo-Bank had worked in the pharmaceutical industry prior to banking. Like the banks, the pharmaceutical industry had been brought under the government's wing some years earlier. Congress's decision to confiscate nearly every penny of pharmaceutical-industry profits forced the industry's companies to slash costs to stay solvent.

Invariably, the first area cleaved by the pharmaceutical industry's cost-cutting axe was research and development. What followed was a parade to market of misfit and marginally useful niche drugs. One of the most successful of these *accidental* drugs had been a pill that induced arm tremors. The drug had been shockingly useful for the artists employed to paint the countless murals depicting the BELOV'D UNITERS and their reigns in power. The drug-induced tremors increased an artist's painting productivity by 79% over those who worked without medication.

Another serendipitous substance induced interactive-cartoon hallucinations in children. The drug initially caused widespread panic until sociologists realized that the medication was a perfect fit for those families that couldn't afford a television.

The niche drugs hadn't generated sufficient revenue to keep drug companies solvent. Soon, the American pharmaceutical industry began to collapse. The heads of every pharmaceutical company trudged to Washington, D.C. on foot. Each of them pushed a wheelbarrow containing a very large stone. The exhausting feat was meant as an act of contrition aimed at convincing Congress and the Administration to allow them to maintain the profit margins necessary to stay viable.

Instead of finding actual elected officials, the drug industry executives found a tape recorder that played a looped message. "Your greed has been your undoing. America is better off without you. Go home," the message repeated.

The Yellow Lapdog Gazette ran headlines applauding the implosion of the pharmaceutical industry. On DAMPMEN, the banner beneath the news-kittens read, "Hurrah! Now we can get our prescription drugs from Canada, Europe, and China." Unfortunately, the euphoria was short-lived. The words "unexpected medication shortages" soon made daily appearances on the same news-kitten banners that had been used to laud the American pharmaceutical industry's demise.

As she had on most other mornings since her hiring, the Puppetgrad Federal Pseudo-Bank's compliance officer arrived early. The silence the empty building offered made it easier to slog through the complicated Federal reporting forms. *Unlike* other mornings though, the compliance officer was surprised to hear every telephone in the building ringing as she opened the front door. Even more surprising—the end of one call made way for the start of another.

At first, the compliance officer tried to ignore the telephones. Then she began to worry about the source of the unusual call volume. The branch wasn't due to open for a few hours. That fact made the flood of calls even more puzzling. *This is spooky,* she thought.

From down the hallway, the branch manager appeared and said, "Good morning. What's going on with the phones?"

"I have no idea. They haven't stopped ringing since I got here."

"Have you taken a call yet?"

"I was a little unnerved by it all. I've never seen anything like it."

"Do you want to grab a call or should I?" the branch manager asked.

"Why don't we go to my desk, and I'll take a call. It will give us some idea of what's happening. And I'll have access to my computer too," the compliance officer said while she walked to her desk and switched on her computer. She pushed the hair back from her face and readied herself to pick up a call. Then, wearing a smile that belayed her anxiety, she grabbed the receiver. "Hello, Puppetgrad Federal Pseudo-Bank, how may I help you?"

The caller wasted no time. "What happened with my account?" he raged. "I check my balance every morning, and I lost forty thousand dollars last night! How is that even possible?" the caller demanded.

The bank manager watched as the color drained from the compliance officer's face. *Oh, no! This is not good,* she thought.

"I'm so sorry, sir. If you'll give me a moment, I'll bring up your account records, and we can see what happened."

"I'm sorry for taking that tone," the caller muttered. "That was my whole life savings. Seeing it gone was scary. I appreciate you checking for me."

The compliance officer took a deep breath and silently cursed her computer. She hoped the mess would have a reasonable explanation. While she waited for the account software to load, she scribbled a note on a piece of paper for the bank manager to read. "A serious transaction error has occurred," the note read.

The bank manager swallowed hard as she read the note. *Did a massive series of transaction errors trigger the high volume of calls?* she asked herself. Then she felt a knot of fear clenching itself within her gut. There wouldn't be any easy solution for that kind of problem. *It's going to be a long day,* she told herself.

"Oh, no—" the compliance office muttered as she dropped the telephone.

"What is it?" the bank manager asked.

"Forty-thousand dollars was deducted from the caller's account. There's no transaction log to explain where it went. The money just vanished."

Chapter 27

The troubles seen at Puppetgrad Federal Pseudo-Bank were a tiny sliver of the colossal cow-pie of a meltdown that crippled the nation's banks. In the aftermath of the bizarre event, bank executives from across the country—each of them dressed in their mandatory orange prison jumpsuits—flocked to Washington for what they expected to be a group flogging.

In truth, Congress hadn't actually called for them to report. The migration—born of long-standing habit—had become something of a reflex for bankers. But instead of driving hybrid cars or flying on corporate jets, most of the bankers crawled on their hands and knees while shouting "Unworthy" as they slunk along the ground. As each of them arrived in Washington, they made their way to the *Cage.*

The Cage was another innovation born during the New Dark Ages. As Congress tried to micro-manage most of the economy, its members were shocked by the number of hearings required to keep their interests on course. Scheduling meeting times and providing adequate space for all their witnesses became a logistical nightmare. They had an overcrowding problem, and they needed a solution—fast. At the rate they were holding hearings, they risked being overrun by those called to testify.

The Cage had been envisioned by a Congressman from New York and one from California. The two had been eager to get their hands on the Federal Government's fair share of revenue generated by garage sales. They held hearings and called thousands of garage sellers to testify. A crush of common people filled the hearing room to bursting. The New Yorker turned to his colleague and whispered, "We need somewhere else to hold these ... *ugh* ... people."

The Californian whispered "Maybe we should build them a pig pen." Both of them laughed.

The following morning, a bill authorizing the construction of a large, open-air cage was introduced. The cage was intended to house Congressional witnesses during their testimony. The cell was constructed with a rusty metal skeleton and had chain link fencing for skin. A tin roof capped the facility. The cell also featured rough-hewn benches made of sliver-dense wood and a drinking fountain that always seemed to dispense warm, faintly-orange water. The Cage even contained a rack to provide chiropractic care to dissidents.

Of course, not everyone was held in the Cage when they were called to testify. When actors, rock stars, or other cultural luminaries were asked to share their wisdom, they were always accommodated in more traditional meeting rooms. When asked about the preferential treatment afforded to celebrities, the Congressman from California stated, "There are three hundred million people in America. How could we possibly fit them all into our hearing rooms? There are far fewer celebrities. Our hearing rooms can accommodate them nicely."

There was rarely a spare inch in the Cage when bankers were called to testify. Today was no exception. When images of the President appeared on the television monitor that had been installed on the far end of the holding pen, the bankers retreated until they formed a quivering mass in the corner. Few of them had forgotten the Stalinesque purge of the troublesome car dealers some years earlier. Resigned to their fates, the bankers whimpered as they awaited the calls for investigation and the threats of mass firings. Nothing less could be the outcome after the countless banking bungles.

Instead of anger, President Mannequin's expression appeared joyful as he strode to the podium. He wore a navy blue suit with a gold colored tie instead his customary sequined jumpsuits. He'd even declined to sing his presidential anthem. *Today was far too important for such theatrics,* he told himself. The events of the past twenty-four hours had validated everything Mannequin had ever believed about the evils of capitalism.

An aide had called him to deliver the good news at seven the previous morning. "You're never going to believe what happened," the aide began. "My bank balance …it's like twenty thousand dollars bigger than it was yesterday. And like, I called the bank, and there's like no way to know where the money like came from. So it's like mine now, right Mister President?"

The news chased away any trace of drowsiness the President had been feeling, but he still asked the aide to repeat the story so he could know he wasn't dreaming.

The aide repeated her story and then stated that she wasn't the only person who had been blessed—*or cursed*—by the mysterious banking transactions. Similar incidents had happened across the country.

Possibly even more surprising, President Mannequin had learned from the aide that Vice President Spendini had already gotten out in front of the banking miracle. Spendini had even coined the term, "Immaculate Redistribution" to describe the changes wrought upon America's financial landscape.

Mannequin had spent the majority of the day doing interviews to discuss the so-called "miracle." Though Mannequin initially refused to attribute the events to a supernatural force, as the day wore on, he began to wonder whether the redistribution had been a divinely-inspired omen.

"This event," Mannequin told a reporter "demonstrates the good fortune that can only occur in a fair and just nation. Rest assured that what has happened across America today is a direct rebuke of those selfish few who have chosen to believe in the lies that have been spreading over these past few weeks."

By the time today's news conference arrived, Mannequin knew what he had to do. He had even written his own speech. This was the right time for him and the right time for America. So while the bankers huddled together inside the Cage, President Mannequin began to speak. "Today is a momentous day. Too many Americans went to bed two nights ago unsure about how they would make ends meet. Their prayers were answered."

"Too many Americans laid awake wracked with guilt over the good fortune life had bestowed upon them. Their anxieties have been allayed," he continued, assuming the style and cadence of a preacher.

"I faced my own crisis, and I paced the halls of the White House, wondering whether I had chosen wisely in naming Charles Spendini as Vice President. My decision has been confirmed." Mannequin turned to face Spendini who was sitting directly in front of the podium. "Would you come up here, Vice President Spendini?" Mannequin said in a voice filled with warmth.

Spendini rose from his chair and walked to the stage. He waved presidentially to the assembled members of the FGNB and to the millions of Americans watching on television. When Spendini arrived at the podium, President Mannequin shook his new Vice President's hand. "I have a little gift for you, Vice President Spendini. It's time for me to announce my retirement. Effective immediately, I resign the Presidency," Mannequin said. "I have complete faith in you, President Spendini. America should have that faith too."

The timing of Mannequin's retirement took Spendini by surprise. He hadn't prepared any remarks, but he never turned down a chance to get the word out—particularly this close to election time. He smiled and began to speak. "As President Mannequin said, this has been a very important day. For some of you, this has been a day of second chances. This has been a day of reprieve from the financial woes that have plagued you. For others it has been a day of sacrifice in the name of a brighter future for America. For all of us who believed in a better day for America, I would tell you that your faith has been rewarded. But this is only the beginning. Some have called this an 'Immaculate Redistribution.' I would call it economic justice. For the first time, all Americans have been given equal access to wealth and level footing upon which to stand. For the first time, there are no rich and no poor. There are only Americans." Spendini stopped to fold his hands and raise them to the sky, as if giving silent thanks to the unseen engineer of the mysterious financial events.

"My advisors have told me that many Americans—those who have been called upon to sacrifice their riches for the collective good—have been wondering how my Administration intends to address this situation. I am happy to report that this Administration will make no attempt to undo what has been done. In time, everyone will see this event as a sign—a validation of America's movement towards fairness."

The reporters shouted their adulation for the new President. Spendini raised a hand to acknowledge the cascade of cheers. And from streets across America, those people who saw their bank account balances grow could be heard chanting "Spendini! Spendini! Spendini!"

From their vantage point in the Cage, the assembled bankers

exchanged confused glances. *What just happened?* they might have asked one another. Millions of dollars had changed hands in what appeared to be a massive meltdown of the banking system. Yet there was no call for investigation. No one demanded a purge of bank executives. No one talked about the need for more oversight. The only explanation offered was divine intervention.

Then the bankers—most of them bearing bloody wounds on the palms of their hands and shredded skin on their knees—shook their heads in disbelief and shared a silent consensus as they filed out of the Cage. *Something's rotten in Washington.*

Chapter 28

Giddy best described President Spendini's mood. The Bank Balance Juggler had worked better than even he could have imagined. He'd hoped the redistribution would give him a bump in the polls as he headed towards the election. However, Mannequin's proclamation that the "Immaculate Redistribution" was a validation of the former senator's rise to power was too good to be true.

Flushed with excitement, Spendini decided to visit the White House. He wanted to spend a moment in his new office before he went home for the night. He sighed as he stood outside the door to the Oval Office and stared inside. He'd waited his whole life for this moment, and the time had finally arrived. *Maybe I should go sit in the chair for a minute. Just to see how it feels,* he thought.

When he flipped the light switch and stepped inside, a surprise awaited. Neil Kugler—the designer of the Juggler—sat behind the new President's desk. Clearly Kugler had been waiting for a while.

Spendini's body ached after the long day filled with handshakes, pats on the back, and requests for favors. The rush of excitement had finally begun to wear off, and he was in no mood for surprises, particularly from Kugler.

The DJSM software designer looked a mess. A fright wig would have improved the appearance of his hair. Five o'clock shadow covered his cheeks and chin. Red-eyed and reeking of alcohol, Kugler hadn't even noticed that his white Oxford shirt—looking more like a bed sheet than a garment—was only partway tucked in. "I thought I was going to be exempted," Kugler mumbled from his seat.

"Exempted from what?" Spendini laughed, feigning innocence. He sat in a chair across from the desk.

"Exempted from the redistribution virus—the Juggler—Mister President," Kugler spat. "You told me that my bank account would be protected—I lost more than a million dollars."

"I'm not sure what you're insinuating, Neil, but I know I don't appreciate your tone. You heard President Mannequin. The Immaculate Redistribution was a miracle."

"Don't treat me like a fool, Spendini," Kugler growled. "That was my virus. I initiated it myself after you sent me the exceptions file. I saw it run."

Spendini sighed and shook his head. "You are choosing a very dangerous path. You never want to make accusations before you have all the facts. I called your server room after I sent the exceptions file, and I asked them to shut down your server farm. I had second thoughts. I no longer wanted to run the program. I didn't think the time was right."

"You'refullofshitMisterPresident." Kugler's eyes had crossed and his head wobbled as he slurred the insult.

Spendini stood now and leaned across the desk. He whispered his words through gritted teeth. "You better listen carefully. Yesterday's events affected bank accounts across the nation. Anyone who suggests that the transactions were anything but miraculous, risks making themselves my enemy—and an enemy of America. I make it my business to ensure that America's enemies find *no* safe haven. And it wouldn't take a lot of persuasion to convince me that *your* finances should be investigated. I mean, how did a low-level bureaucrat such as you manage to amass such a hefty bank balance? That doesn't sound fair does it—someone like you having been paid so much?" Spendini sat back down again. "In fact, after I've finished with you, your supervisors will realize that you've been embezzling from DJSM for years. Plus they'll see that you programmed your own skim into the Hand of Equity. Which of us do you think people will believe?"

Spendini smoothed his suit coat and straightened his tie. "Neil, neither of us wants this to get ugly. I lost a ton of money in the redistribution too. Don't you think I would have exempted myself if there were really any accounts that escaped economic justice? Trust me when I tell you that your virus was never launched. I checked with about thirty banks this morning. There was no trace of any tampering in any part of the banking system. This truly was a miracle."

Neil shook his head and sighed. "I can't believe I just did this …I am so sorry, Mister President. I hope you will forgive me. I just assumed that since we talked about the virus yesterday that the entire redistribution was the result of my program. I didn't mean to cause any trouble … I was just shocked when I saw that my entire savings had been lost. I hope you understand." Kugler rose from Spendini's chair, wobbled around the President's desk and staggered towards the door. Before leaving the Oval Office, he turned towards Spendini and said, "This is quite an impressive event to kick off your bid for election. It's hard to believe that a miracle like this doesn't signal more good things ahead—right Mister President?"

"Sure thing, Neil," Spendini said before he smiled and waved. "Remember, you should be proud of the role your funds played in this miraculous event."

As Kugler left the White House his brain struggled against the effects of the alcohol he had consumed. Before he'd weaseled his way into the Oval Office to wait for Spendini, he had hacked into the new President's bank records. Spendini's sizable account balance *grew* by more than fifty million dollars during the Immaculate Redistribution. Clearly the President had been the one who was running a private skim. Kugler only needed to decide how to use that information.

Chapter 29

Sweat had already formed on Lafayette's brow. Yet his show hadn't even begun. He had never suffered preshow jitters before the Fairwaves Edict, but the law had changed everything. The safety Lafayette once found in mobility had vanished. Before every show, a car with Federal Government plates pulled alongside the converted semi-trailer and motioned for the vehicle to pull to the side of the road. Once the rolling studio had stopped, the Designated Victims climbed aboard to perform their monitoring duties.

Surprisingly, those fairness watch dogs had yet to fulfill their mission. Not a single cane-pole blow had been struck. Lafayette knew that the day of his punishment would eventually arrive, but he still hoped to avoid it if he could.

The initial euphoria of the Immaculate Redistribution had faded. The men and women who'd been penniless prior the miracle had eagerly waited outside stores. They wanted the chance to spend their new-found riches. They were certain that wonderful things awaited them at the heads of the long lines that slinked out of the few remaining retail stores and wound along—sometimes for city blocks. But once these new customers received their chance to enter the stores, they were shocked by what they saw.

Instead of seeing shelves lined with goods and staffed with employees who offered to provide services, the shoppers found nothing except for the stray pieces of junk that no one else wanted. In one book store, the only item left on the shelves was a "budgeting self-help book" written by one of the BELOV'D

UNITERS. The very brief work consisted of three sentences: "Make sure someone else limits the amount you can spend. If you can't stay within your limit, force someone to lend you money with no expectation of repayment. It's always worked for me."

Riots erupted as the formerly poor demanded their goodies. "We've been duped," some said. "We finally have money, but we don't have anything to spend it on."

Business owners could only beg the forgiveness of the "moneyed mobs" that scoured the countryside looking for items upon which to spend their money. It quickly became apparent that the Immaculate Redistribution had been fool's gold. There hadn't been any increase in goods or services to accompany the large shift of money. The suddenly available wealth—given the dearth of willing merchants—did little more than drive up the prices of the few existing goods and services.

Lafayette had also felt the sting of the Immaculate Redistribution. Not only did he lose millions of dollars, but his in-studio phone line was barraged by callers. The callers accused him of spearheading "the plot to deprive the formerly-poor of their rightful access to goods."

In the midst of the harassment, a cryptic message appeared in Lafayette's private voice-mail box. The caller alluded to the "truth behind the Immaculate Redistribution" and asked for a return call. Lafayette paced within his studio. Times like this made him crave a cigarette to steady his nerves. *This has to be a set up. They want me to call this guy. Then the guy tells me some "secret." When I talk about the call on-air, the Feds come and cane me,* he told himself.

Unsure about how to proceed, Lafayette picked up his telephone and pressed it into his ear a dozen times. Each time he hung up before dialing any numbers. *I should just stay out of this. There are some things that I don't want to know. And if this is true, I don't want to know the truth. People get dead over this kind of thing.*

Then, while ignoring the potential danger of his choice, Lafayette snatched the telephone from its cradle, dialed the digits, and waited for the phone line to ring.

Neil Kugler sounded insane when he answered the call. He launched himself into a rambling explanation of his peril. To Lafayette, Kugler spoke as if he expected someone to kick down his door at any moment. The man was hurrying to unburden himself of the truth.

Lafayette tried get him to calm down, but it was too late for that.

"They're going to kill me!" Kugler ranted. "They're probably sending someone over right now," he said before he began to sob.

"Neil…Neil…I need you to explain this to me one more time. Start at the beginning," Lafayette whispered, trying to soothe Kugler's tattered nerves.

Kugler paused a moment and seemed to regain a shred of control over his emotions. He talked about the day the Hand had first been proposed. Then he spoke about the call he'd received from Spendini. "It's clear that you are a very bright young man, Neil," Spendini said. "I can see big things for you in the future if you remember who your *friends* are." It was then that Spendini asked Kugler to develop the Bank Balance Juggler.

Kugler smiled to himself as he recounted the memory. He'd never felt as important as the day he completed the Hand. *Not bad for some geek,* he told himself.

Then Kugler explained the real force behind the Immaculate Redistribution. He told Lafayette about the virus that secretly examined the balance of every bank account in America. Once a total had been calculated, the program simply shuffled the deck—taking money from the full accounts and depositing the liberated wealth into empty accounts. All of the transactions were executed without an electronic trail, which was important. With no trail, the effects of the redistribution could not be undone.

When Kugler mentioned that Spendini had authorized the launching of the account-balance-shuffling virus, Lafayette's blood ran cold. The story left him speechless. "Are you aware of an organization called the Underground Light Rail, Neil?"

Kugler said that he'd never heard of the group.

"Pack a bag and head south, but go now. If you make it to the border, ask around—but don't ask public officials or anyone like that. Just ask typical people until you find some of the Light-Railers. It's possible that if you make it far enough, they'll find you. They can get you out of the country. I'm guessing they're your only chance right now."

"I don't want to leave," Kugler protested. "Spendini screwed me, and I want my money back."

"Spendini screwed all of us, but if you don't leave right now …" Lafayette paused and thought about the scrapes he'd had with the speech bullies. "There are people who will find you and kill you. And they won't think twice before they do it."

Kugler remained silent for a moment. "Okay. I'll go. You can't let Spendini get away with this," he said before Lafayette told him to hang up the telephone and go.

Kugler felt nauseous. The world was about to collapse on top of him, and he knew it. He ran to his bedroom, snatched shirts, socks and shorts out of his dresser drawers, and shoved them into a travel bag. He pulled up a loose floor board in the corner that concealed stacks of cash. He grabbed all the money he'd squirreled away and his passport. He hoped he'd have time to disappear.

After he snatched the bulging rucksack off the bed, he moved quickly towards the front door. Soft scratching sounds greeted him from the outside of the door. *No. Not yet*—Kugler said to himself, but it was already too late.

A deafening crash shattered Kugler's eardrums, and a hammer-like force tossed his body across the small apartment. After he bounced off the far wall, his shattered body—no more than a bag of bones—slid a foot before stopping. Jagged slivers of wood, chunks of what—moments earlier—had been the front door, protruded from his skin. Smoke and a band of men wearing the combat uniforms of EEFF poured into the wrecked apartment through the ragged hole in the wall. "Guilty," one of the camouflage-clad Teachers grunted as he grabbed Kugler's neck and wrenched it to the left. The chorus of crackling bones left no doubt about Kugler's fate. Within minutes, the computer-prodigy's brain shut down for the last time.

Inside the semi-trailer in Florida, Lafayette just couldn't get comfortable in his chair. It was the same seat that he'd always used, but today it just didn't feel right. *They don't dare touch me. This is America, not some Third-World banana republic. People won't stand for it if they attack me during the show,* he reassured himself. Deep down, he knew he was whistling in the dark.

He couldn't take his mind off Neil Kugler. He wondered whether the young man had managed to escape. Even the arrival of the Designated Victims—an event that had come to make him smile—failed to lighten his mood. The activists formed their customary semicircle, weapons in hand, around his chair. He knew that each of them yearned for the insult that would allow them to strike.

After what seemed like an eternity, show time finally arrived. "If anyone doubts that your government is more interested in protecting its own power than in protecting you, I don't know how you can explain the events of the past forty-eight hours. The wide-spread theft and redistribution of your life's savings has been called an 'affirmation of your government's efforts to ensure economic justice.' The event was called a validation of President Spendini's rise to power. I am wondering where the conspiracy theorists are hiding today," Lafayette said. He knew he was taking a risk by opening his show in this manner. "You people know who you are. Anytime there is the slightest hiccup in business, you go into hysterics. Where is your outrage today?"

"I know what you Demagoblicans are thinking," Lafayette continued. "There he goes again; it's always the same old stuff. But I can tell you that Greta Government has stooped to a new low. I received a call this morning from a man named Neil Kugler—" The mention of Kugler's name elicited a gasp from the assembled activists. Suddenly, each of them turned towards the studio door and hurried out.

Lafayette stopped talking while he watched the exodus. *What's going on here?* he asked himself. Then he shook his head before he resumed his hosting duties. *I guess they need to have another discussion. It figures.*

"Neil Kugler worked for DJSM—the same agency that collects your taxes," Lafayette resumed, "and he was instrumental in the development of the software that runs the Hand of Equity. But this young man developed more than just the Hand of Equity. On the direction of now-President Charles Spendini, Kugler also developed a top secret, oh, no—"

Lafayette knew immediately that today would not be like all the other days. Three men and three women—a textbook case of gender equity—barged into the studio without warning. Lafayette tried to swallow but his mouth had gone dry.

Without a word of explanation, the group descended upon the talk-show host. There was neither argument about who would strike the first blow nor war cries. There was only a hailstorm of blows and a rain of blood. The ugly sounds the Teacher's fists and elbows made while striking Lafayette's face and body resonated across the radio waves. The echoes of the grim assault reached the show's listeners in every corner of America. The beating continued until Lafayette had fallen to the floor and quivered in a pool of his own blood. One of the attackers bent down to wipe his blood-stained fists on one of the few clean patches of Lafayette's clothing. Another of them spat in the battered-man's face.

The sounds of the assault had been allowed to go out over the airwaves to send a message. The message was a warning to anyone who dared speak out against the Federal Government.

Once the one-sided melee was over, the sounds of fists and boots striking flesh were replaced by dead air.

That night at a Tallahassee bar, the Designated Victims toasted the lucky few who had given Lafayette such a ferocious beating. "It was a blow for free speech," one of them shouted. Others bragged about the number of times they would have hit the talk-show host had they only been given the chance.

And later, when those activists climbed into bed for the night, each of them whispered a silent prayer to Mother Nature that Lafayette, who now lay in a coma, had suffered enough brain damage to keep him off their air for good. A message had been sent this day. Next on their list was Ray Watford.

Chapter 30

A few hours later along the California coast, Kevin Meadows had fallen asleep on his couch instead of in his bed. The cell phone's clattering atop the Italian marble end table jolted him from his sleep. "Talk to me," he said.

"The capers are in the omelet." It was Mick Boyle with a situation report. Boyle had been instructed to stake out the Los Angeles International Airport until Watford's flight landed. The *capers* were Watford and the *omelet* was the airport, Boyle explained before asking, "What do you want me to do now?"

"This operation is a go. The Foursome for Fairness is in the game," Meadows said. He was the one who had decided that the group needed a nickname. He believed the moniker gave their efforts credibility and thought the name might make a good movie title some day. "Follow him, but don't let him see you," Meadows said before he hung up.

But Meadows wasn't finished. He dialed a series of numbers, but while the line rang, he couldn't remember if he had dialed Sunny Davis or Davis Sunny. In truth, the distinction between the two was really no distinction at all.

Sunny Davis was the current Chairwoman of the Demagogue Party and a woman who had worked her way up through the party. She graduated summa cum liberal from the Massachusetts School of Indoctrination and received her first taste of politics during an internship with the Demagogues. The existing party hacks had been shocked to see the college girl spearheading an unprecedented expansion of the party's scope and mission.

Davis said that the *Fifty States Movement* in the Demagogue Party was "lazy and uninspired." In its place, she mapped out the *Three Thousand One Hundred Forty Counties Campaign* and urged the Demagogues to "ensure their dominance in every county in the nation." While proposing the ambitious plan, Ms. Davis suggested that the party needed to "dig even lower than the grass roots. We need to be willing to root through the dirt if we must. America's number-one political machine shouldn't act like it's being run by slackers. Let's get out there and stomp some elephant tail!" she'd shouted from a table top while pitching her idea.

In addition to her rousing oratory skill, Sunny was a striking beauty. She had deep blue eyes and an improbably perky smile. At first glance, she was the girl-next-door that every boy dreamed of meeting, until you looked a little closer. Her Nordic blonde hair always looked brown—she rarely bothered to wash it. She routinely wore psychedelic sun dresses that showcased her unbelievably furry armpits. And up close, she stank—she detested deodorants.

Sunny had been raised on a Maine commune by her mother, Love Davis. In her youth, Love had been a world-class quick-change artist. Sunny grew up captivated by her mother's artistry. Sunny then learned her mother's secrets by helping to prepare costumes and watching her mother rehearse.

Sunny made good use of the skills she'd learned during her foray into politics. While working on her first social-justice project—a movement to unionize honey bees—Sunny had her first encounter with Senator Spendini. Spendini explained to Sunny that he had been invited to speak at both the *Ethyl-Noleo Growers Annual Corn-Festival Dinner* and at the *Unpoor Friends of the Poor's Annual Conference on Hunger*. Unfortunately both events were scheduled at the same time. Spendini needed the support of both special interest groups, so he asked Sunny to share some of her special expertise.

Sunny gave Spendini a crash course in the art of the quick-change. The Senator had been an apt student. After only a few hours of instruction, Spendini could perform basic quick-changes. The techniques allowed him to shift from husking the corn to hustling the poor almost effortlessly. As he shuttled between the two events, he shucked like a huckster for the corn growers and did his best "Mother Teresa" for the unpoor Friends of the Poor. His successful twin-bill had been worthy of a golden statuette.

Sunny's contributions to Spendini's success earned her the Senator's patronage. Spendini agreed to shepherd the *Winged Workers Act*—a law Sunny had written which created a four-day work week, shorter hours, and established a union pay-scale for honey bees. Unfortunately for bee keepers, honey bees did not deal in American currency. The farmers were left on the hook for the payment of the bees' wages, payroll taxes, and union dues.

Marxists around the world praised the Winger Workers Act and wished they'd concocted the scam themselves. The Yellow Lapdog Gazette reported that bees everywhere observed a "minute sans stinging" as a gesture of their gratitude.

Spendini continued to support Sunny's career beyond the Winged Workers Act. The Senator even backed Sunny's rise to the seat of Demagogue Party Chairwoman. But chairing the Demagogue Party wasn't enough for Sunny.

She decided to use the spirit of bipartisan cooperation in Washington to her advantage. She used her quick-change skills to become Chair*man* of the FauxPublican Party, on top of her post with the Demagogues.

Sunny had realized that the FauxPublican Party had been

running from its conservative principles for more than a generation. Instead of advocating for individual liberty, smaller government, lower taxes, and a strong national defense, the FauxPublicans had adopted the Santa-Clausey politics of the Demagogue Party. Both parties eventually played the same game of big-government *top this* to win over voters. Both Demagogue and FauxPublican alike would often be found at local shopping malls—constituents, with wish list in hand, perched atop each candidate's lap. Sunny only needed tiny tweaks in her patter to transition from Sunny Davis, the Demagogue, to Davis Sunny, FauxPublican. She even achieved substantial cost savings for both parties. She moved the FauxPublican headquarters into a building already occupied by the Demagogues. Though the two parties maintained separate addresses, the arrangement allowed them to share the same group of staffers—and the same set of philosophies.

In contrast to her name, Sunny had a reputation as a diamond-hard political operator. Rivals within her own parties knew that she would put her foot across a man's throat before she allowed him to get ahead at her expense. But the treatment she extended to fellow Demagoblicans—the now-aligned Demagogues and FauxPublicans—was a gentle breeze compared to the murderous contempt she held for conservatives.

Kevin Meadows had hoped to appeal to Sunny's killer instinct when he made his first contact with her. Meadows called Sunny and told her that "he and some friends could make her Watford problems disappear." All Meadows asked for in return was a promise of future patronage if his plan succeeded.

"How do you plan to make that happen? I've seen your movies. You're not even that good an actor," an incredulous Sunny challenged.

"I don't know if you realize this, but I do all my own stunts." Meadows lied, "I'm also one of the stunt coordinators in my films—it's in my contract."

"What do you intend to do?"

Meadows explained the plan, and Sunny reluctantly signed on. *How bad can things be?* she asked herself. *If they mess this up, I just say they were overzealous actors—problem solved.*

That conversation occurred two weeks ago. Tonight *Operation Fairness* was underway. Meadows had called Sunny to update the status of the plan. The decidedly unsunny, Sunny, growled when she heard Meadows on the line. "Why are you calling me? I can't have you getting me tangled up in this." She wanted to kick Meadows in the balls for his inability to follow simple instructions. "I appreciate your desire to keep me informed, but I need plausible deniability. I can't have you calling me. Do you understand this?" she snarled. "And don't even tell me you're using a cell phone, you nitwit. I'll come out there and cram that cell phone into your ear if you use it to call me again."

Meadows couldn't help but become turned on as he spoke with the fiery party chairwoman. He found Sunny to be terribly hot and hoped there might be a chance for the two of them to get together when this was over. But for now, all he could do was try to calm Sunny's angry mood. "No, Ms. Davis. I won't call you again, and I promise I won't call you using a cell phone."

"Good boy. Don't screw this up, Meadows. Try to be discrete. We can't have you out there stumbling around and making a mess. When you've secured the author, call me from a land line. Someone will contact you with instructions. Your only job is to keep him safe and out of the spotlight until after the election. Do you understand me?"

"Yes, ma'am."

"If you pull this off, you'll have the undying gratitude of the Moral Compass Society. We're a good group of people to have in your debt, Mr. Meadows. You'll be on the "A" list in no time. So, go make this happen."

Chapter 31

As Ray entered Los Angeles International Airport for the first time, the stench of rotting food and garbage filled the air. Small heaps of trash lay scattered along the walls. Garbage overflowed the top of every trash can. A blanket of soda cups, snack bags, and pieces of rotten fruit that had been discarded by other travelers covered the corridors. *This is even worse than Puppetgrad,* Ray thought. The sight typified the state of the union.

Not only had the inside of the terminal become an eyesore, the incessant racket of Greta Government made Ray's ears sore. "Attention! Attention!" Greta blared. "Be sure to have your travel papers ready *before* you reach the screening station. You will not be allowed to board your flight without verification of your work status."

Ray reflexively reached down to his hip pocket and patted the folded stack of papers. He thought back to the days when Americans were able to go on a trip without carrying evidence of the Jobs Czar's consent.

Then, as he stepped around a pool of unidentifiable spew, he pulled his cell phone from his pocket to call Sarah. Greta interrupted his call with yet another announcement. "Physicians, please ensure that you have proof of your *guarantee of return* bond," she said. "The bond value must be ten million dollars or 95 percent of your assets, whichever is higher. Failure to show proof of a valid guarantee of return bond will negate your tickets and will prevent you from boarding any flight for travel outside the continental U.S."

Ray couldn't help but pity doctors. If private-sector workers thought the Jobs Czar was tough, the Health Care Czar was a harsher taskmaster. The implementation of socialized medicine triggered a flight of physicians. Some doctors fled the country. Others went into hiding and opened secret, *cash-only* clinics. A few of them disavowed their medical training and disappeared.

The Federal Government responded with the *Doctors Dispersal Decree*. The decree provided a method to ensure that physicians were equitably located throughout the nation. The U.S. was divided into a series of health care zones. Doctors were allocated to zones based on a location-lottery. The lottery determined which zone the doctor would settle within to open a medical practice. Each doctor then became responsible to deliver medical care within that zone.

The decree was a nice idea, but it failed to solve the doctor-disappearance problem. Some doctors told the Healthcare Czar that they were going on vacation and simply never returned. The Health Care Czar responded with the very French-sounding *Doc-Jacques* system. It was the same technology used to reacquire stolen automobiles. Doctors simply wore a tracking bracelet.

As an added measure of insurance, the Czar decided that doctors who left their assigned zone would also be required to post a bond to ensure their return. The bond amount virtually guaranteed financial ruin for any doctor who decided to skip town.

The combination of the tracking system and the bonds had effectively ended the exodus of physicians. But that didn't mean that all physicians had accepted their fate. Ray saw security officers hauling at least two doctors out of the terminal in handcuffs. The black, house-call bag both of the physicians were carrying might have been a dead give-away.

Once Greta had finally zipped it about the bonding issue, Ray pulled out his cell phone and called his wife. "Hey, Honey. I made it," he announced.

"How much time do you have until you need to be at the studio?" she asked.

"I have a while. I'm not due there 'til this afternoon. I'll have plenty of time to do some sight-seeing."

"Break a leg tonight. I'm proud of you."

"Thanks. I'll see you tomorrow," Ray said as he ended the call.

The trip to California had been an unexpected surprise. But the same could have been said for many of the events that had taken place since the day he'd left his novel at Kerwin Publishing. His reputation had become a fire hydrant for the Yellow Lapdog Gazette's daily use. He was DAMPMEN's favorite piñata. Networks that typically aired entertainment-based programming even devoted portions of their programming day to reading from the FGNB's, "Ray Watford is a villain," playbook. Even Presidents Mannequin and Spendini had taken swipes at him from behind their bully pulpit.

Because he'd also been fired by Compassion County and had his bank account frozen, the call from the producer of the Echolalia with Edgar Cockatiel seemed like a Godsend. The show's producer said that he'd heard of Ray's financial struggles and wanted to offer him a chance to make some money—cash under the table to "help him feed his kids."

Ray asked about the catch, but the producer told him, "There's no catch. We just want to see you be part of our panel and debate our host on the merits of your book. It'll be as easy as that. When you're finished, you'll go home with a pocket full of money, and it will be great television."

Ray had seen snippets of Cockatiel's show, and the content caused him concern. The show consisted of a predictably-tired monologue, followed by a trite, cliché-ridden panel-discussion. Colorful profanity seemed to be the high-water mark of show's intellectual brilliance

The show's host, a self-proclaimed comedian and satirist, was the one-way street of political thinkers. Suggesting that Cockatiel was a liberal populist was like saying that Pete Maravich had once played basketball.

And though Ray had been surprised by the invitation itself, he'd been confounded by the level of importance which seemed to have been attached to his appearance on the show. The AirFair Airlines Czar issued Ray's ticket to travel within a matter of hours. *Why all this fuss for a show with an audience that's this small?* he asked himself as he boarded the plane. *They must have to measure Cockatiel's ratings with an electron microscope. Whatever the reason, it can't be good,* was all he could come up with.

Chapter 32

Mick Boyle had been watching from his seat as Watford emerged from the jet way. He tailed the author at a distance. There were few travelers nearby. He didn't want his quarry to suspect that he was being followed.

If Watford rented a car, Boyle was to contact Jimmy Forest with a license plate number and a description of the car. It would be Forest's job to tail the author until the group made its move. They couldn't afford to have Watford get lost on the way to the studio and see their chance blown.

Will Williams had been placed on standby in case of an emergency. He was due to relieve Forest from shadowing duties, if the change was practical, in the afternoon.

Boyle knew that the success or failure of the plan now rested on his shoulders while he waited for Watford to emerge from the men's room. He had been chosen as the initial shadow because he was the group's least recognizable member. The assignment—like all the criticisms he received from the Hollywood press—hurt his feelings. Some tabloids called Boyle "Kevin Meadows's shadow," saying he couldn't make it in Hollywood without the zombie-movie actor. Others whispered that Boyle and Meadows were gay but wouldn't come out of the closet. None of it was true.

Boyle had been born in California, but he didn't grow up dreaming of a career in acting. His start came when he was asked to serve as an extra in a low-budget film. He found that he enjoyed the commotion and atmosphere of the movie set. He began to go to auditions and tried to hold onto some type of life in the movie industry.

His big break came when he earned a speaking role in *Lobotomized American Zombies*. His character's brains had been eaten inside the film's first twenty minutes, but he'd met Kevin Meadows during the shoot. The two became instant friends and soon were inseparable.

While Meadows liked to be at the center of attention, Boyle didn't mind standing on the side lines. Meadows was a talker, and Boyle liked to listen. Their friendship fit. And though Boyle hoped their plan would elevate his career, above all other reasons, he wanted to see Kevin receive the validation he so craved.

Boyle knew that his own days in Hollywood were numbered. At some point, the calls would stop coming. If this job prolonged Meadows's stay in the spotlight, for Boyle it will have all been worthwhile.

"Attention all travelers: the AirFair Airlines flight to Stockholm is now in general boarding," the flight information system announced. The announced flight to the capitol of Sweden had become a long-standing phenomenon.

AirFair Airlines—the nationalized American air-travel company—operated the flights as the first leg of an all-expenses-paid tour of Europe. The journey began in Sweden and finished in Greece. The entire trip was a vacation package that allowed a few lucky Americans the chance to relive the BELOV'D UNITERS' first European tour. Thousands had gone on the tours at taxpayers' expense.

The stampede of hopeful AirFair travelers ended Boyle's recollection of misty memories featuring Meadows. He pulled his feet and legs up onto the seat to avoid having his limbs trampled by the crush of travelers seeking a free vacation. Then it struck him. "Where's Watford?" he muttered.

He jumped to his feet and fought the urge to run. He walked into the men's room to check on the author. *Please be in here. Please be in here,* he said to himself as he stepped through the doorway. His eyes darted around the filthy restroom. He even spent a moment peering under the stall doors. There was no sign of Watford.

Boyle left the men's room and strode towards the airport's main corridor. *I should probably call Kevin and let him know what happened ...No. You can't let him down. You just need to find the author. Be calm and everything will be fine.* Then Boyle had an idea.

As he tried to rent a car, Ray learned that nothing fell outside the reach of Federal Government. As part of the *Carbon Footprint Reduction and Fairness in Car Rental Act,* the Feds implemented new requirements which dictated exactly how many joules of power and how much cargo space a car renter could rent.

Since Ray was traveling alone, the law allowed him access to no more than a single-body-mobility-pod. As seemed to be his luck, the Go-Green Rent-A-Car had none of the egg-shaped units available. He was given two options. He could forgo his car rental or volunteer to carpool with a Californian who needed a ride home.

The orange-clad, car-rental attendant processed Ray's reservation and stated, "I can give you a two-person car, but you'll need to make a small detour." *A small detour,* Ray learned, meant a round trip of 660 miles to Alameda. Seeing Ray's frown, the car rental agent added, "Feel free to walk to Studio City, if you like."

"This is turning out to be some trip," Ray said as he took the keys to the rental car and walked to the car-rental shuttle with his new traveling buddy.

Boyle had nearly lost all hope as he approached the last car rental stand in the airport. He'd already pulled his cell phone from his pocket—readying himself to report his failure—when he saw Watford at the Go-Green counter. Boyle didn't recognize the man that stood alongside the author, but he did recognize the BELOV'D UNITER European Tour jacket. *I've got to get me one of those,* he thought as he watched Watford and the second traveler disappear through the door.

He no longer had the luxury of discretion. He ran after the pair and didn't stop until he too had climbed aboard the rental-car shuttle, making it inside only seconds before the bus pulled away.

When the shuttle arrived at the rental car parking lot, Boyle walked slowly to the parking lot and lingered. He needed to report the color, model, and plate number of Watford's rental car to Jimmy. Eventually, his patience was rewarded. Boyle watched Watford climb into the yellow, Federal Government Motors Custom-Deluxe-Clown-Car and drive away. As Boyle wrote the clown car's license plate number on the palm of his hand, he breathed a sigh of relief and then called Jimmy Forest.

He'd successfully completed his task. Now it was Forest's turn.

Chapter 33

Ray checked his side mirror and prepared to make the left turn onto Studio Boulevard. His neck and shoulders ached after spending the entire day in the car. The round trip to Alameda had been tedious and taxing. He had seen photos of the California freeway system, but he hadn't realized that a reprioritization of roadways had occurred. During the trip, he discovered the specially-designated moped and bicycle lane, walker lane, visually-impaired walker lane, pet-walker lane, and the motorized and motor-less wheel-chair lanes. Given the circus-like atmosphere on the roadways, he never noticed the motorized scooter that tailed behind him was being driven by Jimmy Forest.

Forest spat a bug from his mouth as he straddled his scooter. Man and machine waited behind Watford at a stoplight. With the Liberal Broadcasting Network's (LBN) parking lot just up the road, Forest planned to cut around the author at the light. Then he'd arrive at the studio first.

Once the light changed, however, things didn't go as planned. Forest nearly collided with a woman and her poodles as he gunned his scooter and sliced through traffic to make his turn. Fortunately, Watford had steered his car into the midst of the California Organ Grinders Club which was out for its weekly "monkey walk."

Once he'd cleared the congestion, Forest checked his rearview mirror and saw Watford well behind him. He gunned the scooter's throttle and sped off to join the rest of the Foursome while they prepared a little surprise for their prey.

Less than five minutes later, Ray made the final turn of his environmentally-friendly odyssey into the LBN studio parking lot. The studio had been the long-time home of the *Echolalia with Edgar Cockatiel* program. Ray had hoped to have some time to catch his breath, but he'd barely arrived in time. The show was due to start in less than 30 minutes.

A cool breeze washed over his face as he eased his tall frame out of the car's cramped confines. As he moved to close the driver's side door, he realized that he'd forgotten his stack of note cards. He hoped to review the cards before the show. As he reached across the car's front seat, he heard a vehicle skid to a stop behind him. Startled by the commotion, he spun around to see the nose of a windowless, gray cargo van sitting inches from the trunk of his rental car.

Before he could react, the rear doors of the van flew open, and three men dressed in black coveralls and ski masks hopped out. A black leather sap—a chunk of lead encased in a leather pouch—dangled from the right wrist of each of the men. One of them held a roll of duct tape.

Ray stood motionless—too shocked to move—as the scene unfolded. Meanwhile, the masked assailants spread themselves across the open end of the "V" that was formed by the intersection of the clown car and the cargo van. Ray saw that he was trapped.

"Can I help you?" Ray asked the men, wishing that this was just a bad dream. The men said nothing and continued to advance slowly and cautiously toward him.

"I'm not looking for trouble. I'm just here to do a show. I'll give you my wallet," he said.

"You've already made trouble," the shortest attacker grunted.

"Your stinking money isn't going to help you."

"I don't know who you think you're looking for, but this is the first time I've ever been in California. You've got the wrong guy." Ray held up his arms in front of him, pleading to the masked men.

"You're the right guy alright." Again it was the short man talking.

"Will you shut up, Mick," a stocky man—his build like a football linebacker—hissed.

Mick? Ray's mind began to race. He tried to connect the dots, hoping that he could defuse the situation. Then he realized that he recognized the linebacker's voice. "You're Jimmy Forest," Ray blurted, hoping that his recognition of Forest's voice might somehow end the nightmare. "Why are you doing this?"

The tallest attacker then growled, "Let me give you some advice. Shut your mouth and get into the van. You'll be getting inside one way or another. If you cooperate, things will go a little easier. Otherwise, this will be very painful."

Ray bowed his head while his mind searched for an escape plan. *I'm being kidnapped by a group of actors. How weird is that? And to think that I spent money to see their movies. That won't be happening again any time soon.* Without warning, he attacked.

Ray rushed at Boyle, who was the nearest. He balled his hands into fists and threw a haymaker right hand. The punch caught Boyle in the side of his jaw. Boyle staggered and then stumbled backward before falling to the ground.

Next, Ray pivoted on his left foot and delivered a side kick that struck the man he'd identified as Will Williams. The kick struck Williams just inside his knee and caused the joint to buckle. Williams screamed and fell to the ground, holding his damaged limb.

Ray turned to Jimmy Forest. He didn't know whether to fight Forest or try to run past his grasp. Hoping to buy himself some time, he said, "I don't want to hurt you, Jimmy." He gasped, trying to catch his breath. "You saw what happened to Mick and Will." Secretly, Ray wished that Forest would just climb into the van and drive off. But *that* wish never came true. Forest held his position. "I'm not getting into that—"

The van's driver was Kevin Meadows. Seeing that the abduction had gone sideways, Meadows had climbed out the passenger's door on the unseen side of the van. He moved around the vehicle's hood and slid through the space where the hood of the van and the trunk of the clown-car met. Ray never had a chance.

Once Meadows had snuck in behind, the show was over. He walked up behind Ray and slammed his leather sap into the back of Watford's head, knocking the author unconscious. After Ray had fallen to the ground, Meadows rasped at Forest, "Get over here and help me get him taped up." Forest immediately obliged. "We can't have the studio rent-a-cops coming to see what's going on." Meadows grabbed the roll of duct tape out of the fallen Williams' hand and started wrapping Watford's ankles.

Once Ray's hands and feet had been bound, Meadows placed a piece of tape over the writer's mouth. He and Forest carried Watford over to the van and dumped him into the back.

While Forest helped Boyle and Williams into the vehicle, Meadows slid behind the wheel. By the time the van's cargo doors had been yanked shut, the vehicle's tires were already screeching.

After leaving the parking lot, Meadows pulled a cell phone from his coveralls and made a call.

Chapter 34

Back in Puppetgrad, Sarah Watford grabbed the bowl of popcorn from the counter and walked quickly to the living room. "Justin… Austin…" she called as she flipped on the television. "I made popcorn," she said causing delighted smiles to light the boys' faces.

"Wow!" Justin exclaimed. "Where did you get it?" The use of corn in Ethyl-Noleo made popcorn a luxury that only the most elite could afford.

"Don't tell your father, but I dipped into our savings account. I saw one of Senator Spendini's aides carrying a fifty pound bag of it out of the Government Surplus Co-op. I offered him a thousand dollars for a pound of it."

"That's a lot of money," Austin replied.

"I know, but this might be the only time we get to see your father on television. I think *that* makes it a celebration." The three of them settled onto the orange-vinyl couch being careful to avoid the protruding springs. Soon the opening credits for *Echolalia with Edgar Cockatiel* began to roll. Sarah felt goose bumps form on her skin when the announcer mentioned Ray's name. "I can't believe it. Your dad is on TV." At the moment, she wasn't sure who was more excited, she or Ray.

With Sarah and her sons looking, Edgar Cockatiel strode out onstage and began his customary monologue. The host's white suit and lime green tie—when coupled with his large nose and the plume of white hair which had been teased and gelled until it pointed skyward—made the host closely resemble his name-sake.

Once the side-splitting monologue had ended, Cockatiel

called out his panel of guests. First to arrive was actress Sunny Cleanair. Next, the host introduced rock-n-roller, Ima Bettawurld. And finally—accompanied by a chorus of boos, catcalls and shouts of derision—the host presented "Ray Watford."

Sarah was the first to react. She blinked, looked away from the television, and then looked back again. "What's going on here?" she asked. She couldn't believe what she was seeing.

With a look of shock pasted onto his face, Austin asked, "Where's dad?"

A fog of confusion enveloped Ray's memory. He'd begun to regain consciousness, but the process was slow. He tried to touch the painful lump that had formed on the back of his head but discovered that his hands had been bound. When he tried to move his legs, he discovered that his legs had been hobbled as well.

Slowly, the images of the altercation returned. As the attack played out, Ray remembered that he'd been able to identify his attackers. But that didn't clear up their reasons for kidnapping him in the first place. Nor did it give him any clue as to what would happen now that they had him. *Could this be part of some practical-joking television show?* He considered his predicament. His head ached and he was bound in the back of a moving vehicle headed to just about anywhere. *No. There's too much potential liability for this to be a gag.*

Could this have anything to do with my appearance on the show? He pondered the unexpected invitation from the producer and the rushed travel arrangements. *It's hard to believe any of this is a coincidence. I come all this way only to be kidnapped by a bunch of actors.*

A bump in the road caused his aching head to bounce off the floor. Though excruciating, the blow helped to clear his mind. *Neil Kugler leaked information about the Immaculate Redistribution and he was killed by a mysterious natural-gas explosion.* He needed to connect the dots. *Buster Lafayette mentions Kugler's name and then gets assaulted and the incident goes out over the air to his entire audience. I come here and get kidnapped.* Then an explanation crystallized for him. *Maybe they're trying to silence me too …*

While the genuine Ray Watford bumped along in the back of a cargo van, Edgar Cockatiel and his kangaroo court put their "Ray Watford" on trial. The imposter that had been recruited to play the role of Ray Watford was given one million dollars and instructions to "say anything that enters your mind as long as it offends the members of some protected community." The actor played his role brilliantly. He managed to cram a lengthy list of slurs—hurtful insults uttered against Blacks, Mexicans, Puerto Ricans, Jews, Muslims, Gays and Lesbians, people with red hair, bottle blondes, unwed mothers, Asians, chimpanzees, people with disabilities, environmentalists, and the homeless—all in a span of less than twelve minutes.

When "Watford" finally finished spitting venom, he slithered out of the studio to another cascade of boos and a shower of popcorn. Cockatiel and his panel spent the remainder of the show savaging all conservatives.

Having already tuned out Cockatiel's in-studio antics, Sarah searched the Internet until she found a phone number for LBN. She was relieved when the call was answered by a *real* person. "HimynameisSarahWatfordandmyhusbandwassupposedtobepart ofthepaneltonight," *Breath* "butthemanontheshowwasn'thim," *Breath,* the agitated Mrs. Watford blurted.

"I'm sorry ma'am, but I didn't understand a word you just said. Could you say that again?"

This time Sarah paused and took a deep breath. She told the LBN studio receptionist that the Ray Watford who had appeared on the show wasn't the *real* Ray Watford.

"The show is on the air right now," the receptionist replied. "Are you sure you're tuned to the correct channel. The show is only on premium cable."

"I get LBN, and I was watching the correct show!" Sarah shouted. "I am trying to figure out why my *husband* didn't appear on the show."

"According to my notes, Ray Watford was on the show—Oh wait. He just stormed out of the studio. Is it possible that you missed his appearance?"

"The man on the show WASN'T my husband!" Sarah screamed into the telephone.

"Ma'am, it doesn't help the situation when you talk to me that way. Is it possible that your husband isn't the Ray Watford who was supposed to be the guest on the show? Maybe your husband isn't really an—"

Enraged and frightened for Ray's safety, Sarah slammed the telephone down onto its cradle. She tried to be strong in front of her sons, but the tears soon won the battle. She put her face in her hands and cried. After the jag subsided, she picked the telephone up again and tried to reach Ray's cell phone. The call went to voicemail immediately. *He didn't appear on the show, and he's not answering his cell phone. What else can I do?* Sarah asked herself. Clouds of dread had begun to gather on the horizon.

Wait—I can call AirFair, she realized. *They can tell me for sure whether or not he made it to California. Maybe he boarded the wrong flight by mistake.* She spent the next three hours calling AirFair Airlines, Go-Green Rent-A-Car, and the Los Angeles Airport. None of them had seen her husband or could offer any information about his whereabouts. The airline hadn't even been able to find a ticket for any Ray Watford in their system.

Sarah stared at the floor after she'd hung up the telephone. She fought the urge to cry again. Ray had disappeared without a trace, and she had no idea how to get him to reappear. Justin walked over and rubbed her back—a small gesture to try to ease his mother's suffering. "Have you tried to call the cell phone company? Maybe they can tell you where Dad called from this morning." Sarah smiled for the first time in hours before she kissed her youngest son on the forehead and snatched up the telephone.

Chapter 35

Agents who worked in EEFF's Cyberspace Manipulation (CM) Department made the impossible possible. Those agents were hired for their exceptional keyboarding skills, ability to remain calm under pressure, a peerless familiarity with the capabilities of the Internet, and the ability to hack into the countless computer networks that flowed onto the information superhighway.

The exploits of the Cyberspace Manipulation team—when they were performed correctly—were untraceable. Software *glitch, ghost* or *floopiness* were some of the terms that were used to describe successfully manipulated cyberspace. Given the planned abduction of Ray Watford, there was nothing floopy about the assignment that awaited Mike Hanks today.

Each time the phone in the CM duty center rang, Hanks tensed. He knew the call was going to come soon. He was ready to do some business. A sealed envelope sat on his desk. Inside was the list of tasks he'd be asked to perform. All he needed now was the green light.

Hanks was the fastest Cyberspace Manipulator in the world. No one could match his skill. But whenever he received a critical assignment, a single flaw revealed itself. While he was cool under pressure, he wasn't immune. Prior to critical assignments, Hanks was forced to relieve certain bodily pressures with such a frightening degree of regularity, the other duty-center agents had taken to calling him "Old Faithful" behind his back.

The aptness of the nickname was to be demonstrated again today. "Hey, can you do me a favor and listen for my phone?"

Hanks asked the only other agent on duty.

The man—his back turned to Hanks—smiled broadly upon hearing the question. He'd just won a bet for $100.

"I gotta take a leak," Hanks announced as he left the duty center.

A few hundred miles away, the gears were already turning. Kevin Meadows called Sunny Davis/Davis Sunny at Demagoblican headquarters. He reported the successful capture of Watford.

Sunny Davis/Davis Sunny then called President Spendini who was busying himself on a fact-finding mission in Nassau. Spendini hoped to resolve the age-old question on bikini construction. How much material was too much?

Spendini—irritated with the interruption of his data gathering— quickly saw the importance of the call and relayed the message to General Welfare at EEFF. Because Welfare had been busy shaving strokes off his golf handicap with his twin, Swedish caddies, the President's call had to be routed from EEFF's main switchboard to the green of the eleventh hole at Elitist Pines Country Club.

After receiving the green light from Spendini, Welfare sent the "Go" code to Mr. Dannyo, the current CM Duty Chief. The final link in the chain was a shouted warning to Hanks—who was still in the men's room—telling Hanks to "get your ass down here. It's time to roll."

Hanks' foot falls could be heard all the way back to the duty station. The agent ran from the men's room—a string of toilet paper still stuck to his shoe—straight to his chair. After he'd taken his seat, Hanks' fingers darted and dashed across his specially designed keyboard. The keyboard's modifications allowed EEFF's cyberspace manipulators to squeeze a few extra words per minute out of their exceptional keyboarding skills.

Within the first minute, Hanks had already hacked the database for Go-Green Rent-A-Car. An EEFF agent had already been dispatched to the LBN studio's parking lot to retrieve, sanitize, and then return Watford's rental car to the airport. Even beneath the closest scrutiny, the tiny car would look like it had remained in its parking stall all day. Hanks had been assigned the more difficult task of erasing all record of Watford's rental from Go-Green's database.

Once Hanks had finished erasing the car rental, he eliminated the record of Watford's trip west on AirFair Airlines. Over the years, Hanks had worked miracles to earn his reputation as the top gun in Cyberspace Manipulation. Today, he intended to demonstrate that wizardry once again.

Chapter 36

Grateful best described Sarah's emotional state after the fifteen minutes she'd spent speaking with Janie Beck. Beck worked as a customer service representative for American Cellular Technologies. Though Janie had never told anyone, she read Watford's novel so she felt an instant empathy for the author's wife.

"Ray called me on his cell phone from the airport this morning, but I haven't heard from him since. No one seems to know anything about where he is … or at least that's what they're telling me. I'm hoping you know where Ray's call came from this morning."

"If you can hold on for a minute, Mrs. Watford, I'd like to get my boss on the line," Beck said before she waved at her supervisor, Buck Lewis, indicating that he should be part of the call.

"Hello, Mrs. Watford. I'm sorry to hear about your husband," Lewis said. "We'll give you any help we can." Beck and Lewis watched while the computer loaded the record of Ray's call. "Okay, I see the call, and it originated from Los Angeles, California this morning at—"

Hanks leaned back in his chair and cracked his knuckles. Other EEFF agents had crowded into the duty-center to watch him in action. When he had finished deleting every record on the list, the gathered agents cheered. "Hanks! Hanks! Hanks!" The cyberspace king bathed in the adulation.

However, the cheers had momentarily drowned out the

shouts from Mr. Dannyo, who had been yelling to catch Hanks' attention. "I just got word from Surveillance," Mr. Dannyo shouted. "The Watford case required one more record-delete. Watford used his cell phone to call home after he got off the plane. Get rid of that call before anyone sees it."

"That wasn't on my task list, sir," Hanks protested.

"I know it wasn't on your task list. Somebody screwed up. Just find that record and get it deleted."

Beads of sweat had formed on Hanks' face. This was a scenario that truly matched his skill. In most cases, he was given IP addresses and passwords in advance for the computer networks he hacked. This time, he had to make his hack from scratch. His eyes glazed over like a shark in a feeding frenzy. His fingers flashed as he barged his way into the American Cellular network and commenced to wreak havoc. A handful of keystrokes later, he was ready to put his assignment to bed. "See ya, Ray," Hanks whispered as he executed the delete function. The final trace of Watford's trip to California vanished with the push of a button. As far as the Federal Government was concerned, Ray Watford never left home.

Back at American Cellular Technologies headquarters, Buck Lewis blinked his eyes. He couldn't believe what he had just seen. "What happened to the call? You saw it, Janie? Didn't you?" Lewis asked.

"What's going on?" Sarah asked. She heard the alarm in Lewis' voice. For a moment she thought the cell phone company employees were going to give her some information, but now—

"I don't know what happened, Mrs. Watford. I saw the call record. Janie saw the call record. And then it just vanished."

Chapter 37

President Spendini smiled when his secretary announced the call from Sarah Watford. *If you would have told your husband to keep his mouth shut, you wouldn't be in this situation.* The call hadn't surprised him. The Watfords had been Spendini's constituents when he'd been serving in the Senate. He guessed that a call from Sarah would eventually arrive. *These people watch too many movies. They think the government is just yanking people off the street all the time. They need to learn that such events only happen in dire emergencies—like this.*

Spendini made Sarah wait for a few minutes before he picked up the call. He didn't want to appear too available. "Hello, Mrs. Watford. What can I do for you?" he asked, working to sound fatherly.

"I don't know where else to turn, Mister President. My husband has disappeared, and I can't get any help trying to locate him. I'm beginning to wonder if this has something to do with his book."

"And what is your husband's name, Mrs. Watford?" Spendini asked, using the old *just play dumb* approach.

Sarah explained the situation regarding the book, Ray's trip to California and his disappearance. She told the president about the calls she'd made to try to locate Ray, the imposter on the Cockatiel show, and she even told him about the cell phone record that had disappeared.

"Have you told anyone else about this information?" Spendini was alarmed to hear about the cell phone call. He'd been assured by General Welfare that every trace of Watford's trip had disappeared. *Apparently some of the evidence didn't disappear soon enough.* "And how did you learn about this cell phone record?" Spendini asked.

Sarah shared the story about Janie and Buck at American Cellular Technologies. When she finished her story, she said, "I don't want people to think I'm crazy, but I'm beginning to wonder whether someone wanted Ray to disappear."

There was a pregnant pause between the two of them; Spendini unsure how to respond, Sarah confused by Spendini's silence. "Mrs. Watford, in spite of some tall tales to the contrary, the Federal Government is not in the business of abducting its citizens, if that's what you're implying."

"I wasn't implying anything. All I know is that Ray's gone, and no one has been any help in finding him," she said before she began to cry.

"I will do some checking, Mrs. Watford. If I learn of anything, I will pass it on to the authorities. I'm sorry your husband is missing. Hopefully we'll be able to find him soon."

With that, Spendini hung up the phone. He had no intention of telling anyone anything. His only concern was ensuring that Watford stayed gone until after the election.

Chapter 38

After his call with Sarah Watford ended, Spendini wasted no time before calling General Welfare. Welfare had been small of stature as a boy. The other children teased him mercilessly throughout his school years. He'd run for student council in an attempt to change things for students like himself, but he never won.

Later, after he graduated from college, he had a burning desire to right the wrongs he'd felt as a child. He swore that no one—except for conservatives and they deserved it—would ever experience teasing again.

Welfare was still small of stature as an adult, but he used towering effort to compensate for his lack of physical height. During his rise in the military, Welfare had denied himself any semblance of normalcy. He dedicated virtually all of his non-sleeping hours to his work. "I won't rest until I'm at the top of the chain of command," he told himself every night after he'd brushed his teeth.

Few Americans had the power to intimidate General Welfare any longer. But as his phone line began to chirp, the EEFF Czar groaned when he realized that one of those people waited at the other end of the line. "Hello," the general answered, wary about Spendini's intentions.

"We have an issue, General," President Spendini said, his voice taking the form of a steely dagger that stabbed into Welfare's ear.

The general's face turned red in an instant, a reflex from his days as a boy who could do nothing right. "What is it Mister

President?"

"I received a call from Watford's wife today. She told me that a couple of employees from American Cellular saw the record of the cell phone call Watford made from California. Imagine my surprise at hearing that news, particularly since my *EEFF Czar*—the man I hired to keep things like that from happening—dropped the fucking ball!"

Welfare swallowed hard. He felt sick and began to grovel immediately "I'm so sorry, Mister President. I thought we had cleaned every trace of Watford's trip. I can't imagine how something as simple as a cell phone call slipped past us."

"The simple things seem to have a way of tripping us up, don't they, General?" Spendini stopped talking, allowing his Czar to twist in the wind for a moment. "I promise you this—if that cell phone call comes back to bite me, I going to send a group of Teachers to *reeducate you*. NOW FIX IT!"

Chapter 39

Janie Beck knew she was in trouble. The eyes of her coworkers followed her every move from the moment she arrived at the office. Three corporate hatchet men had been camped out in her cubicle for hours. "We need to speak with you, Ms. Beck," the three men said in unison using a voice loud enough for everyone to hear.

"Could one of you tell me what is going on?" she asked.

None of the men acknowledged the question. They had already turned and begun a march to the *gallows*—a glass-walled conference room that was used to discipline, embarrass and/or terminate the employment of misbehaving employees. The tallest of the *suits* held the door for the group and then closed it behind them.

Inside the conference room sat the entire upper-management sector of American Cellular Technologies. Each of them— pinched of face and tightened of buttocks—glared at Beck with an expression that struck a perfect balance between indignation and contempt. At the far end of the room sat Buck Lewis.

Janie felt a fleeting impulse to smile. She was relieved to see Buck's familiar face, but the serious faces arrayed between the two of them quickly extinguished her relief.

Silence filled the room and left the air thick—almost heavy. Janie struggled to remain calm in the face of the imminent inquisition. *You've done nothing wrong. This is all a misunderstanding,* she tried to reassure herself. But instead of starting the meeting, the assembled managers waited, hands folded upon the table. *What are they waiting for?* she wondered.

Suddenly the door burst open, and the silence was broken. "Alright, where are they?" the tiny man in the navy suit shouted. General Welfare had decided to present himself to the group of managers as if he were a law enforcement officer. He'd seen photos of Lewis and Beck in advance, but he made a show of scanning the room. He wanted to demonstrate that his trained eye could recognize an evil-doer at a first glance. Even if he hadn't seen the photos, the seating arrangements—Buck and Janie at the opposite ends of the table and no one seated within five yards of either of them—immediately told the tale.

Janie tried to swallow but her mouth felt like it had been filled with a cup of dust. She could hear her heart beating up in her ears.

General Welfare fixed Janie with his gaze. He stroked his chin thoughtfully. Then he turned his head slightly and stared at Buck. "Can either of you tell me the punishment for embezzlement of taxpayer funds?" He let the words lay there, waiting to see whether either would crack.

Every soul in the room remained silent. All of them feared making even the slightest sound. They had no wish to draw the interrogator's fiery gaze. "I will tell you what the punishment is. It starts with sweating it out in a tiny box with me," Welfare said before he slammed his fist down onto the cheap plywood table. Then he began to speak in a whisper. "Clearly, neither of you is willing to be an honorable person by standing up to confess what we already know. Both of you have been caught trying to embezzle over a million dollars from your own company. But more importantly, you have stolen the rightful property of the United States Government—the reluctant owners of this company. With a little bit of cooperation, we might be able to find some leeway in your sentencing. But let me be clear, any chance for leniency ends when we walk out of this room." He let the words dangle, hoping to get a confession in front of the audience.

Both Janie and Buck remained silent. They floundered in a sea of confusion, trying to fathom how they could have been implicated in an embezzlement scheme when neither of them had stolen a penny.

"That's fine," Welfare said. "If you're not willing to confess to your own people, you leave me no choice. I'm taking you downtown. Let's go," he said before he threw open the door and ushered Beck and Lewis into the corridor. "Hold that elevator!" he yelled. "I'm on official Federal Government business!"

Janie nearly fainted while she contemplated being hauled off to jail. She thought about confessing in hopes of making things go easier on her, but she didn't. Going to jail was going to be bad enough, but she couldn't imagine how embarrassed her parents would be if she was charged with embezzlement.

If Janie could have seen the future, she wouldn't have wasted a single moment worrying about jail. Neither she nor Buck was going live long enough to see the inside of any jail.

Chapter 40

The successful abduction of Watford had given President Spendini his first restful day in weeks. The seditionist's novel had gone viral in spite of the Computer Czar's efforts to halt the book's distribution. The Czar's minions crashed the Kerwin Publishing servers repeatedly. And when Kerwin managed to get his servers back online, the Computer Czar had the servers crashed again.

Undeterred, citizens had begun to share the images of Watford's novel using flash-drives and other memory cards. *What could be driving the mistrust these people have for the work we do?* Spendini asked himself. He lifted the copy of the novel he'd received from Edward Tramsoot. *Maybe I'll find some answers in here.*

But instead of reading from the beginning, Spendini fanned the book's pages until he saw an interesting chapter. He leaned back in his chair, put his feet up on his desk and began to read.

In the Hall (Reflections on America)
Chapter Five

I had no idea what to expect inside the next door. It had already been a long day, and I wanted to move things along. So I asked the Iron Fist and the Invisible Hand if I could sit down with both of them at the same time. *"They're body parts,"* I said to myself. *"How much can they possibly have to say?"* How wrong I was.

I knocked at the door and waited for an indication that that they were ready for me to enter. After standing around for what felt like fifteen minutes, I knocked again and then pushed the door open.

I saw the Iron Fist first. He sat at the table, tapping his index finger impatiently. When he saw me enter, he began to type on a keyboard that sat in front of him. "What took you so long? Aren't you smart enough to realize we couldn't call you inside? We don't have mouths—Duh!" His typewritten message appeared on a monitor that sat in front him.

I fought to hold my tongue—and failed. "Why didn't you just open the door? You've got a hand don't you?"

The Iron Hand clenched itself into a fist as though he were preparing to strike. I ignored the threat. "Where's the Invisible Hand?" I asked.

In the far corner of the room, I heard the chatter of another keyboard. I walked towards the noise and saw keys popping up and down as if by magic. "Ah, so you're the Invisible Hand."

"At your service," was the message that appeared on a monitor suspended above a seemingly empty chair where the Invisible Hand presumably sat.

"I apologize for the confusion, and I'm sorry for getting snippy with you, Mr. Fist. No hard feelings, alright?" I looked at the Iron Fist and extended my right hand towards him.

The Iron Fist unclenched itself, and then abruptly turned its palm away from me, showing me its knuckles—a spoiled child turning away from a grownup. I shook my head and muttered, "I knew this was a bad idea."

I plopped into a nearby chair. I stared at the Fist trying to get a read on him. "I know Karl Marx has been running around telling everyone to avoid me, but I had to meet with you. You both have played important roles, in one way or another, in the development of every nation. I know there's a lot that I can learn from you."

"I've never been a fan of you or your tactics," I said. Then I watched him grow tense and begin to clench. "But that's why I'm here. I wanted to give you a chance to share your side of the story." He relaxed slightly and nodded his approval.

"The Invisible Hand allows willing buyers and willing sellers to come together so they can negotiate deals that work for both parties. Certainly there are times when one party has more information, a greater ability to walk away from a deal, or more resources at its disposal, but when we talk about the Invisible Hand, we are still talking about instances when people have the ability to say no to a transaction." I heard chattering from the corner and turned to see the words, "Right on!" appear on the monitor above the Invisible Hand.

The Fist began to type at his own keyboard. "There are way too many times when one party takes advantage of the other!!!" The Iron Fist shot back. "That's why the working classes need me!!!"

"I'm not sure who could really argue that a free market system isn't superior to an economy that is managed by a central government, whether the government is elected or dictatorial. Look at the trouble even socialist countries find themselves in."

"I can argue that, you simp!!!" The Fist replied. "Remember the no-bid contracts that the FauxPublicans handed out during the Iraq War? If I had been in those meetings, none of that would have gone on!!!"

"What about the cozy loan terms that Demagogue Congressmen received while they pushed the mortgage market into the abyss? What did you do to stop those, Rusty?!!!" the Invisible Hand said. He loved this.

The Fist glared at the Invisible Hand. I realized that the two of them had their own history. "Why don't you come over here and say that to my hand, chickenshit?!!!" the Fist replied.

"Alright, maybe we can tone this down," I said as I stepped into the space between the two rivals. "Let's get back to the point of this conversation. And while we're at it, can you cut the crap with the triple exclamation points. You're angry. I get it." I shook my head at the triteness of it all.

"I know that we can point to past abuses by capitalists and Marxists alike. What I came here to ask for was some kind of explanation from you, Mr. Fist, which explains how you can believe that you're smart enough to make better decisions than the millions of consumers making the best use of their limited resources. These are people who are just trying to make ends meet. They want as much value as they can get from their scarce resources. They have no political axe to grind. They don't want to try to control other peoples' lives. They just want to buy their paper towels at DealMart because they can get five rolls for the same price they'd spend on three rolls at some other store. Where's the evil in that?"

"They should be using cloth towels. They're better for the environment," the Fist muttered. He began to sulk.

"Saving the environment is such a scam. It's just another excuse that you and your progressive bag-men use to hide your desire to control other people's lives. Look at what you've done to the cost of food with all your hysteria. Do you think a starving man honestly cares whether or not his food is 'organic?' He just wants something to eat."

The Iron Fist yawned.

"You really think you know best in every area, don't you?"

"People can't be trusted to do the right thing!" the Iron Fist erupted. "People are only concerned about themselves. None of you would have even bothered to lift a finger to try to save the planet until I had the courage to make gasoline too costly for you to afford. You had no intention of doing the right thing on your own!"

"Your ban on gasoline only proves my point," I shot back as I turned to face him. "Gasoline was a legal product. We needed it to power the economy, but you turned your back on the American people. You failed to execute one of your most basic responsibilities—securing liberty. You sat and watched as the supply of oil tightened while world-wide demand rose. You threw up roadblocks to domestic oil production in spite of the billions of barrels of oil that were available for drilling. You remained idle while the available supply of this precious substance become concentrated in the hands of nations— many of which were openly hostile to American interests. Then as the cost of a gallon of gas surpassed ten dollars, you laughed and patted yourself on the back and said, "Americans drive too much anyway." I stared at him now, challenging him to reply. He said nothing.

"There was nothing wrong with gasoline until a small group of activists decided to kill America from within. Then they turned to you to enforce their will. And being the power-hungry narcissist that you are, you were only too happy to oblige. Now America languishes in a slow and painful bleed out. The United States has grown weaker with each passing year. Have you checked to see how hard it is to get on an airline flight these days—if you aren't a public official and you don't qualify for a *Government Hardship Travel Voucher*—that is? That was your doing. Should I come and kiss your ring now?"

"No. But you can kiss something else," he replied. Then he began to clench and unclench himself, sending me an unmistakable message about his willingness to resort to violence.

"Go ahead and threaten me," I said. "I'm not going to take it anymore. You throw around words like *sacrifice*, but who gave you the right to decide which of us are going to make that sacrifice? Were you there when my wife and I had to trade down to a two-door hatchback so we could afford to buy a house? Were you around when I was delivering newspapers in the cold of winter to make ends meet while I was sick with influenza? Were you there when I left my wife and newborn son to go work my *second* job only minutes after getting home from my full-time day job? You were—but only to reach into my pocket—you insignificant ball of tinfoil!" I taunted. "You're a thief and a petty coward hiding behind your cloak of false compassion. You harness men with a yoke, like they are oxen, and you do it out of jealousy and spite. It's all part of your failed attempt to keep your magical rainbow of fairy-dust promises—promises that you never had any business making."

The Iron Fist sat motionless, unfazed by my

rebuke. I saw his fingers twitch for an instant. Maybe he had considered a reply and then changed his mind.

"You're the child who has refused to grow up and join the real world—a place where actions have consequences. You're always looking for the taxpayer to come and clean up after you." I pointed to the other side of the room. "Is the Invisible Hand perfect? He certainly isn't. Businesses have lied. Some have broken the law. But so have you, Mr. Fist. Maybe every American should get a letter from DJSM that explains in plain English the exact state of all those retirement funds we were forced to send every payday." My faced had turned red by now, and spittle was flying from my lips. "Maybe you can tell me about the real state of Manny Faye and Meddy Frack. You haven't been very transparent in either of those instances," I chided.

The Iron Fist began to type again. He seemed more relaxed this time. Maybe I'd finally reached him. "Liberty is terribly unrewarding," he said. "Why would I allow people to choose for themselves? Why should I allow them to keep what they earn? What does that do for *me*? How does freedom help to keep me in office? How does it help me to secure *my* legacy and allow me put *my* name on a bridge?"

I shook my head. The meeting had been a complete waste of time. "You're power drunk.

You don't even see what's going on around you. Go ahead. Take what you want. Don't say *please*. Don't say *thank you*. Every time we give you a penny, just demand more. If we object, give us the good ol' government guilt routine, or use us to grease the tread of your tanks. I'm sure that will work for you," I taunted him.

The Fist simply nodded his agreement and typed, "That sounds like a good plan. Maybe this meeting wasn't a complete waste of time."

Spendini closed the book and scratched his head. "Why is everyone so upset? This Watford really seems to get it. That Iron Fist was spot-on."

Chapter 41

While President Spendini spent his time reading, one of his flunkies was out doing damage control. The EEFF Czar had turned to a friend of the family for some assistance.

"I'm Sheena Glitzy, and this is DAMPMEN's Nuanced Worldview. Tonight's topic: Embezzlement and a double suicide. Our guest is General Welfare. Welfare was the chief investigator on a multi-million dollar embezzlement case involving two low-level employees at American Cellular Technologies. Hello, General."

Welfare had been trying to avoid eye contact with the lovely hostess. When he finally looked up to see her, he panicked. "Uh— what was the question—um, Sheila?" he stammered.

Great! Not another babbling boy. Sheena silently raged. *I'd better not have to carry him for the whole show. Maybe we should be screening these people better. I don't need these guys to start drooling all over themselves when the cameras come on. And if he calls me 'Sheila' again, there's going to be trouble.*

"We seem to be having some technical difficulties. We'll have the general back with us in a moment," Sheena said. Meanwhile, the show's assistants scolded Welfare, telling him to "get it together."

When the show resumed, Sheena glared at General Welfare and wondered whether he'd be able to actually speak. "Could you explain what happened with Janie Beck and Buck Lewis?" Sheena asked.

Welfare held his fists by his side and clenched them hard. He gouged his fingernails into the palms of his hands and drew blood while trying to maintain his composure. He'd always frozen around beautiful women, and Glitzy had proven to be too much for him to handle. *Get a grip,* he told himself. *You need to convince these people that Beck and Lewis killed themselves. Now do this.* "During my investigation of Beck and Lewis, I found that the two young people in question had been betrayed by the system. They were baptized in the corrupted font of big business. Unfortunately, they drowned within the same pool."

"So what happened to them?" Sheena's team of analysts had already been given all of the details from the police investigation. The FGNB had stressed the importance of detailing the deaths of the two embezzlers.

"It was tragic, really. As American Cellular Technologies' managers will attest, I was forced to bring the two embezzlers in for questioning earlier today. I had already gathered more than enough evidence to send both of them away for a very long time. And they knew it. As I was transporting them back to the station, they tried to escape."

"What happened then?"

"Lewis, who we now know owned a storehouse of illegal weapons—including assault rifles—pulled my service pistol from its holster and shot himself." The general's statement was a total fabrication woven by the FGNB. "As the pistol fell from Lewis' hands, Beck grabbed the gun and killed herself."

"Oh my goodness," Sheena said, gasping to show the shock she felt upon hearing the sordid details. "Did you have any idea that they had intended to kill themselves?"

"I heard them whispering in the back seat of my car, but I had no idea what they had planned. If I'd only left my weapon at home today, this disaster could have been averted. This only shows how valuable our national gun ban has been."

"Disaster, General?" Sheena thought her guest had gone a little too far with his last comment. "Remember, these people were embezzlers after all. Some would say this was a case of poetic justice," the hostess suggested.

"It's sad, but true," the general agreed. While his face wore a frown, he was smiling on the inside. He'd just clipped the last loose end of Ray Watford's case. Everything would be fine now.

Larry Lemonpants watched Nuanced Worldview from his office suite and smiled. It looked like General Welfare had successfully sold the Beck/Lewis double-suicide. If Lemonpants hadn't seen the video himself—EEFF possessed images of the general putting a pair of .38 slugs into the back of Lewis' head and then Beck's— even he would have been convinced by the general's tale.

Lemonpants clicked off the television, but remained seated behind his desk. He pushed his hands together and allowed his fingers to form steeples in his best evil genius fashion and smiled. Though it was late, he still had one more issue to resolve. He'd heard the news of Sarah Watford's attempts to locate her husband. There was no reason to believe that Mrs. Watford's attempts would cause any harm, but the woman was still creating a lot of smoke. After spending a moment admiring the stars in the nighttime sky, Lemonpants jotted some talking points onto a sheet of paper. A few minutes later, the FGBN had been successfully armed to douse Mrs. Watford's fire.

Chapter 42

Sarah had cried herself to sleep the night before. It was the fifth day since she'd learned about Ray's disappearance. No one had been able to uncover any trace of him, and she'd heard that the first two days following the abduction were critical. Secretly, she wondered whether or not she would ever see him again.

Silence cloaked the house while she walked from the bedroom to the kitchen. Austin and Justin had stayed home from school again. Neither of them was able to concentrate on their school work. Neither boy wanted to think about their mother being left alone.

"I need some coffee," Sarah muttered to no one in particular. Instead of retrieving a can of fresh coffee grounds—a luxury they couldn't afford—Sarah pulled a cloth bag from the cupboard. The bag held recycled gold—used coffee grounds that she had saved from earlier days. A few minutes later, she walked to the battered living room sofa with a cup of watery coffee in her hand. She clicked on the TV and saw a *breaking-news* edition of Nuanced Worldview. She listened intently to the host.

"A few weeks ago, Ray Watford created quite a stir. Watford's novel generated an intense outcry, but today it appears that the author is grabbing headlines for another reason," Sheena Glitzy began. "A spokesperson for the Watford family has told DAMPMEN that the author has gone into hiding."

The television screen cut from Sheena to footage of the "Watford-family spokesman," a man Sarah had never seen before. He wore a wrinkled suit that seemed three sizes too large, and his face looked dirty. Not much of a spokesman was he. "I think Ray has finally realized the damage his book has done," said Peter Gimble. Gimble had identified himself as a longtime family friend.

Glitzy returned to the screen. "Gimble was quoted as saying that he had no information about Watford's long-term plans, except that the author intended to stay out of the spotlight until after the upcoming elections." Glitzy smiled a broad smile. "It looks like Ray Watford has finally realized that elections are about the *candidates*, not about the American people—" Glitzy immediately cursed herself for going off-script. "I meant the other way around."

DAMPMEN immediately cut to a *For Your Own Good Announcement*—well-intended advice from the Federal Government. There were too few advertisers left to fill all the empty time. The break allowed Sheena's analysts some time to prepare for the next segment.

When the show returned, the guests formed a constellation of Washington's brightest stars, all of whom had made a statement commending Watford for his decision to back away.

Sarah threw her coffee cup against the wall. Brown liquid and porcelain shards redecorated the dingy wall. Soon both of the boys appeared in the living room. "What's wrong, Mom?" Justin asked.

"Something is going on, and I need to find out what it is," she said.

As she stomped across the living room to grab the telephone, she was alarmed when she heard it begin to ring. She picked up the handset and heard a moment of static before a warbling voice began to speak. "We know that you have been trying to contact high-ranking officials," the electronically-modified voice droned.

"We're disappointed to learn that. No one can help you find your husband except us."

"Where is he? Is he safe? Tell me!" Sarah shouted.

"Your husband will be returned unharmed but only if you cooperate. You must follow our instructions exactly, or you will never see him again. Is that clear?"

"I'll do anything; just send him home."

"Good. Stop contacting elected officials. And don't contradict any of the media reports about your husband's condition. Follow these instructions and everything will be fine. Disobey and—well, you can imagine the harm we can do. Is that clear?"

Chapter 43

The waters of the Mississippi River gently slapped against the side of the *Thomas Paine*. The boat's owner had painted a large red circle with a line though its center over the American patriot's name. The painted touch-up had been meant to suggest that the boat's true name was *"Down with Thomas Paine,"* so the owner could avoid harassment from river patrols.

Though the Thomas Paine belonged to a former Congressman from Minnesota, French Garamond had the wheel. Garamond was headed north, steaming somewhere between Bellevue and Clinton, Iowa. The buzzing of his cell phone dragged him away from the serenity of the cool river water and back to the hot water he found himself in. He didn't recognize the caller's number and knew he should just let the call roll over to voicemail. The many attempts on his life had forced him to adopt cautious habits around the most mundane activities. A simple decision about whether or not to answer a telephone call sometimes felt like a life or death choice. Ignoring his urge to play it safe, he answered the phone.

"Please listen carefully. This conversation is being monitored," the caller began without identifying herself. "It's critical that we meet. I have information that would be of great importance to you."

"But who are you?" Garamond asked.

"I can't reveal that right now. I'm endangering my own life by contacting you. A secret government agency has mobilized itself to silence you … permanently."

Garamond stared at the deck of the *Thomas Paine*. "How will we meet?"

"Continue to move along your current heading. Keep your current mode of transportation. If I've been able to unravel your false identification, you can bet that my colleagues will soon do the same. I have to cover your tracks, and then I'll join you. Just watch for me."

"How will I recognize you?" Garamond asked. He received no reply. She had already hung up.

During his years financing and cultivating the network of safe houses, volunteers, and other assets that formed the foundation of the Underground Light Rail, Garamond always told himself that he was safe. "No one can catch me. They don't know where to find me," he often told friends when they expressed concern for his safety. The mysterious caller shattered that confidence. He wondered whether the call had been intended for misdirection. Maybe the Feds wanted him looking in one direction so they could swoop in from another.

Almost 60 years-old now, Garamond knew that his days of running from trouble were nearly over. He had evaded detection on countless trips back into America. He wondered whether his luck might have finally run out. He didn't dread capture or even death. He only wondered whether the Light Rail would survive without him.

As Garamond rehashed the telephone call, he failed to see that his boat had nearly come to a halt in the water. When he finally realized that his motor needed *refueling*, he grabbed a long steel bar. The length of steel served as a lever that allowed the boat's skipper to twist the large bundle of rubber bands that actually powered the boat.

When the rubber bands were sufficiently twisted, their release would spin a paddle at the boat's stern. The rubber-band-powered boat was modeled after the power-train that had once been used to propel balsa wood rockets along lengths of clothesline at meetings where young men dressed in uniforms and learned stuff.

Though the rubber-band motor was inefficient and made for glacial travel speeds, it was one of the few Government-sanctioned options available to the boater who didn't want to row. *Maybe there's a bright side to this after all,* Garamond thought. *If there is an ambush ahead, this stinking motor will give me a few extra hours to live.*

Chapter 44

Back in Puppetgrad, Calder's supervisor was livid. "I've finally got that lying hag!" Dingo Clark growled. Menace dripped from his words like foam from a rabid dog's mouth. "She's going to pay for leaving—" Clark shook his head, realizing that he had been thinking about his ex-wife, rather than focusing his attention on Calder. *Calder's going to suffer too. She betrayed me and she's jeopardized my career.*

Clark was part of the covert surveillance team that EEFF had tasked with tracking Calder's movements. Though she hadn't known it, Calder had been under EEFF's constant eye-ball witness surveillance since she'd destroyed the scanner in Watford's bathroom. Though EEFF never recovered any footage that disproved Calder's account of the events inside Watford's PHU, General Welfare decided that it was safest to assume that Calder was guilty in the absence of evidence proving her innocent.

*Calder thinks she's so smart. She thinks she can take my house and half of my income and—*Clark felt the sting of hot tears as they formed in his eyes—*she even took Pepper.* Pepper was the dog that Clark and his wife had raised together. *But I still love her. Why won't she just come back? I'd forgive her and take her back in a minute if she'd only talk to me. I'd show her that I can be a better man ...* "Oh, shit," Clark whispered. This time he had a small chuckle at his inability to keep his focus on Calder.

"Clark!" It was General Welfare standing in the doorway. The Czar's presence wiped the smile off Clark's face. "What in the name of Millard E. Fillmore are you doing in here?" The image was comical. The diminutive EEFF Czar screamed at the monstrous Agent Watcher. And even though Clark towered over his boss by nearly a foot and carried at least one hundred additional pounds on his muscular frame, it was the giant who cringed and appeared ready to wet himself. "I could hear you down the hall. Good grief, are you coming unglued on me?" Welfare demanded. "Don't make me demote you, you giant ape!" Welfare had moved in close and wagged his cocktail-weenie-sized index finger into Clark's beefy face. "You mess this up and I'll have you doing beehive surveillance for the rest of your career!" the beet-faced general shouted before he abruptly turned and stormed away.

"But sir—" Clark said while he chased after the Czar. "I have some new information on the Calder investigation."

Welfare quickly turned around, his manner softening a smidgen. Welfare had people to whom he answered, and any information on Calder was helpful. "Good man. Call a meeting in my office in thirty minutes. Let's get everybody up to speed on what is happening with that traitor."

Exactly thirty minutes later, Dingo Clark had taken a seat in the Czar's office. Also there was Mr. Dannyo from Cyberspace Manipulation, and the latently terrifying, Razor. Razor was a ranking member of EEFF's Teacher's union, and as tough a man as the Federal Government employed.

Razor's height measured six inches shorter than Clark, and the Teacher possessed a fraction of the taller man's mass, but no one dared anger the educator. Razor's muscles rippled at the slightest movement. Jagged scars—evidence that seditionists didn't always accept their reeducation like lambs—crisscrossed his face. A baseball-sized crater on the back of Razor's head offered a constant reminder of a particularly violent encounter. He'd had a confrontation with a cleaver-wielding butcher who needed a little extra persuasion to crack open his fair speech textbook. Razor—though injured in the fight—then used the cleaver to crack open the butcher's skull.

Most of the Teachers assumed that Razor's nickname stemmed from his affection for a straight-razor. However, the name arose from far more innocent circumstances. The young Razor had been on his college's wrestling team. During road trips, he'd rarely needed to shave his boyish face. His roommate—on the other hand—grew a beard quickly enough to put most lumberjacks to shame. After a seemingly endless string of days when his hairy roommate yelled, "Hey, you got a razor?" the grizzly teammate finally abbreviated by saying, "Hey—Razor," and the nickname was coined.

By the time Razor's undefeated, collegiate-wrestling career was over, the moniker had spread beyond the boundaries of the team's locker room. Crowds repeatedly chanted, "Razor! Razor! Razor!" as he punished a series of unfortunate foes.

Joining Razor and the others in General Welfare's office via teleconference were Larry Lemonpants, President Spendini, Rita the Clown, and Sunny Davis/Davis Sunny. "Hello everyone," General Welfare said as he rose from his chair to start the meeting. "Thank you for agreeing to meet on such short notice." He paused, hoping that someone would give him a compliment for his appearance on Nuanced Worldview. No praise came, so he continued. "As you all know, we've had one of our own—Agent Shawn Calder—under surveillance for some time now. She was the agent assigned to the Ray Watford case—" Welfare was forced to stop speaking when Rita the Clown went berserk at the mention of the author's name.

Welfare had no choice but to mute Rita's microphone so he

could continue. He then told the others about Calder's decision to betray EEFF. "Agent Watcher Clark recently uncovered footage of a cell phone call between Calder and French Garamond," General Welfare said. "Garamond was on a boat which was moving up the Mississippi River at the time Calder made contact with him. Unfortunately, by the time Agent Watcher Clark found this evidence, it was too late to act. The fugitives had already abandoned the boat near the Minnesota border. We lost contact with them at that point."

Welfare reached over and grabbed a stack of printed sheets. "A few minutes ago we received this from our Cyberspace Manipulation Department." He handed a sheet to Clark and Razor and faxed the page to the others before he continued. "This is the text of a *Blabber* message sent less than an hour ago by Garamond. For those who don't know, Blabber is the social networking website that allows ordinary Americans to feel like they know celebrities and others of importance by subscribing to exclusive *boilerplate* updates sent out over the celebs' Blabber accounts." Welfare stopped speaking to give the others a chance to read the message.

> Do you feel tired of being pushed around, insulted, and taken for granted?
>
> At one time, Las Vegas was a place where Americans would go and enjoy a few tiny liberties they couldn't find at home. But over time, Congress taxed away that ability. Now only the wealthiest and most powerful Americans can even enter the city.
>
> Tomorrow is the day we take back Las Vegas and the day we start to take back America. I've

been living in Garamondia for long enough. I'm
ready to come home. Join me in Vegas at noon.
It's time you saw the faces of all of those who
feel the same way you do.
    French Garamond

"How could you allow a message like that to go out on
Blabber?" Sunny Davis/Davis Sunny demanded of the EEFF
Czar. "You have to shut that guy up."

"How did you expect me to stop that message when I'm here
with you?" the general shouted.

"You should be thankful that I'm *not* in there with you. I'd
come over and chew your nose off, General."

Pandemonium ensued. Shouts, threats, and epithets flowed
across the Internet and into the EEFF meeting room. After the
shouting match had raged for nearly five minutes, Razor pursed
his lips and whistled. The whistle's volume startled the others into
silence. "We know where we'll find Garamond and Calder. It's
time we stop pissing and start planning," he said. Without waiting
for approval, Razor outlined a plan and instructed everyone to
report to Karl Marx International Airport by sundown.

Chapter 45

The smell of lemon—ricotta pancakes wafted through the narrow opening at the bottom of the door. The delicious aroma made Ray's mouth water. His stomach growled, and he hoped his captors might offer him a few of the fancy flapjacks.

Considering the possibilities, Ray decided that he'd had a pleasant enough stay in California. Aside from the assault in the studio parking lot, the actors had treated him well. They gave him food at meal times. His room had a comfortable bed and a bathroom. A television was mounted on the wall. It was far nicer than his PHU in Puppetgrad.

Since his captors didn't force him to wear a blindfold, Ray took full advantage of his situation and watched television whenever he could. He kept the volume turned down low and shut the TV off whenever any of the actors entered the room. If the TV had been a mistake, he didn't want to draw attention to the error.

DAMPMEN's ad nauseam coverage of *his* appearance on Echolalia with Edgar Cockatiel left him scratching his head. On a good day, Cockatiel's show might have had 312 viewers. So anything that transpired during the virtually unwatched show was, by definition, irrelevant. But if you judged by the news coverage Ray Watford's political doppelganger was receiving, you'd guess that the fake Watford had mapped out a strategy that ensured Middle-Eastern peace. Even scarier were the news stories about how he had decided to withdraw from the public eye. There weren't many entities that could make a person *disappear*.

And he had gotten the impression that the most likely of those entities—the Federal Government—was somehow pulling the strings behind his abduction.

He worried about Sarah and the boys. How had they reacted to his disappearance and all of the lies, he wondered? *I wish I could call her and tell her I'm fine,* he thought. Unlike the readily-available television, Meadows and the others had ensured that no telephone had been left within his reach. Powerless to do much else, Ray enjoyed the smell of the pancakes and began to channel-surf. *I wonder if Sarah will make her pan—*

Beyond the door a heavy crash made the walls shake. Next Ray heard a flurry of shouts, cries, and smaller collisions. Ray rushed to the door and pressed his ear to the wood. He hoped to overhear some clue that would help him decipher the commotion.

In the next room, French Garamond, Shawn Calder, and members of the Underground Light Rail Chapter of Los Angeles had engaged the enemy. A rescue operation was underway. The home invasion was the result of days of preparation and planning.

When Calder discovered that she was being used as bait to lure out Garamond, she packed a bag and drove north into the wilderness. Once she was safely outside the city, it took her a satellite telephone and a few hours of wrangling to make contact with Garamond. The industrialist happened to be in country and on his way up the Mississippi River.

Calder arranged to board Garamond's boat in Iowa. Once onboard, she explained the series of events that had caused her to defect from EEFF. She talked about EEFF's surveillance network, her visit to Watford's home, Neil Kugler's role in the Immaculate Redistribution, the successful abduction of Watford, and EEFF's plans to ambush Garamond himself.

After he listened to the story, Garamond sat in stunned silence. He had long believed that each time he entered the country he ran the risk of capture. He guessed that the Federal Government would have loved nothing more than to see him silenced for good. But he had never heard those suspicions validated—until now. In truth, the knowledge that a bumbling behemoth like Greta Government could monitor the activities of its citizens impressed the Garamond. He never would have guessed her to be so capable.

Garamond stroked his chin and digested Calder's story before he made his own confession. "I got Watford into this mess. I insisted that Kerwin publish the book even though I knew the reaction would be harsh. I was foolish enough to believe I could protect Ray, but now I know that I couldn't. His family has no idea where he is or if he will ever make it home. I owe it to Ray, and I don't care if I have to call in every favor I'm owed; I'm going to get him home to his family."

"I was hoping that you'd say that," Calder whispered. "I'm responsible too, and I don't care what it takes; I'm helping you get him back."

It had been those sentiments that led Calder, Garamond, and the members of the Underground Light Rail straight into the melee being fought inside the luxurious home of zombie-movie star, Kevin Meadows. Calder had used a metal ram, borrowed from the Teacher's supply locker in Puppetgrad, to blast the door open. Once the door had been breached, she tossed in a flash-bang grenade—also courtesy of the Teachers. Then she and the rest of the group stormed into the home.

The sneak-attack caught Meadows, Forest, and Boyle by surprise. The sudden commotion caught Forest off-guard and caused him to drop the entire platter of pancakes onto the floor.

Calder had been first through the broken doorway. "We're here for Watford," she shouted.

Boyle—given his repeated exposure to Hollywood special effects—was unfazed by the flash-bang grenade. He ran across the room and stopped directly in front of Calder. Boyle knew that they had to hold on to Watford if their plan was to succeed. Their careers hinged upon their ability to fend off the attackers. For an instant he was unsure how to defeat the woman who stood in his way. Then he had an idea. He waved his hand slowly in front of Calder's face and said. "Feel free to leave Ray Watford with us."

Calder looked confused for a moment. Then in the midst of the standoff, she turned to French Garamond and said, "We should feel free to leave Ray with them."

Garamond smiled and nodded his head at Calder. "*Sure*, we *should* feel free to leave him," he repeated back.

A short-lived smile briefly lit Boyle's face. His expression abruptly changed as he saw the sole of Calder's combat boot on its way to deliver a crushing high kick. The blow struck the right side of his head, catching him just above the temple. Knocked unconscious by the kick, he collapsed to the floor.

Without pausing, Calder wheeled and delivered a kick to Meadows' ribs. Meadows grunted as the kick forced the air from his lungs. He too fell to the floor. Once down, the actor writhed and moaned, his face contorted by the agony.

Jimmy Forest had been a different story. After he dropped his plate of pancakes, he leveled three of the five members of the Underground Light Rail with a series punches and forearm blows. As Forest lifted the fourth Light-Railer off the ground and prepared to slam him onto the floor, Calder saw the actor turn his back to her. She darted across the room and approached Forest from behind. As she neared the burly actor, she set her feet squarely and executed a straight-ahead football kick that would have made Lou Groza proud. Her foot slammed into Forest's groin with the force of a sledge hammer. After absorbing the blow, Forest managed little more than gurgling noises as he crumpled to the floor and curled into a ball, cupping his hands over his violated groin.

After surveying the house for any other threats, Calder, Garamond, and the only Light-Railer left standing wasted no time in locating Watford. Within seconds, the author was free and being ushered towards the front door. No one in the group wanted a second go-around with the actors. So Calder, Garamond, and Watford helped the injured Light-Railers to their feet and the group made a speedy exit.

Outside the home, Will Williams pulled into the driveway shortly after the battle began. When he saw the bulldog of a truck parked there, he knew something was wrong. Williams made appearances at European auto shows a few times each year. The arrangements allowed him to make some extra money and gave him a chance to rub—*hmmm ... elbows* with a host of beautiful models. He also got to see the next-generation autos. It was at one of those shows that he first saw a vehicle like the one parked in Meadows' driveway.

That's a Garamond Utility Vehicle, he said to himself. *But it's against the law to even possess a Garamond, let alone drive one. Oh, shit,* he thought when he realized what the vehicle's presence most likely meant. He dropped to the ground and he craned his neck to look towards Meadows' house. He saw the front door hanging open.

Checking first to make sure that no one was watching, Williams ran back to his own car and rummaged through glove box. He hoped to find a knife, a pair of scissors, a screwdriver— anything he could use to puncture the burly vehicle's tires. Then he remembered the corkscrew that had fallen underneath the passenger-side floor mat. *I guess this will have to do,* he said to himself.

He scuttled back to the Garamond Utility Vehicle, looking more like a crab than a man, and regretted what he was about to do. He took a final, admiring glance at the rugged beauty of the forest-green rig and jammed the corkscrew into the side wall of the first hulking tire.

When Calder and the rest of the group stepped out Meadows' front door, they saw no trace of Will Williams. However, Garamond immediately knew that something was wrong. "Somebody's slit our tires," he grumbled.

"How is that even possible?" Calder asked

"I don't know who could have done it. I just know the truck is sitting too low for its tires to be fully inflated." A quick examination confirmed that each tire had been punctured.

"So what should we do now?" Calder asked.

"Watford and I will catch the subway and take it to the airport. I have a few cars parked in the lot—just in case. Calder, you go with one of the Light-Railers. Take a bus to the Universal City safe house. Once you get there, grab a car and get to Vegas. You three," French said as he motioned to the remaining Light-Railers, "torch the truck and then vanish."

Garamond and Watford watched as Calder and the Light-Railers disappeared down the street. If everything went well, they would see her again in the morning. None of them turned to watch as a flare was lit and then thrown into the GUV. A few minutes later, the vehicle exploded, leaving nothing for EEFF when they arrived to investigate.

"I need to call Sarah and tell her I'm okay," Watford said as he and Garamond walked towards the subway station.

"I can understand why you'd *want* to call her, I honestly do. And I'm not going to *stop* you if you try to call her. But if your goal is to see her again, giving her a call now would only endanger both of you." Garamond's expression remained stern. "That woman who helped free you was part of an organization has been assigned to spy on *everyone* in America. They knew about you and your book before you even gave it to Kerwin."

Ray sighed and hung his head as Garamond continued.

"These guys are going to try to get you back. Do you really want them listening in as you tell your wife that your free? Not only would we be in danger, but so would she. Your best chance to see her is to keep moving so we can make it to the airport. What do you say?"

Ray nodded his head while he and Garamond slunk northward towards the subway station on Vicarage Road. The pair shielded themselves behind trees, parked cars, or whatever cover they could find. In the distance, they saw MacArthur Park and knew that the subway station was near. If nothing else, reaching the park would put some much-needed distance between them and the still dangerous, Foursome for Fairness.

Three blocks away and hidden safely inside a hedge row of shrubbery, Williams sat on the ground and pulled a cell phone from his pocket. He didn't want to do it, but he had to assume the worst. Williams dialed the emergency number.

Sunny picked up the call on the first ring. "Meadows! How

stupid are you? I told you not to call me from a cell phone. I can hear the cars in the distance. Clearly you're too stupid to follow simple instructions."

"I'm sorry Ms. Davis—*uh*—Mister Sunny, but I need to report a problem," Williams stammered.

"Who are you? Where's Meadows?"

"I don't think it's a good idea for me to use my name, but let's just say that a certain *Frenchman* and some of *his* friends paid *my* friends a visit this morning. Then the Frenchman and *his* friends grabbed a certain package that *my* friends had picked up at the airport. The Frenchman is in the process of taking the package into the desert … in Nevada."

The stream of profanity that flowed out of Sunny Davis/ Davis Sunny's mouth made Williams blush. By the end of the call, his face was the color of a fire hydrant.

After Williams finished reporting Watford's escape, he returned to Meadows' house. He stepped through the doorway and saw Boyle, Meadows, and Forest struggling against the tape that bound their wrists and ankles.

Williams was relieved to see that his friends were well. He worried that they might have been seriously injured or even killed. He quickly freed them from their bonds. Once each of them was back on his feet, they grabbed the keys to their cars and immediately left the house. None of them spoke about what had happened. They knew that they had been given a rare opportunity to impress some friends in high places, and they had blown it. All that could be done now was to try to salvage their failure by recapturing the author again. After each of them had climbed into a car, they fanned out to search the area.

After four hours of driving and looking, each of them knew what none of them wanted to admit. They weren't going to find

Watford. They drew straws to determine which of them would be forced to endure Sunny Davis/Davis Sunny's wrath.

Chapter 46

Sunny Davis/Davis Sunny tried to sleep. She hoped that some shut-eye would allow her to keep her mind off the bungling actors. But she couldn't get her mind to relax.

At the moment Sunny, President Spendini, Rita the Clown, Larry Lemonpants, General Welfare, Dingo Clark and some of EEFF's deadliest Teachers were westbound towards Las Vegas aboard Lemonpants' private, luxurious airliner.

Within minutes of take-off, the jet's cabin had erupted into a cacophony of shouting and blame-throwing. EEFF blamed the Demagoblicans for failing to keep the American people from rising against its government. "You should have thrown them a larger bone. That would have gotten them to shut up!" General Welfare shouted.

The Demagoblicans blamed Tramsoot, his Yellow Lapdog Gazette, and the bubble-heads at DAMPMEN for butchering the Demagoblican messages of fairness and economic justice. "If you dunces knew how to spin a story, no one would have even bothered to read Watford's novel. You blew it, Tramsoot," Sunny Davis/Davis Sunny exclaimed.

Tramsoot blamed Lemonpants for suggesting that Watford be allowed to run free. "You should have taken Watford into custody and beaten the dissent right out of him," Tramsoot argued.

Lemonpants blamed Rita the Clown and President Spendini for failing to properly ensure that the Reclaiming Our Fairwaves Edict was enforced. "If Lafayette had been silenced right away, the people would have been too afraid to speak out," Lemonpants raged.

Then an impromptu brainstorming session began. "Napalm—definitely. I think we should give the whole city a napalm paint-job," Tramsoot suggested. Rita the Clown honked her horn repeatedly—a noisy show of her approval for the idea.

"I have an even better idea," said General Welfare. "We should stampede cattle through the city. The cattle could trample all those hicks—just like they're trampling our vision for America. That would be poetic, wouldn't it?" Welfare smiled at his ingenuity. Then the ideas came in bursts. It became impossible to determine who was doing the suggesting. "What about a flood? We could destroy Hoover Dam and drown everyone. We should nuke the city and wipe out those rednecks. What about a nice plague?"

After he allowed the group to vent, President Spendini took control of the discussion. "As much as I'd like to *nuke* all of them, we need to be a little more surgical," he said. "Our aim was to take out Garamond all along. In fact, they've made it easier for us to grab all of them at the same time, so let's calm down a bit with all the nuking talk. I happen to like Las Vegas—I mean Sacrifice City. And it's finally my turn to host the annual Despots and Dictators convention. This year I'm going to change things up a bit. I'm going to invite the assembled despots to call out how they've been aggrieved by the United States, and I will respond by making an apology. It should be pretty exciting because I'm going to really open the floor. Nothing will be off limits, so I don't want to hear any more talk about flooding or stampeding the city either."

Spendini rubbed some drowsiness from his eyes. "The Immaculate Redistribution hasn't been as successful as I'd hoped. People are bitter about having all this money and nothing to spend it on. We need a bit of positive PR. Let the people gather. It won't change anything. We've know that we can control them. But before it's all over, let's just make sure we get Watford and Garamond into custody. We know where to find them. We'll have the element of surprise. How hard can it be?"

"I can help you, Mr. President," a lone voice said.

The assembled group turned to face Razor. He'd been silent for the entire flight.

"The Teachers and I will neutralize *all* of the traitors for you, sir."

Chapter 47

During the drive from Los Angeles to Las Vegas, Calder saw a bound-paper copy of Watford's novel. The book sat on the back seat of the Garamond Utility Vehicle that carried her and a handful of Light-Railers to Las Vegas. It had been years since she'd actually read from a book. She couldn't resist the urge to pick it up.

In the Hall (Reflections on America)

Chapter 6

I had been anticipating this meeting all day. I spent most of my life avoiding books written about men like Nicholaus Copernicus and Karl Marx. I paid little attention to Adam Smith's invisible hand and worried even less about an iron fist.

All of the other historical figures seemed free to come and go as they pleased, but when I arrived at this man's suite, I saw a prisoner. He was locked in a cell. Clearly this one was dangerous.

Though I could scarcely see him through the glass, he looked tired. His shirt was rumpled and his tie hung somewhat off center. Five o'clock shadow covered his cheeks and chin, and his eyes looked bleary. He stood and faced me from behind the pane of hazy, floor-to-ceiling glass.

"Hello. Do you mind if we talk?" I shouted. I hoped he could actually hear me through the thick, glass wall. I leaned in and strained to hear a reply.

It had been a long day already. My legs felt like lead and my head ached, pounding out its own rhythm. But I had to know his story, and I needed to tell him mine. "I get so angry sometimes when I hear politicians talking down to us ordinary people. They seem to think that being elected to public office qualifies them to decide how we should think, how we should spend our time and what we should believe." I pulled up a chair and sat down near the man's cell.

"I've never been to France, and I might never get the chance to go. But I'm supposed to devote *my* time and learn to speak French so that I don't embarrass the president? Maybe it's time ordinary Americans were allowed to go on television to vent their frustration or talk about the embarrassment that presidents have heaped upon us."

"Then we get to see presidents glad-hand and gush while they talk about the wonderful citizens of other nations. Meanwhile, they treat Americans like we're the equivalent of a pile of dog shit stuck to the bottom of their shoe. Do they forget that we're the ones that pay for their stay in the White House; we pick up the tab when they go globe-trotting; we are the ones that put food on their table by allowing them to take it from ours?"

"But why would I be surprised by any of that?" I asked. By now, I had become so incensed that I was asking and answering my own questions. "I'm not surprised by it at all," I replied. "That's what makes this so frustrating. When you can see this kind of behavior coming from a mile away, it no longer seems like an accident or a slip of the tongue. It just seems like the people who are running America have distaste, a disdain or even an open hatred for those of us who don't want to buy their snake-oil-surprise version of liberty. And that attitude starts at the top, I've noticed."

"You know I didn't come here to sell any kind of lifestyle or try to convince people to do things my way. I only came to say—and I think a lot of people feel the same way—that I'm tired. I'm tired of elected officials who think they own me," I said to the man behind the glass. "Feel free to join in if you know the words," I joked.

"I've had enough of the victimhood-by-proxy attitude that is passed out like candy in every "community" around this country. I am *not* the cause of your problems, and I'm tired of being blamed for every problem that arises. Maybe each of us could look into a mirror some time when we want to see who's responsible for the state of our own lives."

"Most Americans are generous to their core,

and I would bet that the vast majority of people would step up and do whatever they could to help others if they believed that this agenda of false compassion was going to end. But instead of throttling back on their play-money schemes, the President and the Congress have dreamed and schemed new ways to pull money out of the pockets of producers. There isn't even a glimmer of hope that this rush to Marxism is anywhere near its end."

"Then they wonder why we become bitter and cling to guns and religion. We see no hope that America will ever reject its growing obsession with collectivism. These elected officials take and take and take. And in the end, what do the producers get? We get shamed and blamed and guilt-tripped from pillar to post. When have taxpayers gotten a simple *thank you* from Congress? We're the ones who allow members of Congress to go on making their empty promises."

I stopped speaking and rubbed my hands through my hair. The insanity of it all left me exasperated. I looked at the man behind the glass and hoped to receive some response— any response. Then I took a closer look at the hazy image in the glass. Then I finally saw it. The wall was a mirror. I had been talking to my own reflection. I was the *bitter clinger.* I was the *typical white person.* I was the one that no one in Washington seemed to want to hear from.

"I could have had this same conversation at home and saved myself a trip," I said with a chuckle. And at that moment, I knew I had seen everything I had come to see. I turned and started towards the exit. Then, while lost in the recollection of all that I had seen and heard, I nearly ran headlong into him as he stepped around the corner.

"Sorry about that, Mister—" I recognized him instantly. "You're My Favorite President," I exclaimed.

"I am? We'll I'm flattered to hear that. And you're Mr. Watford; may I call you Ray?"

"I would be honored, Mister President."

"It sounds like you stirred things up with old gray-beard. The Iron Fist and Mother Nature are pretty mad too," My Favorite President said as he smiled.

I couldn't help but smile back. His charm was infectious. "I wish you were still around, Mister President. We could use someone like you in the White House, sir."

"That's very kind of you to say, but America is doing fine without me. She will continue to be fine. Let me tell you why. No matter how many times these activists and would-be messiahs try to crush your spirits, they can never strip away what it means to be an American. They can try to saddle you with a mountain of debt. They can demonize the successful. But as long as a single person remembers the ideals that made

America great, the spirit of America will live on."
He patted my shoulder. "It's easy to become
anxious when the people in power use fear to
try to control you. But remember—as long as
the people keep their faith, the nation can do
great things."

"I know, but it's so hard when all you hear
from politicians is 'if only the government had
the power to do this or that, then we'd be all fine.'
How much more control do they need?"

"It doesn't matter what they say. Just
remember that the government has never
been the source of America's greatness. The
American people make America what it is. And
the nation is poorer for leaders who try to trick
and bully the citizenry for political gain." The
president shook my hand before he continued.
"It's never been lobbyists, political contributions,
or catchy slogans that win elections. It is citizens
that win elections. Elect leaders that share your
commitment to freedom. And remember that
there is no quick fix to achieving prosperity. It's
only hard work and a commitment to liberty that
will get this nation back onto its feet. Blaming
Peter for having the audacity to be successful
and then confiscating his wealth to give it to
Paul will never be the answer ... And, P.S. You
might not want to let them trick you like this
again—just a thought."

Chapter 48

As he waited in the predawn darkness, Razor knew the Teachers would handle themselves well in the battle to come. He also knew that he would have to hand-hold the rest of the group. Before they had even assumed their positions outside Monaco Joe's Resort and Casino, Lemonpants and President Spendini strutted and preened during a pre-melee pep talk. Both men shouted about their eagerness to go and "kick some ass for freedom" and encouraged the rest of the group to do the same. But that was then. The time for posturing had ended. Now, they waited silently in the shadows of a replica of the Arc de Triomphe.

"Did they think that we'd just give up and let them live?" Lemonpants asked, breaking the group's silence for the fiftieth time. "We're going to get rid of Watford at any cost."

Razor shook his head and wished that Lemonpants would shut up. The showy environmentalist had arrived for the fight dressed in a black-leather jumpsuit, a brown belt, and black shades to conceal his eyes. *Doesn't that asshole realize we'll be hitting them before it gets light? He'll be the first person to land flat on his face when he fails to see a curb through those glasses,* Razor told himself.

"I want to get me some," Lemonpants hissed.

If he doesn't shut up, I'm going to strangle him myself, Razor silently raged. *We'll have to see if you even have the guts to break a nail once the fight starts. Those Light-Railers aren't going to just hand Watford over. And I'm walking into a fight with a guy who suddenly thinks he's a lounge singer.*

Razor took a final look at his band of warriors. The Teachers wore the standard EEFF camouflage. The members of the Foursome for Fairness also wore EEFF camouflage. Razor didn't even bother asking them how they managed to get their hands on the uniforms.

Lemonpants stood up against the wall, smiling like a fool in his jumpsuit. Sunny Davis/Davis Sunny looked like a peppermint-swirl candy in her go-go girl outfit. A red and white swirled hat and red boots completed the ensemble. President Spendini looked like he was on his way out to the golf course with his tangerine polo shirt, khaki trousers, and presidential windbreaker. He'd smeared mascara under both of his eyes, presumably to make himself look like a football player. Tramsoot must have thought he was giving a lecture as he arrived in corduroy pants that were clearly a size too small, a large brown belt, a denim shirt, and a tweed jacket. Dingo Clark—content to be seen rather than heard—just leaned against the base of the Arc and whispered to himself. Presumably, he was preparing himself to show his *ex-wife* who was boss.

Edgar Cockatiel, wearing his signature white suit, reached his position late. He'd nearly revealed the group's hiding place as he riffed on his comedy routine while they passed the time. "Hey, everybody…what's the difference between a conservative and a cow pie? No, I can't think of one either." He rolled on the ground racked by spasms of laughter.

Razor shook his head and said a word of silent thanks that none of them had guns. He shuddered to think about what might have happened if Lemonpants had arrived holding a firearm. *He'd have already gone Hollywood and shot off his own foot.* That mental image made Razor smile. *At least he would have been out of the way—maybe I should have brought weapons after all.* He smiled again.

Now that they had gotten into place, all that was left was the waiting. Razor was a patient man, but once a job needed doing, he preferred to get on with it. Their primary aim was to snatch up Watford and Garamond, but Razor wanted to take Calder and Kerwin too. He believed that the best plan was to wait until Watford, Calder, and Garamond were in close proximity. After they'd dispatched the traitors, he and the Teachers would dispose of as many of the Light-Railers as possible.

Razor tensed, sensing the moment was near. As he prepared to give the signal to attack, he couldn't help but admire the courage the seditionists showed. With Calder among their numbers, they knew about the forces arrayed against them. And yet, they showed up and prepared for their rally just the same. Under different circumstances, he could have respected their cause. He hoped that Watford, Garamond, and particularly Calder, would eventually come to understand that his actions weren't personal. He was just following orders.

As the earliest traces of sunrise began to light the horizon, Razor knew it was time to attack.

Less than thirty yards away from the lurking Teachers, and still unaware of their presence, Garamond stood in the bucket of the cherry-picker and stared down Sacrifice Street. The stretch of road had once been known as the Strip, but a lot had changed since then. He slowly inhaled the cool morning air. The sensation left him feeling invigorated.

Sunrise had nearly arrived, and only a few preparations remained undone. Soon, his fellow countrymen would arrive for the rally—or at least he hoped they would. Only the shrill cries of Greta Government broke the silence. "You should all go home before this gets ugly," she called out as Garamond and the others decorated the boulevard. "You're not going to like today's lesson plan. Disperse—you rabble." When the threats and insults became too much to stand, Garamond used the cherry picker and a bolt cutter to clip Greta's wires.

The Feds clearly know that we're here. The only question is when will they show up? Garamond asked himself. The Teachers could descend upon them at any moment, and he knew it. There was no attempt to recapture Watford between Los Angles and Las Vegas—a fact that both pleased and worried Garamond. He knew that Lemonpants and his goons couldn't afford to have Watford's story leaked before the election. The truth of the author's abduction and EEFF's spying would have certainly turned the people against the whole of the Federal Government.

Maybe Lemonpants has gone soft and given up, Garamond speculated. He knew it was no more than wishful thinking. Lemonpants was here; he could feel it. He just didn't have any time to dwell on the danger. Work needed doing.

This once vibrant strip of road had been ignored for years and now lay in disarray. The pavement had cracked and buckled. Stringy weeds poked through holes that had developed in the roadway. Garamond shook his head at the shameful sight. *We'll do our best to make it look pretty for today. Who knows, maybe somewhere down the road it will be Vegas again,* he said to himself.

When he'd finished hanging his banners, he lowered the basket of the cherry-picker to the ground. On his way down, he admired the replica of the Arc de Triomphe. Given his childhood affection for France, the monument seemed an appropriate backdrop for the triumph he expected today. He smiled as he watched a few of the Light-Railers setting up barricades and hanging red, white, and blue signs. Down the street, a few more of the civilian-soldiers made last-minute preparations near the sound stage. Garamond was proud of them all. *Today will be a big day in American history. Today we will start to take this country back.* Then he stopped to admire their work.

Red, white, and blue bunting hung from the front of the abandoned Emperor's Digs (it had been closed due to its imperialistic theme) and the still-open Firenze Freddy's Fun Factory. The managers at the Fun Factory had tasked a few of the resort's maintenance workers to hang the bunting and star-spangled banners from the building's exterior. The managers had long memories of the slights former presidents and members of Congress had hurled towards their fair city in the past.

The decorations extended southward along the Strip until they reached President Puppet's Paradise. In the latter days of her Administration, President Mary O'Nett had become quite sensitive to the terms illusion, hallucination, fantasy, imagining, mirage, half-truth, deception, and lie. She then demanded that the Apparition Hotel and Casino close its doors—that is unless the casino was given a less incendiary label. The Apparition's owners—not wanting to see their operation closed and their workers thrown into the street—reluctantly agreed to make the change. The new name, President Puppet's Paradise, had been O'Nett's idea, in homage to her mentor.

When the final bit of bunting had been hung and the last sound check finished, Garamond smiled with satisfaction. He called to Watford, Calder, and the group of Light-Railers approaching and said, "What would you say to some breakfas—"

Calder saw them first. "Teachers! Run!" she shouted. Dread turned her legs rubbery as she watched the Teacher's burst from the shadows. She had seen EEFF's enforcers in action, and she knew well the harm they could inflict. She waved her arms at her compatriots and shouted, "Go that way!" pointing south along the Strip. She'd even had to shove some of the Light-Railers who'd remained frozen in their tracks like startled deer. Once everyone was on the move, Calder ran too. She only hoped they could reach Pinky's Casino in time.

"Lets Go!" Razor bellowed, as he the other Teachers and the members of the Moral Compass Society charged the traitors. Razor saw Calder's head jerk to attention as the attack began. She was sharp, and he knew that he would have to deal with her before the battle was over. *Some of them are panicking. Good. Let them panic. Hopefully they'll stumble over one another. That would make our job easier.*

In an instant, the Teachers were on the traitors' tails. Fortunately for the pursued, their head start gave EEFF's enforcers some ground to make up. Razor wished they had been able to get closer before they charged, but he knew that you could never control all the variables in battle.

As he closed the distance to his prey, Razor heard Calder urging the Light-Railers to run faster. *Calder realizes what's going to happen when we catch them. She knows that if any of them try to surrender, they won't get any mercy. That will keep them fighting hard.* In the distance, he saw the entrance to the abandoned Pinky's Casino. The door had been propped open. *Looks like they were expecting an ambush—I would have done the same thing if I had been in their shoes.*

As Calder and the Light-Railers disappeared into the building, Razor knew that they would have to find the fugitives in total darkness. And that was the best case scenario. The worst case was that Calder and her comrades had set up an ambush inside the darkened building. *Why didn't we bring our full kit?* Razor scolded himself. *I was no less a fool than Lemonpants. I never should have underestimated them—underestimated Calder. She's the key. If I can take her down, the whole bunch will crumble.* Razor did a mental inventory while he chased. The flashlight in his thigh side pocket gave him an idea. *But I'll have to be careful about how I use it.*

When the Teachers and the members of the Moral Compass Society reached the doorway to Pinky's Casino, they paused to catch their breath. "Anyone else have a flashlight?" Razor asked. All the Teachers took flashlights from their pockets and checked to make sure they worked. None of the others had thought to pack a light. Razor realized it was probably a good thing. A flashlight would not only help its wielder locate the enemy, but it would also reveal his own position. It was a high-risk high-reward proposition. "We don't know what we're going to find when we step through this doorway. They might have ducked into this building only to escape out another door. But since it appears that they were expecting us, they're probably *waiting* for us inside. Be careful. This is probably going to get rough."

"I'm ready to get rough," Lemonpants growled.

"I'm ready to get rough, too." Cockatiel echoed.

"Yeah, let's dance," Kevin Meadows said, repeating his zombie-movie catch phrase.

Razor took his position outside the door frame and motioned for the group to follow. He stepped into the darkness and then sidestepped out of the doorway. Sensing danger, rather than seeing it, he dropped to the floor and rolled to his left. He felt a rush of air above him and heard a metallic clank as a heavy, steel crow-bar struck the door frame where he had been standing. "Ambush!" he shouted to warn the others. He kept rolling across the floor until he reached the wall. The tiny tongue of early-morning light that had penetrated the doorway flickered as the rest of the group dove in through the door and rolled across the hard, concrete floor.

After he remained still for a moment and listened to his

surroundings, Razor got to his feet. His eyes had begun to adjust to the darkness, but he still saw little. The sounds of combat raged around him. Unseen feet shuffled across the floor. The clash of metallic objects rang. Whispered threats, and the *Swish! Swish! Swish!* of chains being swung with deadly intent, filled his ears. Occasionally the homicidal symphony was punctuated with a sickening thud or a thunderous smack—signaling that a makeshift truncheon had found its mark.

As more combatants joined in the fight, the level of confusion snowballed. It was impossible to distinguish friend from foe. The effectiveness of some of the attacks made Razor wonder whether the Light-Railers were using night vision goggles. Even Razor with all his experience in this kind of environment had only been able to land glancing blows at unseen passersby. He needed to take a risk.

When Razor heard slow shuffling sounds to his left, he turned on his flashlight and shined it directly at the noise. Less than five feet away, a Light-Railer—a length of pipe in his hand—froze in the midst of the unexpected and unwelcome spotlight. Razor extinguished his torch and took two running strides to close the distance to his prey. He slid to a stop and then delivered a leg-sweep with all of his strength. The painful jolt of his shin striking the Light-Railer's knees told him that his attack had been a success The Light-Railer, knocked clean off his feet, fell to the floor—all of his weight slamming down onto the unforgiving concrete. Razor pounced on the defenseless man and quickly realized that his enemy's collision with the floor had left him unconscious. Razor considered inflicting a fatal blow but decided against it. *He's done fighting. If he recovers, I'll deal with him later.*

Razor got to his feet and decided to try the same tactics again. He moved a few paces to his left and heard someone nearby. *Click—*

on came his flashlight. *Click*—off it went. In that illuminated instant, he saw another Teacher. The man had suffered a gash that ran from the corner of his right eye to the corner of his mouth. Blood covered his cheek. Even in the darkness he appeared pale from blood loss, but he was still fighting.

Razor continued to move to his left, leaving the relative safety of the wall. He stumbled over a body—prone and motionless on the floor. He nearly fell over the casualty but instead righted himself. As he struggled to regain his balance he fully expected a surprise attack that never came.

In the distance, he heard a chorus of grunts and cries. *Calder. It has to be her,* he told himself. He crouched and began to creep towards the fight. *She must have night vision goggles,* he thought as he continued a slow and steady crawl forward. *How can I get to her before she sees me with those goggles?*

Then it hit him. The plan would leave him at risk, but it seemed like his best option. He raised his arm high above his head and pointed his flashlight straight into the air. He clicked on the light and allowed it to stay lit for a full five seconds. After he extinguished the torch, he shouted at the disgraced EEFF agent. "Calder—I'm over here—"

Calder heard a voice calling to her from the darkness. She couldn't resist the urge to look. Then as she turned to face the cry, her brain registered the possibility that she was falling into a trap. By then, it was too late.

The beam from Razor's flashlight caught Calder squarely in the face and lit up her night vision goggles like an Independence Day fireworks show. She yanked the device off her face, but the damage had already been done. Stars danced before her eyes and she staggered, trying to regain her equilibrium in the aftermath of the overwhelming light. She panicked for an instant, unsure how to protect herself. That instant gave Razor more than enough time.

Calder heard herself grunt as the Teacher's tackle forced all of the air out of her lungs. She raised her hands to her head and tried to cushion the blow as her skull struck the concrete floor. Fortunately for her, the force of Razor's blow knocked her backwards. She slid when she landed, rather than falling straight down onto the floor. The force also pushed her beyond the area where Razor expected to find her.

She rolled over onto her hands and feet and heard Razor grunting and pawing at the floor. He was mere feet away and clearly trying to finish her off.

Calder knew she needed time to recover. Shaking her head to try to clear her mind, she rolled to her right, hoping to put as much distance between herself and Razor as possible. She then began to bear crawl away. As she moved, she gave a fleeting thought to Watford and Garamond. She'd promised to look after them, but they'd quickly become separated in the early moments of the ambush. Right now though, she had her own hands full. *I hope they're alright,* she silently wished. Then she forced herself to concentrate on her own danger. *I'll find them when I'm done—if I make it.*

While she crawled, her hand found a puddle of thick, sticky liquid on the floor. Reflexively, she wiped the blood on her pants, but she kept moving. Suddenly, Razor's light found her again, this time shining across her back and casting a shadow in front of her. *He's shining the light and then attacking,* she realized. Without hesitation, she sprang to the left and seconds later heard Razor grunt as his lunge carried him into the area where he expected to find his quarry. She hated to leave the fight, but she knew that she was at a huge disadvantage against her powerful and deadly pursuer.

Her vision was starting to return by now, and she could see the finger of sunlight that poked inside through the still-open casino door. She stood and ran for the exit. She heard footsteps giving chase behind her. As she entered the door's threshold, she shoved her right hand into the door frame. The push allowed her to change direction abruptly. The maneuver also allowed her to slow down and turn to face Razor as he followed her outdoors.

Chapter 49

Still inside Pinky's Casino, Ray Watford took his breaths in labored gasps. He was exhausted. The left side of his face ached—courtesy of a glancing blow from a baseball bat. The impact destroyed his night vision goggles and left a cut near his jaw line. The blood still felt sticky on his face as he gingerly patted the wound.

With the sound of scattered fighting around him, he sat huddled near the wall. He knew that Garamond was out there somewhere and so was Kerwin. Without his night vision goggles, he was of no help to either of them. So he stayed where he was.

A short distance away, Kerwin and Garamond whispered back and forth to determine a strategy to survive the fight. Thus far, they had used their night vision goggles to work in tandem. One would get their prey off balance and vulnerable, the other would swoop in for the kill. The tactics allowed both of them to avoid injury. Unfortunately, that was about to change.

The Teachers quickly realized that the Light-Railers were using night vision goggles. So when a Teacher found a Light-Railer, instead of using blows to the head, the educators began to use a tacking technique. The method allowed the Teacher's to confiscate the Light-Railer's night vision goggles for their own use. The tactic allowed EEFF's fighters to quickly even the odds. Of the twenty Light-Railers that started the fight, only a handful remained standing. The rest lay bruised and broken.

Garamond saw Calder run out the casino door a few moments earlier. He noticed that she was being followed closely by a Teacher. He had whispered to Kerwin that the two of them should try to help their leader. But as the pair methodically worked their way towards the door, the plan hit a snag. Kerwin spotted the quartet of Teacher's approaching on a run. "French—" he whispered.

Garamond quickly spotted the looming figures. Without a moment's hesitation, the Teachers threw themselves upon Kerwin and Garamond. Garamond unsuccessfully tried to protect his gut from the first punch. He groaned from the force of the blow and dropped to the floor. Then a storm of unseen punches and kicks rained down upon him. A few yards away, Kerwin received a similarly brutal lesson from his own pair of instructors.

After Razor had barged through the door, he saw Calder waiting for him. He readied himself for the confrontation. He knew that once he'd subdued Calder, he and the other Teachers could mop up the remaining Light-Railers and then grab Garamond and the author. He hoped they could arrest a few of the Light-Railers—instead of killing them all. Then the jailed traitors could serve as an object lesson that might discourage anyone who believed they could defy the government. Razor growled and clenched his fists.

Calder had raised both of her arms into defensive positions as she prepared for Razor's attack. Suddenly her eyes widened and her eyebrows rose up her forehead. "Who are you?" she asked as she lowered her guard slightly.

The question took Razor by surprise. He too lowered his guard a fraction and took a closer look at Calder. Then it hit him. He reached into his thigh pocket and retrieved a battered photo. A moment later, he abandoned any attempt to defend himself.

First, he looked at the faces in the photo. Then he looked at Calder, unsure whether he could believe his own eyes. Another glance at the picture and a long stare at Calder followed. "You're her—" he blurted.

Tears had formed in Calder's eyes. "Yes, I am." She reached out and gingerly took the photo from Razor's hand. She held the tattered snapshot as though she were afraid she might break it. She gasped as she looked at the faces of the man and the woman embracing one another in the image. Then she began to sob and threw her arms around Razor's muscular shoulders. She held him tightly and kept the photo of her parents clenched between her fingers.

When Razor was finally freed from Calder's embrace, he gazed at her, trying to make sense of what was happening. Calder saw the confusion on his face and began to explain.

"Shortly after I was born, my mother and father learned that they were going to have another child. They didn't have enough money to make ends meet, and my mother used to cry herself to sleep at night. She worried about how she and my father would keep a roof over our heads. People told her, 'go and have your pregnancy interrupted. Clearly, this is a case of premature pregnancy, following your daughter's birth so closely.' But my mom wouldn't hear any of it. Eventually, after a lot of tears, my parents agreed that they would give their son up for adoption after he was born." She paused for a moment, watching as the truth dawned upon Razor. "Where did you get the photo?" she asked.

Razor's eyes began to glisten. He looked down at his feet for a moment, trying to hide the tears that had formed in his own eyes. He sniffled. "My parents never wanted to tell me they had adopted me. They were the best parents I could have ever *dreamed* of having. They taught me about duty and loyalty. They loved me even when I made mistakes. But as I grew older, I realized that something about me was different. My mother and my father both had blonde hair and freckles. My mother had green eyes and my father blue." Razor looked into Calder's face for a long moment. She had the same raven-black hair and brown eyes as he did. "After a day in the sun, my mom and dad looked like a pair of lobsters. My skin turned bronze."

"Just like me," Calder replied.

"When I was eleven, a bully at school kept teasing me, telling me that I was adopted. I didn't believe him, but I could see the difference between me and my parents. I didn't know what to say." Tears now ran down Razor's cheeks. "When I got home that day, I asked my mother, and her reply changed my life. I loved my adoptive parents, but when my mom told me that my birth mother had given me away, I was devastated. It was as if someone reached inside me and turned me inside out. 'Why had my birth parents rejected me?' I asked myself. And the conclusion I reached was that I hadn't been good enough or that I didn't try hard enough. Even when my mother told me that I had been adopted as a tiny baby, it still didn't make it any easier. I swore that I had been a terrible baby and that my adoptive mother was lying to spare my feelings."

Calder reached over and touched her new-found brother on the shoulder. "You know that's not true, right?"

"It didn't matter whether it was true or not. That's what I believed. I started to punish myself. My dad had introduced me to wrestling, and I started to force myself through painful, endless workouts. I ran until I puked, and then I ran more. I tried to inflict enough pain upon myself to drive those feelings of rejection out of my mind." Razor sat down on a patch of weed-riddled concrete. "I never really wanted to hurt anyone, but I had to do something with the pain. When I wrestled, I made my opponents pay. I never lost a match. Later, I learned that EEFF had been keeping an eye on me. I found one of their representatives outside my dorm on college graduation day. They explained the nature of being a Teacher, and it fit for me. I've been a Teacher ever since."

Then his face turned to stone. "But I have *never* turned my back on an assignment—and I don't know how I can do that now," he whispered.

"I know you're dedicated to your duty," Calder said. "But today, I'm asking you to think for yourself. Think about the law you're being asked to uphold. General Welfare has ordered you to silence Ray Watford at any cost. Why is that? Is it because Ray asked people to open their eyes? Is it because Ray asked people to think about all the garbage the Federal Government News Bureau has been shoveling on top of them? Aren't those good things to do?"

Razor sighed. "I don't know what to tell you, but I'll help you find Watford. Then we can sort things out when this is over." He walked over and embraced Calder for a long moment before he turned and walked back into Pinky's Casino. Along the way, Calder handed her brother a set of night vision goggles before she followed him into the dark space.

Razor quickly found the members of the Foursome for Fairness. The actors brandished lengths of pipe at a group of fallen Light-Railers. In less than five seconds, Razor had knocked Mick Boyle unconscious with a single punch to the jaw, left Kevin Meadows doubled over, moaning in agony from a kick delivered to his solar plexus, and had Will Williams spitting out blood and teeth after the actor took a knee flush on the mouth. Jimmy Forest had mustered enough courage to take two swings at the deadly Teacher. The actor's reward had been an overhand right to the cheekbone that felled the aptly-named Forest—like a piece of tall timber.

While Razor busied himself with the actors, Calder

dispatched President Spendini, Sunny Davis/Davis Sunny, and Edgar Cockatiel. The trio had been trying to sneak out one of the casino's side doors. Calder left the three of them immobilized after treating them to a variety of punches and kicks.

After he'd finished with the Foursome for Fairness, Razor came upon the quartet of Teachers who had been pummeling Garamond and Kerwin. He knew that once he attacked a fellow Teacher, there would be no sorting *anything* out. He would be just as guilty of aiding and abetting a seditionist as his new-found sister. Nonetheless, he wasted no time delivering a front kick which sent one of the Teachers sprawling and howling in pain. The blow had been Razor's own declaration of independence. Then he used a flurry of fists, elbows and kicks to leave the remaining Teachers heaped in a pile of bruised flesh and blood-speckled clothing.

A minute later, Calder found Ray Watford struggling against bindings that held fast his wrists and ankles. Watford had tried to rescue Garamond and Kerwin from the Teachers a few minutes earlier, but he had been no match for a single Teacher, let alone a group of four. The educators quickly subdued Watford and took special care to leave him alive but incapable of flight. Standing guard over the Teachers' prize was Dingo Clark.

"Hello, Kristen," Clark growled. Kristen was his ex-wife's name.

Calder scowled, shook her head, and then performed a flying scissors on her former boss. With both of her ankles wrapped around the monster's neck, she dragged him down to the ground. Clark's face was the first thing to collide with floor.

"I'M NOT KRISTEN!" Calder shouted at the unconscious oaf before she moved to free Watford.

Once Watford got to his feet, Calder cut the cord that bound the author's wrists and ankles. After she'd finished, she surveyed the room for threats. Seeing none, she and Watford found Garamond, Kerwin, and Razor. The group crossed the blood-streaked floor together. Smiles formed on each of their faces as they stepped back into the sunshine, each of them thankful to have survived the ordeal.

The Battle of Las Vegas, as future Americans would come to call the confrontation, was over.

Chapter 50

French Garamond couldn't help it. Smiling felt like murder on his swollen lips, but it was the most enjoyable pain he'd ever felt. From onstage, he stared at the sea of faces that had gathered. The crowd stretched from Firenze Freddy's Fun Factory down the Las Vegas Strip past the Emperor's Digs and on to President Puppet's Paradise. *This is just like those rallies they used to hold before the crack down on free speech,* he silently recollected. Pride welled within him, and the sensation made it difficult to breathe.

"I want to thank you all for coming," Garamond said into the microphone. "Let's get this celebration started with a young man who'd like to sing us a song. Please welcome, Nick Brickman."

Brickman strolled to the microphone, his guitar hanging from his broad shoulders. He wore his brown hair closely cropped. He shaved daily but always left a skim of stubble on his chin and jaw. He liked the ruggedness it gave his boyish face. He smiled and waved to the crowd as he adjusted the microphone. "Hello, Las Vegas! It feels good to be back." He paused and strummed a few chords on the guitar. "I wrote this song about a group of people who were the greatest people to have ever walked this earth. Rain or shine, hot or cold, light or dark, they and their followers were there for you. Or that's what the papers tried to say anyway." Then he began to sing.

Congress fouled the mortgage market
Laid claim to all the banks
They troweled out pork sandwiches
Taxpayers got no thanks

They wrecked the auto makers
With all their greenie laws
They spent all their time taking
Like some greedy Santa Claws

But we'll just hope for a brighter future
We'll hope for a better day
Then we'll beg the BELOV'D UNITERS…
To come and hope our cares away.

They made us don the orange
As they sent us off to slave
They'll snatch the pennies off our eyes
When we're dumped into our graves
They'll say it's for our own good
That they truly know what's best
Tell me where to find a can of spray
To ward off those Sove-yet pests

Meanwhile, we'll wait for a brighter future
We'll hope for a better day
Then we'll beg the BELOV'D UNITERS…
To come and hope our cares away.

Our soldiers got bent over
Made ready for some peace.
They were told the Oh-pressed terrorists
Might just desist and cease.
Instead of firing bullets
Soldiers smiled and waved as friends
But the bombs just kept explodin'
Seems some jihads never end

But we'll just wait for a brighter future
We'll hope for a better day
Then we'll beg the BELOV'D UNITERS...
To come and hope our cares away.

Some days I look at TV
And wonder where we've gone
Following the man-gods' paths
To the promised great beyond?
Karl Marx must be their father
Mother Earth their lovin' mum
If you tend to buy their snake-oil rap
Chances are you might be—a little bit gullible.

But you can wait for a brighter future
You can hope for a better day
And you can hope the BELOV'D UNITERS...
Will come and hope your cares away.

Stunned silence greeted Brickman. The BELOV'D UNITERS
had been treated as deities from the moment they first emerged
onto the political landscape. It was considered very bad form to
criticize those former presidents. Though he'd been surprised by
the audience's zombie-like response, he still shouted "Thank you,
Las Vegas!" before he ran offstage.

It would have been hard to blame those in attendance for
their silence. Many of them had unspoken anxieties about the
state of America. No matter the indignities that had been heaped
upon them, they feared the power of a Federal Government—the
beast that seemed bent on fulfilling its agenda over the citizenry's
wishes.

As the day wore on, Garamond recognized the unease within the crowd. They'd been bullied, and they'd been lied to. They'd been called insulting names if they ever tried to object to the treatment that had been heaped upon them by Greta Government.

While Garamond walked to the microphone to introduce the final speaker, he wondered whether the United States had changed more than he thought. Maybe *no one* wanted a return to the nation where you could rise as high as your dreams and ambitions carried you. Maybe the price of hard work and risk was too high for this generation of Americans. So it was with a heavy heart that he grabbed the microphone and said, "I know we've had a great day so far, and it is almost time to wrap things up. We have had some of the leading voices of conservatism here. Let's give all of them a big thank you." Once again only polite applause rose from the crowd. "Up next, we don't have a giant of conservatism. We have a man who grew up in a family that didn't have a lot of money and didn't wear any of the names of American royalty. He just did the best he could with what God had given him, and here he is. Ladies and gentlemen, here is a *citizen* of the United States of America, Ray Watford."

Ray approached the podium with a smile on his face and butterflies in his stomach. His legs quivered. His jaw felt like it weighed a thousand pounds as he tried to form the words to speak. He paused for a moment. He remembered the sadness and outrage he felt—watching his sons growing up during a time when they were taught to hate their own country. And he couldn't remain silent any longer.

"My fellow Americans," he began. "It is with great humility that I speak to you today. I have never pretended to have all the answers. I simply believe in the beauty of the nation that was lent to us by those who came before us. It was their hard work and sacrifice that made this nation what it became."

"However, I believe we have waited too long. There are people who believe that access to power gives them the right to shred the legacy that Americans bled and died to protect. These progressives—as they like to call themselves—are little more than bullies who have taken advantage of our generosity and trust."

"They call us racists for trying to protect the last shreds of *American* heritage they haven't already destroyed. They call us greedy when we try to defend a Constitution that we believe is as brilliant, and still holds as much value, as the day it was written."

"Arrayed against us is a network of professional activists, lobbyists, bureaucrats and a judiciary who have hijacked control of the government. They have done so in collusion with the faux-news industry and those elected to serve. Their aim is to redistribute as much wealth as they can lay their hands on and amass as much power as they can grab."

"It's time that these politicians learned that enough is enough. It is time that we establish a new American tradition at election time. If your candidates sound more like Santa Claus than Thomas Jefferson, then something is wrong. If your candidates aren't down on their hands and knees—the spittle flying from their mouths—while they beg and plead for the chance to go to Washington D.C. to protect your freedoms, it should be clear that the candidate is not fit to hold office."

"But we can't blame the members of Congress for all of their failings. It was our silence which led us to where we are. This is *our* responsibility to share. We simply can't trust these people to work without our close supervision."

"This isn't a FauxPublican issue or a Demagogue issue, this is an American issue. Both parties have special interests that they protect. Stop and consider the impact that those decisions have had on your life. Think about the choices that you are no longer allowed to make for yourself. Then consider a choice that you can make as easily as throwing away an old pair of shoes. Decide whether those changes have improved American life."

"Look at the amount of your paycheck that gets taken out every time and decide whether those tax payments have actually made things better. We have a runaway government that is bent on protecting its own power. And they are doing it at our expense. It's time that we all cleaned house. The problem isn't *just* the clowns in someone else's district or someone else's state. If these elected officials aren't begging for the chance to protect our freedom, they should be pursuing other career opportunities."

"No one has ever suggested that helping people end their dependence on government would be easy. No one ever said it would be painless. But that doesn't make it any less necessary. Greta Government is happy to see you enslaved. It gives her power. It guarantees that she will be able to stick around for as long as the duped voters dutifully show up on Election Day and keep her in office. She wants us to be sheep. She wants us to bleat along with the crowd so that instead of kicking her and her kind out of office, we'll thank her for her *generosity* and *compassion*."

"We the people ate snake-oil-surprise by the bowlful. We believed the empty promises about *green* energy. We cheered while the rampant demagoguery broke achievers and producers. We looked the other way while the Constitution was shredded, believing that those in power could actually be trusted. And look at where it has gotten us."

"We have a lot of work ahead of us, but history shows that once Americans make up their minds to do something, not a host of environmental-alarmists, vocal Marxists, or clowns in pancake—"

Gunshots interrupted Watford's remarks. "Get out of my way or you're dead!" The shouts came from somewhere within the crowd. Men and women panicked and ran. Within an instant, the assembled crowd had scattered.

Watford stood alone on the stage. He regretted his own inaction. He knew he should have run, but now it was too late. He looked down at the empty stretch of boulevard and saw the masked assailant. A feeling of dread—mixed with a hint of déjà vu—washed over him.

The gunman wore leopard-print coveralls and a ski mask. He pointed an assault rifle at Ray. "You're dead, Watford! You should have kept your mouth shut!"

The assailant's threats made Ray's blood run cold. He raised his hands above his head and wondered whether he would be lucky enough to make it out of another confrontation alive. "Please put the gun down. We don't need to settle things that way."

"You've destroyed everything I have. You, with your stupid book and your stupid rally; it's your turn to see how it feels to lose, *Ray*."

As Ray listened to the attacker, he soon recognized the voice coming from behind the mask. He sighed and said, "C'mon, Larry, take that mask off. If you're going to kill me, at least have the courage to show your face."

"It's not Larry," Lemonpants said, trying to mask his voice. After a moment, he relented and yanked the disguise off his head. His eyes were large and filled with rage. He kept his jaw clenched tight. "I can't let you do it," he growled.

"Do what, Larry, ask people to think for themselves instead of blindly trusting politicians? We're not supposed to ask questions or form opinions any longer? It seemed like not too long ago, disagreeing with the Administration was the highest mark of patriotism. Now it makes someone a seditionist? I guess life *is* all about timing."

"You people are destroying the planet—"

"Have you noticed how cold the winters have been lately?"

"Your greed is going to tear down this nation—"

"Congress has redistributed billions of dollars in the name of ending poverty. Go hang around a homeless shelter and then tell me whether Congress has made the problem better or worse." Ray looked down and saw that Lemonpants had started to cry. *Maybe I can sneak off the stage while he isn't looking,* he said to himself. Then he crept silently, one step at a time, towards the edge of the stage.

Ray kept his eyes fixed on Lemonpants as the environmentalist continued to weep uncontrollably—a rush of tears, slobber and snot running down his face. When Ray finally arrived at the metal stairway leading to the ground, he took a final look at Lemonpants and then jumped. As Ray's feet hit the asphalt, they landed in a patch of sand. The sound of shoes sliding across the grit jerked Lemonpants from his trance. "Where do you think you're going, *Watford*?" Lemonpants demanded.

Ray didn't reply. He just ran and hoped that Lemonpants was bluffing. Unfortunately, Ray had never been very skilled at poker, and within an instant, Lemonpants began to hose the area with the assault rifle. The weapon's staccato bark—and the sounds of lead screaming past him—filled the air.

Lemonpants shouted, "Die—greedy fascist!" as he tried to correct his aim. Bullets bit into the pavement all around the fleeing Watford. After his first clip had emptied, Lemonpants reached into his thigh pocket for a second.

As Ray continued to run for his life, he heard the firing stop.

Keep running, he's just reloading. A moment later, he heard a rather loud *thunk*—like the improbable sound of a very heavy book striking someone's head. Ray glanced back over his shoulder and saw President Spendini as he stood over the prone figure of Larry Lemonpants. On the ground near the ultra-left-wing gunman's head lay a copy of the *Community Rankings and Penalties List for the Abolition of Prohibited Free Speech*. Spendini had saved Ray's life.

Chapter 51

Ray was shocked to see President Spendini and the incapacitated Larry Lemonpants when he turned around. He stopped running and walked back towards the scene. "What happened?" he asked.

What no one—not Watford or Spendini or anyone else in the brawl—had noticed was that early in the fighting, Lemonpants had slunk out the door and had returned to his airplane to grab some heavier weapons. "I was limping back to Lemonpants' plane after the fight at Pinky's when I saw Larry reach into a rifle case," Spendini began. "When I saw him pull the weapon out, I decided I should probably see what he was up to. When Lemonpants pulled the gun on you," Spendini sat down on the ground and began to rub his temples, "I had some soul searching to do."

"I had originally brought my copy of the List because I thought it would make for great TV. When we finally caught you, I had planned to have the camera man get a shot of me standing over you and reading from the List. It was going to be great— just like in the movies. And it probably would have clinched the election for me."

"So what happened?"

"I don't know ... I saw you and Lemonpants. I remembered that whole scene before the rally, watching you, Garamond, and Calder and the Light-Railers, hanging your decorations even though you knew we would come for you, and I began to think."

Ray nodded a silent affirmation.

Spendini stared down at his feet. "I realized that this wasn't the way it was meant to be. I wasn't supposed to make it to the White House this way. That's when I realized that it was time for all of this to end," Spendini concluded in a whisper.

"What do you mean?"

"I mean all of the killing, and the lying, and the corruption. It has to end. I was the one who authorized the Immaculate Redistribution. Then I had Kugler killed to cover it up," he said before he stopped speaking. He looked exhausted. "I did it so I could become president. I did it because I knew that if I didn't do it, Lemonpants would cut off my money, and I'd lose the next election." He sighed.

Ray walked over and sat down next to the president. "You just confessed to murder, sir."

"I can't do it anymore. The ends don't *always* justify the means. America needs a fresh start."

"I can't disagree, Mister President. I don't think the founders ever intended to give rise to a professional class of politicians. When you wield the power that members of Congress possess, it is far easier to become corrupted by the process than it is to hold onto any semblance of principal. Everyone else is doing the same thing. You know that your opponent in the next election wants your job as badly as you want to keep it. Why would you cut your own throat and listen to that little voice inside when it tells you that so much of what goes on is wrong? And the simple answer, in too many cases, is that you wouldn't."

"Elected officials step in front of the cameras and chastise businesspeople for breaking the law or for being greedy. But you never hear them acknowledge the daily conflicts-of-interest they allow themselves to become enmeshed within. How is it *not* a conflict-of-interest when Congress takes political contributions from a company that makes windmills, and then they pass a law that mandates that a certain proportion of all electricity generated must rely upon the use of those windmills. How does that sound anything but fishy, Mister President?"

"If the shoe fits—" was all Spendini said.

Epilogue

President Spendini resigned the presidency in the aftermath of the Battle of Las Vegas. A day later, he went on television and admitted his guilt in the murder of Neil Kugler.

With Spendini's resignation, Rita the Clown served out the remainder of the disgraced president's term. Rita had suffered a defeat in her own Congressional reelection bid and retired from public office following the inauguration of the newly-elected, conservative president.

In addition to promising a return of conservatism to party politics, the new president pardoned Spendini. No one wanted to see the former president imprisoned in a newly reopened correctional facility. In exchange, Spendini vowed to spend the rest of his life on house arrest, except for the time he planned to spend performing true community service work.

The Demagogue Party Chair, Sunny Davis, retired from politics and moved to Europe where she toured as a quick-change artist. Davis Sunny was fired by the FauxPublican Party and was never seen again.

Milton Kerwin retired and moved to Garamondia.

Larry Lemonpants fled the United States and moved to South America. Upon his arrival, he told a local dictator that the government should curb its petroleum industry. The dictator was so grateful for the advice, he promptly had Lemonpants jailed.

The Foursome for Fairness made a movie about Ray Watford's kidnapping. However, instead of playing themselves, they played the roles of Watford, French Garamond, Milton Kerwin, and

Razor Calder.

Edgar Cockatiel continued to do a television show that no one watched.

Buster Lafayette recovered from the beating he suffered at the hands of the Teachers. In addition to resuming his immensely popular show, he studied martial arts and found and then whipped the ass of each Teacher that had beaten him. He didn't kill any of the now-unemployed educators, but he sure made them wish they were dead.

Edward Tramsoot wrote a string of best-selling novels—an achievement his experience at the Yellow Lapdog Gazette prepared him well to pursue.

Sheena Glitzy made history as the first television anchor—in a very long time anyway—to actually deliver *news*.

Shawn and Razor Calder were wed in a double-wedding ceremony. Both of them married former members of the Underground Light Rail. The two newlywed couples bought houses that sat side-by-side. And for the remainder of their lives, the reunited brother and sister never spent a day apart.

French Garamond returned to America and built the first privately-owned automobile factory since the collapse of the American auto industry. The Garamond Utility Vehicle was an instant success with American drivers. Garamond's former homeland, Garamondia, become a close friend and ally of the United States.

When Ray finally made it home after his California adventure, he spent a month of uninterrupted time with his family before he wrote the *final* chapter of his novel. As he typed the final period, he hoped that he had created a fitting conclusion to the story.

After he printed his novel's final chapter, he dutifully handed the pages to Sarah so she could read them. "I'm not going through that again," she said with a wink as she took the now-unbanned writing paper from her husband's hand.

After receiving his wife's approval, Ray walked out to the street, climbed into his own Garamond Utility Vehicle, and drove to Kerwin Publishing.

Milton Kerwin greeted the author at the door.

In the Hall (Reflections on America)
Chapter 7

After seeing My Favorite President, I finally managed to leave the Hall. The day was exhausting, but I knew I would never be the same. I would no longer stay silent while hordes of activists clamored at the doors of Congress.

Exactly one year later, I returned to the same library where I had found the Hall's entrance. I snuck back into the janitor's closet and stooped down to peer behind the shelves where I'd found the hole in the wall.

Thankfully the books written about the formerly *insignificant* presidents had been returned to their rightful place in the American history and biography sections. A few hundred copies of the BELOV'D UNITERS' biographies had been sent to the bargain bin to make room. It was good to see that even presidents were sometimes called upon to make sacrifices.

I never expected to actually find the entrance to the Hall again. I sure hoped that I would though. When I pulled aside the box of urinal cakes, I saw the same opening in the wall.

I crawled into the hole and then walked down the dirt passageway. But this time I didn't travel empty-handed.

Beneath one arm I held a package wrapped in brown paper and tied with a length of string. After I opened the Hall's door, I heard the same ringing of hammer and chisel. The sounds comforted me. *Progress never stands still, I guess.*

This time I had no need of a map. I strode to my destination and rapped on the door. I was surprised when the door opened an instant later.

Uncle Sam greeted me with a broad smile. His faced looked fit, yet relaxed. He wore a white tee shirt and a pair of blue jeans. His biceps and forearms rippled as he gestured towards a chair. Clearly this was a different man.

I smiled as I sat. "I brought you a gift," I said.

"What could you possibly have that I need? I'm Uncle Sam," he said before winking at me.

I handed him the package and watched him untie the string and open the brown paper wrapping. He reached inside and pulled out the gift. He held the pants and then the coat in front of himself before saying, "You did a good job of guessing my size."

"I had a lot of help," I said. "But there's more."

Uncle Sam grinned while he reached back

into the wrapping paper and pulled out the new star-spangled hat. "You didn't have to do this."

"I know, I just wanted to remind you that there are people who never wanted to see you reduced to a—" I paused, unsure what to say next.

Uncle Sam patted me on the shoulder and said, "I know, Ray...I Know."

About the Author

Nate Roberts lives in the Upper Midwest with his wife and two sons. He has worked in the not-for-profit field, in local government, and as a small-business owner. He has added "finishing a novel" to his list of achievements. Also on that list are feats such as running a sub-five-minute mile, completing a marathon, and winning the fourth-grade tetherball championship back in grade school.

Breinigsville, PA USA
15 December 2010
251480BV00001B/1/P